LISSA: SUGAR & SPICE

The Wilde Sisters: Book Three

by Sandra Marton

COPYRIGHT

DEDICATION

THIS BOOK IS dedicated to the brave men and women of the US Armed Services who so valiantly defend our freedom and our honor everywhere around the world. Thank you for all that you do, and for the endless sacrifices you make on our behalf.

CHAPTER ONE

I T WAS LISSA Wilde's birthday.

Her twenty-seventh, if you were counting, which she was not, and the celebration was in full swing.

A perfect celebration. All a girl could want was right within easy reach.

A gaily wrapped box of See's Truffles. The one-pound box because, what the hell, this was a party.

A long-handled spoon standing in a just-opened pint of Cherry Garcia.

And a vibrator.

Not just any vibrator, but a pink one that had *Pleasure Pleaser* printed all over the tissue paper that enclosed it... Well, that enclosed it once you got it out of its plain brown wrapper.

Lissa patted the vibrator. "Soon," she said. Then she tore the wrapping paper off the box of truffles.

What could be better than a birthday party planned by the

person who knew the birthday girl best?

"Who, indeed?" Lissa said, fingers hovering over the chocolates.

Which would it be? White? Dark? Milk? Lissa shut her eyes, plucked a chocolate from the box, started to take a ladylike bite, thought *the hell with it* and popped the whole thing into her mouth.

Yum.

Delicious.

Amazingly delicious, she decided, and she swallowed, took another piece from the box and bit into it.

A perfect party.

That was the thing about being the only guest. You could concentrate on what really mattered.

"You hear that, *Pleasure Pleaser*?" she said.

The vibrator didn't answer. Not that she'd expected it to. In fact, that was the thing about vibrators. They knew their place in life. They never had to be told what to do or how to do it. Or so she'd heard.

The truth was, this was her first sex toy.

She'd walked by a shop just off Hollywood Boulevard maybe ten times before she'd made up her mind to go inside. She'd thought about wearing dark glasses and a pull-down hat and maybe even a trench coat until she'd noticed women going in and out of the place, not hesitating, not in disguise, and she'd taken a breath, opened the door and found herself in, well, in a sex toy wonderland.

Pleasure Pleaser had been in a case along with at least a dozen others, and by the time the salesclerk had finished taking them out, one by one, turning them on and pointing out the high points of each, not only had Lissa been relaxed, she'd also been giggling.

Selecting one had been about as difficult as selecting one chocolate. The only certainty had been that she absolutely didn't want the one that was supposed to look like a penis.

For one thing, it made her burst out laughing.

For another, the less the thing looked like anything to do with a man, the better.

"I know what you mean," the salesgirl had said. "Who needs a man to get between you and ground zero?"

Lissa ate another truffle.

Who needed that, indeed? The best thing about a vibrator was that after it did its job, it went away until the next time you wanted it.

But then, one way or another, so did men.

Lissa scooped up a spoonful of ice cream and sucked it off the spoon.

"Not ladylike," one of the nannies who'd raised her would have said.

"Man, that is sexy," one of the idiots she'd dated would have said.

Hell. What it was, was the best way to savor the taste of the Cherry Garcia. Nothing more, nothing less.

Lissa put her bare feet on the coffee table in her tiny living room, dug her spoon deeper into the ice cream and watched Humphrey Bogart and Ingrid Bergman gaze into each other's eyes on the DVD. She had the sound muted. Who needed sound when you knew all the dialogue by heart and you could say it along with Ingrid and Bogey?

"*But what about us?*" Ingrid/Lissa said, and reached for another truffle.

Bogey's mouth did that funny little twitchy thing it often did.

"*We'll always have Paris,*" Bogey/Lissa said.

Ingrid wept. Lissa shoveled in more Cherry Garcia.

Bogey lifted Ingrid's chin and they did another round of eye-gazing.

"*Here's lookin' at you, kid,*" Bogey/Lissa said.

Last line, blah blah, then fade to black. Lissa reached for a paper napkin, thoughtfully provided by Pirelli's Pizza, the takeout place that had also thoughtfully provided the nutritious main course for her birthday dinner.

She wiped a tear from her eye and a streak of chocolate from her lip.

Stupid, to cry over a movie that was decades older than she was, to cry over a movie at all, because she knew damn well it had nothing to do with life, but maybe that was the point. Maybe what happened in movies or books or TV shows was the only way anybody could ever even come close to experiencing real, true break-your-heart love.

Not that she was stupid enough to want her heart broken.

Lissa dumped the tissue on the table, swapped the spoon for the remote, clicked the TV off and swapped the remote for the spoon.

It was just the principle of the thing. Feeling down, watching Ingrid fly off with the wrong guy, but then they were all wrong guys, when you came down to it.

Feeling weepy certainly didn't have anything to do with spending her birthday alone.

Another hit of Cherry Garcia. Some of it dribbled on her *What's Cookin'?* T-shirt. So what? That was another benefit of being alone. Yoga pants with a hole in one knee. A stained T-shirt. No makeup. No hairstyle unless dragging. her not-blond-not-brown-who-cares-what-color-it-is   hair   into   a ponytail was a style.

She was alone. And happy.

"I am Alone," she said. "And I am Happy."

Lissa burped.

It wasn't as if she hadn't done the people-and-party thing in the past. She had. The Family Birthday, definitely in caps, at El Sueño, the family ranch, all her brothers, brother-in-law and almost-brother-in-law in attendance, all her sisters and sisters-in-law fussing over her. She'd done the semi-friends and co-workers version, too, where you had the crap embarrassed straight out of you when the who-gives-a-damn staff warbled a painfully loud and generally off-key rendition of "Happy Birthday" over a slab of cake they probably kept in the back for these occasion, because surely nobody was ever dumb enough to actually eat that cake.

And, of course, she'd done the BFBE. The Boyfriend Birthday extravaganza. Fancy restaurants where she'd tried not to think about the fact that if she were the chef, she'd have cooked a better meal or done a better presentation. And then, after the meal, the gift-giving ritual—an expensive but schlocky piece of jewelry that had actually been selected by the BF's PA—Jesus, the world was loaded with initials—or if the

BF had bought it himself, maybe a frothy bit of lingerie that would have better suited a hooker than a girlfriend.

Lissa reached for another truffle.

Not that she'd been anyone's girlfriend for a while.

Catholics gave up stuff for Lent, but you didn't have to be Catholic and it didn't have to be Lent for an intelligent woman to give up men for the duration.

"And more power to you, kid," she said, lisping her way through another bad Bogart imitation.

It wasn't that she didn't like men. She did, as a concept. Men could be fun. They could be charming. Some were amazingly easy on the eyes. They were handy for emptying the occasional mousetrap, fine at holding an umbrella high enough over your head that you didn't get wet running from your door to a taxi or to a car.

And, generally speaking, they were OK in bed.

Mostly, though, they weren't worth the trouble they caused.

They became proprietorial. They became possessive.

Another mouthful of ice cream, and who was she trying to fool?

She'd heard other women talk about those things as a problem. She was never with a guy long enough for him to get all riled up about staking his claim.

The trouble with men was that they lied. They cheated. No matter how they seemed at the start of a relationship, they ended up as one hundred proof SOBs one hundred percent of the time.

Lissa plunged her spoon deep into the Cherry Garcia. It came up empty. Amazing. Were they downsizing the containers?

No problem.

She'd planned ahead. That was the thing about being a trained chef. You know how to manage your supplies.

There was a pint of Chunky Monkey stashed in the freezer.

How could a woman be smart enough to hide ice cream and not smart enough to know that men were not worth her time and trouble?

Well, her brothers, brother-in-law and almost brother-in-law excepted, of course. Jacob. Caleb. Travis. And now, Marco. And, soon, Zach would join the ranks.

Great guys, all of them.

Lissa rose to her feet and went to her tiny kitchen.

Maybe there was a planetary limit on the number of decent men available. Maybe Earth's quota had been reached. Maybe the Wilde men and the Wilde-Men-by-Proxy were it.

"Maybe you need that Chunky Monkey," she said, dumping the empty Cherry Garcia container in the trash and opening the door to the freezer.

She'd never had any luck with men. Not even with boys. Look at the Tommy Juarez fiasco and yes, that had been kindergarten and no, it wasn't foolish to go back that far because lesson were lessons no matter when you learned them.

Tommy had planted a kiss on her cheek while the whole class was playing Duck, Duck, Goose. The very next day, he'd called her a turd bird and kissed Deanna Hilton instead.

Lissa peered into the freezer.

And what about Jefferson Beauregard the Third in high school? Quarterback. Captain. A total hottie. Her steady for eight months until she'd caught him in the girls' locker room—the *girls'* locker room—screwing the brains out of one of the Becker twins, and what a stupid description that was because neither of the Becker twins had brains to be screwed out of and if that sentence had a dangling participle or whatever, she just didn't give a shit.

Where was that Chunky Monkey?

"Come out, come out wherever you are," Lissa said, poking past frozen chicken stock and frozen herbs and frozen something-or-other that she hadn't labeled and who knew what in hell it was now?

How she'd ever gone steady with a boy named Jefferson Beauregard the Third was beyond her. She surely hadn't loved him.

Yeah, but he'd said he loved her.

And of course, who was she kidding? She'd loved him. Puppy love, but still…

And she'd given him her virginity.

Well, OK. She'd been eager to give it to somebody.

Her sisters had clung to theirs as if they were characters in a Victorian novel instead of modern-day Texas females. Not her. She'd been ready, willing and eager to find out what sex was like, and—

"Gotcha," she said triumphantly as she took the pint of Chunky Monkey from where it had been hiding behind a loaf of oatmeal bread she'd baked last week.

And, she thought, popping the lid and tossing it into the sink, she'd found out what sex was like.

It was OK. All right. Fine. Just, well, just no big deal.

It still was and there was nothing wrong with that; it was only that she'd kind of expected it to be mind-blowing, the way books and movies said it was, the way her very own sisters said it was, not that Jaimie or Emily actually talked about what sex was like with their guys, but when Em spoke Marco's name, when Jaimie spoke Zach's, you could almost hear the sizzle.

No problem.

Lissa headed back into the living room and sat down on the sofa.

Sex was what it was, and she was fine with that.

What she wasn't fine with was the BS that went with the sex.

With being involved with a guy.

Which took her straight back to the lies. Oh, the lies! *I adore you, baby. I don't ever want to be with anyone else. You are incredibly special.*

That was what Rick had pretty much said to Ilsa, but he'd let her go anyway. Well, for the right reasons, sure.

Still, Ilsa had flown into the night. And Rick had moved on to deal with his life.

Lissa crammed a truffle into her mouth.

She'd been living in Los Angeles for three years. La La Land, her brothers said. Home to Gorgeous Guys, her sisters said. And both definitions were true. This was the Land of Dreams as well as the Land of Heartthrobs.

She knew that, firsthand.

She'd come here with the dream of becoming a chef. A top chef, one who could put her brand on a restaurant and make it dazzle.

She hadn't come here to find a man, but the men were as plentiful as sand on a beach. Good-looking men. Great-looking, in fact. Who could resist the temptation?

Lissa reached for another truffle. Her stomach gave a delicate roll. Maybe it was time to stick with the Chunky Monkey.

She'd been here three years and she'd been involved with three different guys.

All hot-looking. All fun to be with. All charming.

All actors.

A synonym for dirty, rotten bastards.

"For God's sake, Melissa," she muttered into the silence of the room, "you are either incredibly stupid or incredibly slow."

Truly, she was.

How long should it have taken her to figure out that if men lied, actors—actors fabricated, and even if the words meant the same thing, actors were the worst. Why wouldn't they be? Actors lied by profession. What else would you call acting?

Acting on screen was one thing. Acting in real life was another.

In real life, if you saw an actor's lips move, your best bet was to turn and run.

Lissa stuck the spoon into what remained of the ice cream, tucked the container into her lap and sat back.

If only she had.

But what woman could resist having a six-foot movie god like Carlos Antonioni come back to the kitchen of *The Black Pearl* the night the regular chef had been down with the flu to seek out her, the sous chef, lift her hand to his lips and say that he had expected to find a kitchen goddess but not Aphrodite.

"Why are you not in the movies?" Carlos had said. She'd heard the line before—men liked her looks even though she thought of herself as Typical Texas, meaning she had long legs and big boobs and was, if you liked the type, cheerleader pretty—but coming from a heartthrob like him…

Her knees had gone weak.

He'd wined her and dined her and when he'd made his move, she'd let him. Whatever it was Em and Jaimie were experiencing, Lissa figured she'd like a try at it, too.

With a man this studly, the sex would have to be earth-shaking, wouldn't it?

Nothing. Not even a tremor.

Maybe the sex would have gotten better. Anything was possible…except what had turned out to be most possible was that Carlos's interest had lasted about as long as the shelf life of a soufflé.

So, OK, she'd learned her lesson. Don't be swayed by flattery. By good looks. Get to know the real man.

That was when Jack came along.

Jack Rutledge, every woman's dream, that face, that body, up there on the big screen. If Carlos had been gorgeous, Jack was spectacular. He played small roles, sure, but he was on the move—mostly to the nearest mirror so he could gaze at himself in admiration, except she hadn't really noticed that until it was too late.

The earth hadn't trembled after she'd slept with him, either. Once again, the glassware and crockery were safe.

Not that it mattered.

Turned out that she'd been perfect for quiet evenings—*This is the real me, baby, not the Hollywood guy people see*—but once Jack landed a part in an upcoming Channing Tatum movie—*I'm in four scenes,* he'd said excitedly, *four entire scenes!*—she'd discovered that the real Jack was, after all, that Hollywood guy he'd so disparaged. *Sorry, baby, you're a treasure, but I gotta be seen with names now, like, starlets, you know what I'm sayin'?*

Lissa licked a dollop of Chunky Monkey from the spoon.

Her heart hadn't exactly been broken. It had been dinged, along with her ego, and OK, L.A. was the kind of town that could make you feel really lonely, especially when your brothers, whom you adored, were falling heads over heels in love, which was what had been happening back in the real world.

Then Emily found Marco.

And, at almost the same time, *The Black Pearl* closed.

She'd been surprised, but not shocked. Restaurants had a half-life of maybe twenty months, plus or minus, even the ones that people raved about. A place was hot one minute, not just cold but dead the next. So, no, she hadn't been shocked by *The Black Pearl's* closing.

She'd been shocked that the owner had given neither her nor the staff any warning.

Lissa took a deep breath.

Right about then, she'd met Raoul.

Jesus. Raoul. Hadn't she learned anything about names back in the days of Jefferson Beauregard the Third?

But Raoul was different.

He was—surprise, surprise—an actor, but with a difference.

Good-looking? Yes. Sexy? Sure. He was also well-educated. And rich. Mega rich. They met at a party, he took her for drinks afterward and they talked. And talked. And talked. He was interested in her opinions. In the places she'd traveled as a kid, places he had also lived.

That night was followed by others. They went to dinner. They went to a movie premiere. He held her hand, kissed her goodnight.

And that was it. No moves. No sex. He respected her. She could tell.

He was giving her time to get to know him.

It was the best six weeks she'd spent since moving to the West Coast.

One night, sitting in her living room having coffee after a quiet meal she'd prepared, Raoul told her that he'd been dreaming of something for a long time.

Lissa's heartbeat had quickened.

He'd reached for her hand.

"You won't laugh?"

She'd assured him that she wouldn't.

He'd drawn a deep breath.

"I want to open a restaurant."

She remembered blinking. And saying something really brilliant like, "Huh?"

"A restaurant," he'd said. "The best in Los Angeles. The best in Southern California." He'd brought her hand to his lips, just as he had that first night. "And I want you to be my executive chef."

She'd almost fainted at those words.

Sure, she'd been a sous chef at *The Black Pearl*. She'd been *the* sous chef; her responsibilities had been enormous, but executive chef…

It would make her career.

She'd be responsible for absolutely everything that happened in the kitchen, from purchases to creating dishes and planning menus. She'd be able to put her stamp on things.

People would know her name.

It was the opportunity she'd dreamed of. Tough to come by, especially for a woman, a twentysomething, good-looking woman in a town bursting at the seams with good-looking women.

Even Lissa's agent had been worried about her looks and yes, you needed an agent if you wanted to hit the top.

"Are you serious about a career in the kitchen?" Marcia had asked. "You're sure you won't give up cooking if some producer offers you an acting role?"

It had been an honest question. Ninety-nine percent of the female population between the ages of nine and ninety were in La La Land because they wanted to become stars.

"I'm a chef," Lissa had said. "That's what I studied to be and what I intend to be."

Now, thanks to Raoul, the dream she'd had since she'd baked a batch of pretty decent cookies at age seven had been about to come true.

He would not be her lover, he would be her partner. Well, more or less her partner. She wouldn't have any ownership in the restaurant—he was going to call it *Raoul's*—but together, they would create something grand.

Raoul asked for her input in the design of the kitchen and dining room; he shared his long-term plans for the place. In return, she shared what she knew about the best suppliers of fish, of meat, of produce. She shared with him the much-coveted names of artisans who baked breads to die for, crafted chocolates to kill for, made cheeses to send your taste buds to heaven. She contacted kitchen and wait staff that she knew, from experience, would be excellent workers. She gave him a list of influential people who'd been regular patrons at *The Black Pearl* so he could invite them to their big opening night.

He told her how grateful he was, that he couldn't have even dreamed of opening a top-notch place without her help and she said no, no, that wasn't true, except they both knew that it was.

And still, he didn't make a move on her, but there was something in the way he looked at her that said he liked what he saw.

She liked what she saw, too.

She even had a couple of steamy dreams that starred Raoul. Nothing unusual in that; she had steamy dreams sometimes, dreams that were always better than reality.

Maybe, just maybe, this was her Marco. Her Zach. Maybe Raoul would be the guy who'd make the earth move.

There was more to it than that, though not even torture would have dragged it from her, but lately there were times she felt…

Lonely.

The world seemed full of twosomes and here she was, a onesome.

And so, Lissa did what she had never done before. She played the *What if?* game. She fantasized, not just about sex but about life.

About—did she dare think it? About love.

The more she thought about Raoul, the more convinced she was that he was too much a gentleman, too committed to their friendship to make the first move. She'd have to do it, nothing elaborate, maybe ask him to have a drink after closing once the restaurant had been open a couple of weeks.

Thinking back, she snorted at her stupidity.

Opening night, everything looking perfect, eighty high-profile patrons out front including two food critics trying to look inconspicuous, her staff moving in harmony, each plate leaving the kitchen looking like a painting. Towards the middle of the evening, her phone rang.

It was Raoul.

"Lissa. I'm in my office. Do you have a minute?"

She didn't, not really. She told him that.

"We ran out of fish stock," she said. "Nothing serious—I made more, but I hope it comes out right. I like to let my stock refrigerate overnight, but there isn't time to do that. I tasted it and it seems OK, but—"

"Tell you what," he said. "Bring it with you. I'll taste it, give you a second opinion, and we can take care of a small management issue all at the same time. It won't take long—I promise."

So she poured some of the broth into a small bowl, told her second-in-command to hold down the fort, and she hurried to Raoul's office, tucked into a corner of the basement.

The door was closed. She knocked.

"Come in."

Smiling, she'd opened the door.

"Raoul. It's crazy up there. And I know I'm being silly, worrying about this fish stock—"

The rest of what she'd intended to say caught in her throat.

Raoul was standing directly in front of her, leaning back against his desk, wearing his tux. He was as impeccably groomed as always: hair brushed back from his temples, his handsome face calm. His arms were folded over his chest.

The only jarring note was his hugely-erect penis pointing at the ceiling with urgent importance from his unzipped fly.

"Just shut the door," he'd said, "get down on your knees, and be quick about it."

Lissa had always been an instinctive cook. In that fateful moment, she became an instinctive compendium of rage and anguish.

But not defeat.

One quick twist of her wrist and Raoul was wearing the fish stock. Her last memory was of him jerking back, mouth open in shock, fish bones glinting on his tux…

A fish head first balancing, then sliding off his rapidly-deflating erection.

Lissa groaned, lay her head back against the couch and shut her eyes.

It was also the last memory of her career.

She hadn't been able to land a job, a real job, since that night.

She'd been doing prep work from kitchen to kitchen, filling

in for salad men and sauce men, and one hideous week, she'd even waitressed, something she hadn't done since she'd paid her way through *Le Cordon Bleu.*

It was mortifying.

That whole week, she'd kept praying she wouldn't wait on a table filled with people she knew. Waitressing was honest work, but it would have been a brutal admission of failure in a town that revered success.

That was the same reason she'd flat out lied to her family when she'd gone home for Em's wedding a couple of months ago.

You didn't admit to failure if you were a Wilde.

Wildes were all successful. Incredibly successful. Jacob the rancher. Caleb the attorney. Travis the financial wizard. Her sisters were at the top of their games, too, Emily working with her husband as his VP in international construction, Jaimie holding down the CFO spot at her soon-to-be husband's upper-echelon security firm. Her sisters-in-law, all three of them great moms, were also the best in their fields of law, management and psychology.

Add in the Wilde patriarch, four-star general John Hamilton Wilde, and failure was not an option.

When they'd asked about the fancy restaurant she was working at, she'd said that oh, she wasn't at a restaurant anymore, she was working "on location."

They'd figured she meant on a movie set.

Well, that was better than telling them that she was working at *Grandma's Finger-Lickin-Chicken Coop.* Eight hours a day, she pulled chicken parts out of a huge box, rolled them in a batter that had the color and consistency of cement, then dumped them into a vat of bubbling lard.

It wasn't a job; it was an extended journey through hell. She needed a kitchen again. Responsibility. Creativity. She needed to cook.

The ice-cream container in her lap tilted. She grabbed for it. Too late. It tumbled to the floor.

Amazing, how great Chunky Monkey looked in a carton and how less than appetizing it looked in a puddle on a faded rug.

Lissa shot to her feet, got a handful of paper towels from the kitchen, cleaned up the mess and dropped everything into the trash, even the chocolates.

She couldn't live on what she earned at *Grandma's*. She had car payments to meet and a car wasn't a luxury in L.A., it was a necessity. A roof over her head was a necessity, too. So was food on the table.

So was restarting her moribund career.

Maybe she'd call her agent. She hadn't heard from Marcia in weeks, but there had to be some kind of decent job out there, and wasn't that what an agent was for? To get you a job? *You're developing a somewhat difficult reputation,* Marcia had said the last time they'd spoken, and she'd come within a breath of telling her that it wasn't true, that Raoul had fired her for being a prima donna, which was the rumor he'd spread, but the truth was so ugly, so humiliating…

Brring brring.

Lissa glanced at her watch. Eleven o'clock. Who'd be phoning at this hour? Not her brothers. It was one in the morning in Texas. Besides, they'd called her on Skype early this morning, singing "Happy Birthday," telling her how much they loved her.

"Even if you're gettin' old," Jake had said, and she'd laughed the way she knew they expected even though the truth was that she'd felt maybe a day short of one hundred.

She'd thanked them for their gifts. Wonderful, thoughtful gifts: an autographed copy of Joël Robuchon's version of the *Larousse Gastronomique*, a first edition of Escoffier's *Le Guide Culinaire*, a signed and framed photograph of Julia Child and Simone Beck grinning into the camera from a table at a Paris bistro.

Brring brring.

Her sisters had Skyped her next, singing "Happy Birthday" the same as her brothers had done.

"Except," she'd told them, "you guys sing on key."

They'd laughed and she'd thanked them for all-expenses-and-then-some weekend they'd arranged for her at, as Jaimie described it, "a super-deluxe-oh-how-amazing-you'll-never-want-to-leave" spa just outside San Diego.

"We left the dates open," Emily had added. "We know how busy you are."

Busy frying chicken parts, Lissa had almost said, but hadn't.

Even her father had phoned from wherever he was. Well, not exactly. An aide had placed the call for him. "Hold, please, for General Wilde," an impersonal voice had intoned, and then her old man had said *Hello, Lissa, how are you, happy birthday, did you get my present?* and she'd said *Hello, father, I'm fine and yes, I got the Tiffany's gift certificate, thank you very much*, and she figured she deserved bonus points for not telling him precisely what he could do with that certificate and all the personal warmth it brought with it.

Brring brring.

Where had she left her cell phone? It was right where it should have been, in the rear pocket of her jeans. She grabbed it and glanced at the screen.

Talk about coincidences…

"Marcia," she said brightly, "you must be telepathic! I was just thinking about you."

"Haven't heard from you in a while," her agent said briskly.

"I know. Well, the last time we spoke—"

"Listen, I know it's late, but I have something for you and I need a quick yes or no."

Lissa sat up straight. "Something good?"

"You want some blunt advice, toots? You're not in any position to be asking me questions like that."

"Meaning this isn't something good?"

"Meaning, how about if I ask the questions? Did you ever do any real cooking?"

"What are you talking about?"

"See, you're approaching this the wrong way. What's with the attitude? It gets you in trouble all the time. Mouthing off to Raoul What's-His-Face like you did—"

Mouthing off was precisely what she had not done, Lissa almost said, but it was too late for the truth.

"Never mind. It's all water under the bridge. Just answer the question. Can you do everyday stuff? Forget the edible flowers, the sprigs of rosemary, the goat cheese tarts."

"I have never done a goat cheese tart in my—"

"Lissa. Answer the question. Can you do roasts? Stew? Stuff like that."

Recipes danced through Lissa's head. *Poulet rôti aux herbes. Pot-au-feu.*

"You still there?"

"Yes," Lissa said quickly, "of course I can." She cleared her throat. She could feel hope rising within her, but she wasn't going let it get to her until she knew more. "What are we talking about here? An American-style restaurant?"

"American food. Exactly."

"Upscale, right? Because, you know—"

"Because you attended *Le Cordon Bleu.* Trust me. I know. The thing is, this place needs a cook who can do things with locally-produced ingredients."

Oh God! Lissa felt her pulse beat quicken. Alice Waters. Wolfgang Puck. Tom Colicchio.

"Can you do that? Cook natural?"

"Absolutely!"

"OK. Fine. I'll tell them you'll take the job."

"Just like that?"

"Just like what? They need a cook. You need a job. Put 'em both together—"

"No tryout? No interview?"

"They need a cook, fast. You need a job, fast. You wanna waste time with nonsense?"

Like most good agents, Marcia knew how to get to the point. It was just that this was so far from Lissa's past experiences…

In the exalted world of haute cuisine, meaning meals that

cost what some people paid in rent, you met the restaurant's owner or his rep, you sat for an interview, talked food, talked finances and recipes and customer tastes and management expectations. Then you cooked a meal for the owners, perhaps for a small, exclusive group of steady patrons.

"I need an answer. Yes? No? What's it gonna be?"

Lissa rolled her bottom lip between her teeth.

"What about money? Contract terms?"

"Month-to-month contract."

"Month-to-month? That's not standard. I don't usually—" She didn't usually go jobless, either, Lissa reminded herself. "OK. I guess they want to be sure they're hiring the right person. See, that's why an interview would be—"

"I'm waiting. You in or out?"

A long breath. "What are they paying?"

Marcia snapped out a number. It was a decent one.

"Lissa? I'm still waiting."

"Yeah. OK. I guess that's the good thing about working month to month. We can renegotiate at the end of thirty days. What about bennies?"

"Standard stuff. Medical. Dental. Sundays off."

"They're closed Sundays?"

"You could say that. One other weekday, you'll work it out with the boss. Two weeks of vacation after six months if you last that long. Plus room and board."

"Huh?"

Marcia gave a gusty sigh. "Didn't I mention? This is a ranch."

"A what?"

"A ranch. Horses. Cows. Whatever the fuck wanders

around on a ranch." There was a tiny pause. "In Montana."

"Forget that. I'm not—"

"It's a big place. Several thousand acres. You grew up in ranching country, right?"

Lissa had grown up on El Sueño, a ranch the size of a small nation that had belonged to Wildes for generations, and she'd left it as soon as she could because ranching and ranches were definitely not her thing.

"I did. And I don't like—"

"Nobody's asking you to ride the range."

Lissa chewed on her lip again. "What is this place? A dude ranch? A resort?"

"Listen, I don't have time for Twenty Questions. I got to get back to these people. I promised them an answer tonight."

Lissa had never been to Montana, but she knew a lot about it. Montana was the western state where the mega-rich played at being ranchers. They bought enormous spreads of land, spent fortunes duding them up, visited once in a blue moon and pretended they were cowboys.

And they entertained.

Hollywood glitterati. Directors. Producers. People who could afford to play at being John Wayne for a long weekend. That explained the question about basic cooking. She'd be expected to provide supposedly down-home meals that were actually elegant ones in disguise, and she'd have the pleasure of using mint and haricots verts and kale straight from the garden, eggs fresh from the henhouse.

Best of all, she could make contacts, maybe even connect with guests who'd be so taken with the idea of basic elegance that they'd want to fund a restaurant— and that would be what she'd call it, *Basic Elegance…*

"Lissa? I'm waiting. You in or not?"

"What about staff?"

"What about it? You'll work that out with the owner."

Lissa drew a long, steadying breath.

"OK. I'm in. Just tell me where to be and when."

"They'll send a plane for you. Seven tomorrow morning, at LAX."

"I'll take my car. I'll need wheels once I'm there, Marcia."

"It's a sixteen-hour drive."

"But—"

"I'll have them add a car to that list of bennies. You good with that?"

A decent salary. A roof over her head. A car. A chance to establish herself. And no more I-adore-myself actors littering her life.

"Yes. I'm fine with it. Where at LAX?"

Marcia told her. Gave her the details. And then, just before she hung up, she said something completely out of character.

She said, "Good luck."

* * *

The phone at the Triple G Ranch rang at the same time the wheezing grandfather clock in the hall struck half past eleven.

Nick Gentry, sprawled on his belly on an ancient leather sofa, groaned in his sleep, felt blindly for a throw pillow and jammed it over his head.

The phone and the clock pealed again.

"Goddammit," Nick snarled, rolled over—and landed on the floor.

He cursed again at the sharp pain that radiated through his leg. *It'll get better,* the physical therapists said. Yeah. Right. Maybe in a century or two.

Where the fuck was he? He opened one eye, saw the moose head hanging on the wall, the glassy-eyed grizzly pawing the air in the corner, the mounted bass that had to have been on steroids doing its eternal swim beside the moose, and groaned again.

He was in the den at the Triple G.

Jesus, how he hated this place!

A big wet tongue slobbered across his face.

Nick shoved aside the big-as-a-pony black Newfoundland that went with the tongue. He struggled up on his ass, then felt in the pockets of his jeans, his quilted vest, his plaid wool shirt, and finally found the phone.

"This better be good," he said as he put it to his ear.

"It's Marcia Lowry, Mr. Bannister."

The dog licked at him again. Nick grabbed the huge muzzle and moved it aside.

"Who?"

"Marcia Lowry. The agent. From Cooks Unlimited?"

Nick closed his eyes, then blinked them open. What he'd meant was, who was Mr. Bannister? For a minute there, he'd forgotten the name he'd used when he'd phoned Cooks Unlimited. Hell, he'd more or less forgotten he'd phoned Cooks Unlimited to start with.

"Yeah. Right. So, you have somebody for me?"

"I do, Mr. Bannister. In accordance with your instructions, I told her your plane would pick her up at LAX tomorrow."

Nick grabbed a crutch and staggered to his feet. Bad move; it made his head feel as if it might explode, never mind what it did to his leg.

"What's with the 'she' business, Lowry? I told you, I wanted a man. This isn't a place for a woman."

"I made several calls on your behalf, sir. I'm afraid this was the best I could do on such short notice. If you'd contacted me sooner or if you could just give me another week—"

"I have half a dozen men to feed here. I gave you the same notice my last cook gave me."

"I understand that, Mr. Bannister. And you have to understand that the only person who showed any interest in this job was Ms. Wilde."

Nick found his way to the kitchen, hobbling, bumping against things in the dark, the Newf damn near plastered to his side.

Coffee. He needed coffee, black and strong.

The coffeepot was empty.

He tucked the phone between his shoulder and his ear— that was one of the things he hated about cell phones, how tough it was to tuck the fuckers between your shoulder and your ear and what in Christ was he supposed to do with the crutch? It took a few seconds before he managed to juggle the crutch, the phone and the kettle, but finally he turned on the water and filled it.

"She knows we're in the mountains?"

"She knows you're in Montana, sir, of course."

"She knows she'll be cooking for a bunch of misfits?"

"She is a trained and experienced chef, Mr. Bannister."

"I need a cook, not a chef." Nick plugged in the kettle and reached for the coffee canister. The Newf nosed his thigh and Nick sighed, dug his hand into a tin of dog biscuits that stood on the counter and held one out.

Slurp.

The biscuit vanished into a wet, eager maw.

"She's up for this job?"

"She is."

"Why?"

"Why what, sir?"

"You said she's a chef. So why does she want to work here?"

"She needs a new position."

"Meaning what? Nobody else will hire her?"

"Meaning, *sir*, you need a cook and Lissa Wilde needs employment."

Nick started to measure out the coffee, thought the hell with it and dumped the coffee into the Chemex straight from the canister. The pot was the one affectation he'd held on to, the one link he still maintained between the man he'd been and—*let's be blunt, Gentry*—the cripple he'd become.

"Bravely spoken," he said. "But I'm telling you right now, if this Liza Wile doesn't work out, I'm going to drag your sorry ass up here and hand you a frying pan and a spatula."

"It's Lissa, sir. Lissa Wilde. *W-i-l-d-e.*" Marcia made a sound that might have been a chuckle. "And, believe me, Mr. Bannister, with all due respect, I'd sooner labor in the fires of hell than go to the ass-end of nowhere and cook for a bunch of cowboys."

Nick laughed. The sound was rusty, but he hadn't been doing much laughing lately.

"I told her you'd provide her with an automobile."

"Do I sound like a car dealer?"

"You sound like a man who needs a cook. I thought we'd already established that. Sir."

Nick ran his hand through his hair. What the hell. There were half a dozen vehicles parked around the ranch. Giving the new cook the keys to one of them wouldn't be a problem.

"Yeah. Right. OK, Lowry. I'm gonna hope this works out."

"The same here. Good night, Mr. Bannister."

Nick disconnected. The kettle gave a thin whistle and he picked it up and poured boiling water into the Chemex.

The last cook had simply up and left two days ago.

"This ain't no ranch," he'd said, "it's a hellhole. And you is one nasty son of a bitch to work for, Gentry."

"Thanks for the compliment," Nick had said, "and the name is Bannister."

"The hell it is, but frankly I don't give a crap what you call yourself. I ain't workin' for you no more. I'd rather go to Billings and put in time at a McD's."

Nick looked for a clean mug and found none. No problem. He grabbed one from the sink, gave it a quick rinse, then depressed the plunger on the Chemex.

The woman flying in tomorrow had to be desperate for job. That was pretty obvious. Well, he was desperate for a cook. If she could fry eggs and grill steaks, they were halfway to success.

He'd been away from this part of the country for years, but he'd grown up here. Cooks who worked this kind of itinerant life tended to be old or ugly or drunks, or maybe all three.

Nick poured the coffee, jammed the crutch under his arm, picked up the mug and somehow made it back to his office. The night's bottle of bourbon was on a lamp table. He put the mug on the table, picked up the bottle and added a hefty slug to his coffee.

This Liza or Lisa or Lissa Wilde could be homely enough to scare small children. She could be old enough to have mothered Methuselah. What she couldn't be was a drunk because one drunk per falling-down ranch was enough.

And wasn't that a laugh?

Nick sank onto the sofa. The Newf sank down at his feet and laid his massive head on Nick's foot.

"You're a stupid dog," Nick said, "you know that? Hanging around me. You'd be better off picking on some other sucker."

The Newf looked up and gave a gentle woof. Nick sighed, reached out and scratched him behind the ear. The dog sighed, too, in ecstasy. "Stupid dog," Nick said again, but without any heat.

What did dogs know about winners and losers?

"Nothing," Nick said, and drank some of the bourbon-laced coffee.

Once upon a time, Nick Gentry had been a winner. The Clint Eastwood of the Twenty-First Century, some stupid blogger had called him.

How about a new title? Nick Gentry. The Drunk of the

Decade.

"Don't leave out Gimp," Nick said, raising his mug in salute.

Hell, nobody could leave that out. Not when one of his legs was about as useless as tits on a bull.

CHAPTER TWO

ONE GOOD THING about living alone.
You could pack up your things and leave on a moment's notice.

OK. It took a little longer to get ready, but that was only because you had to spend a little time deciding what to take and what to leave behind.

Lissa took her suitcase from the closet, placed it on the bed and unzipped it. Then she opened her closet and the drawers in her dresser and narrowed her eyes.

Montana. Spring in Montana. A little cool, maybe. Sweaters. A light jacket. Jeans. T- shirts. What else? This place was a ranch. A resort for the rich. OK. Add a long skirt—she had one she'd bought at a street fair last year, denim embroidered with flowers at the waistband and hem. Where the heck was it?

There. Excellent. If she had to mingle with the guests, the skirt and a black cashmere sweater, long-sleeved, kind of low cut, would be perfect. Chefs didn't often make appearances, but one of the things she might do at this place was institute a special buffet night.

"Excellent idea, Melissa," she said briskly, and she added the white silk pants and black silk top she'd scooped up at a resale shop in Beverly Hills a couple of years back.

A buffet night.

Ranch-themed, of course.

A butter sculpture of a horse. She'd turned out to be surprisingly good at butter sculptures. The *pot-au-feu*. A big pot of chili. She'd make it with red wine and call it something ranchy. Cowboy Chili, maybe. Dumplings. Sourdough bread. Maybe trout. Or bass. Or whatever it was she'd vaguely heard people say they fished for in Montana. And game. There had to be game. Pheasants, wild turkey, quail, whatever. She had a recipe for pheasant with a sauce to die for. The sauce included a secret ingredient—90 percent cacao dark chocolate. Not a problem. She could order it online, have it overnighted to the ranch…

And why hadn't she thought to ask Marcia the name of the place?

No matter. She'd find out soon enough.

She packed quickly. Her chef's whites. Her toque. She was proud of the hat; it marked her as a professional.

So did her knives.

"You mean you have to provide your own knives when you work at a restaurant?" Emily had said when she'd found Lissa poring over a catalogue of restaurant equipment a couple of years ago when all the Wildes were home for a long Fourth of July weekend.

Lissa had looked up from a page of gorgeous Japanese carbon steel.

"Well, you don't have to, but serious chefs always have their own knives."

"Why?" Em had pulled a pair of imaginary pistols from an imaginary gun belt and mimed twirling them. "Is it a chef's version of *have gun, will travel*?"

"It's more like a doctor wanting her own stethoscope."

"Huh. I never knew that. I've waitressed in New York," Emily had said, and hurriedly added, "well, not anymore, of course, now that I'm working for an art collector, but when I did waitress, I never saw a cook with his own knives."

"What kind of restaurant did you work in?"

"A diner."

Lissa had grinned. "Diners have cooks, Em. Restaurants, real restaurants, have chefs. And how come I never knew you put in a stint as a waitress?"

"It was only for a couple of weeks," Emily had replied, and she'd moved the conversation on to other things because, as it turned out, she'd worked as a waitress at more than one place and she had, in fact, never worked for an art collector.

But that was history. It had nothing to do with this situation.

Besides, Emily really hadn't lied.

Well, she had, but it had been a white lie, and those didn't count. You told them because you had to. You told them to keep another person from finding out that things weren't as good as they seemed.

Dammit.

A lie was a lie was a lie. She should know, Lissa thought

with a sigh, because she'd been lying to her family for months.

She paused, looked into the suitcase, did a quick check. What more should she pack? Sandals. Hey, spring was on its way, wasn't it? A pair of heels because you never knew. Her sturdy I-can-stay-on-my-feet-all-day kitchen clogs. Sneakers, except she'd wear them instead of packing them.

Same as Emily, she'd been lying as much to keep from admitting her failure as to keep her family from worrying.

Was it really so bad to let them think she'd deliberately left her job at a fancy Hollywood eatery to try her hand at movie set catering?

"No," she said firmly.

No. It wasn't.

The last thing she wanted was her brothers barging in with offers of money and contacts and advice, advice as if time had run backward and she was once again a teenager suffering under the scrutiny and well-meant advice of three big brothers. And she certainly didn't want Jaimie or Emily phoning her a thousand times a day to try to cheer her up. She didn't want pats on the back or checks in the mail or to be told what a great chef she was.

All she wanted was to find a way out of this—this disaster that she'd stumbled into. And heading up the kitchen at a fancy Montana resort was just the ticket.

Her suitcase was full. It was stuffed. She had everything she could possibly need…

No, she didn't.

Lissa reached for the hot pink *Pleasure Pleaser* in its hot pink wrapper.

"We're going on a trip, sweetheart," she told it. "Won't that be nice?"

Then she tucked the vibrator in with her panties, closed the suitcase lid and fought with the zipper until it finally closed.

A fancy dude ranch. Or an equally fancy resort. In Montana, where La La Land's rich elite went for fun.

"Oh give me a home where the buffalo roam…"

Never mind.

They were hiring her for her *pot-au-feu*, not her singing.

And a damn good thing, too.

* * *

By one the following afternoon, singing was the last thing on Lissa's mind.

Recipes? That was different, but she wasn't thinking *pot-au-feu*. She was thinking Marcia the Agent smeared with honey and staked out on an anthill.

"You lied, Marcia," Lissa said. "Dammit, you *lied*!"

Of course, Marcia wasn't there to hear her. Nobody was.

She was standing next to a deserted runway in the absolute middle of absolutely nowhere. Just her, her suitcase, an encircling set of mountains, a stretch of empty land before her, a hundred billion trillion trees behind her, a biting wind, a sky full of snow and in that sky, a rapidly vanishing dot—the plane that had brought her here.

This was a godforsaken wilderness, and if she ever saw Marcia again, she'd punch her lights out the way she should have done with Raoul, whose fault all of this was.

Never mind all that nonsense.

What mattered was the basic, simple, non-arguable fact that if there was a resort here, she'd be damned if she could see it.

The plane that had picked her up at LAX had been a sleek Learjet, shiny and bright on the outside, but not quite what she'd expected on the inside. Lots of leather, lots of plush carpeting, sure, the same as on the Wilde family jets, except here there was the feeling of things let go. The leather seats could have used a polishing. The same for the Lucite tables. Did the ranch fly guests in on this plane? Maybe the slightly worn look of things was deliberate, a way to convince people that they were leaving the glitter of Hollywood for the down and dirty reality of ranching country.

Seemed reasonable.

Still, the slight scruffiness had put her off a little.

Thankfully, there was nothing scruffy about the crew—a pilot and co-pilot who were professional if not very forthcoming.

"Excuse me," she'd said, after her suitcase had been stowed and she'd been told to take a seat and buckle up. "What's the name of this resort we're flying to?"

The co-pilot, whose job it had been to escort her into the cabin, gave her a puzzled look.

"The name of the resort?"

"The ranch," Lissa had said. "I took the job of chef late last night and I never did ask—"

"Chef?"

"Uh huh. The chef. The person in charge of the kitchen?"

"Oh. The cook. Right."

Evidently, the down-home feel extended to titles, too.

"Right," she'd said agreeably. "The cook. And I know it sounds ridiculous, but it was late and I never did get the resort's name."

"The resort," the co-pilot said. The guy seemed to have a problem with repeating things. There was probably a name for it, but right then all Lissa had cared about was finding out the name of the place that had hired her.

"Yes. The ranch. You know. What's it called?"

"The Triple G."

More down-homeyness. Simple. Straightforward. Heck, why not?

Yeah. Fine. But there was such a thing as too much down-homeyness. Such a thing as where in hell was everybody? She'd asked the co-pilot as he'd helped her from the plane, but he'd pointed to the sky, said, "Snow coming. Sorry, but we've got to take off," and the next thing, she was standing here, to all intents and purposes the last human being on the planet.

A golf-ball-sized knot seemed to lodge in her throat.

If this was somebody's idea of a bad joke—

A sudden gust of wind whipped Lissa's hair over her face and, as it did, wet stuff hit her in the eye.

Snow. Just that fast. Snow, not the kind you saw on resort postcards. The kind that meant business. Within seconds, it began blanketing her cotton jacket.

Lissa put down her suitcase, opened her shoulder bag and took out her cell phone. Marvelous things, cell phones. They meant safety. Security. Human contact…

Mostly, they meant they were useless if you couldn't see those miserable little bars on the home screen.

"Hello?" she said. "Hello? Hello? Hello?" Nothing. "Dammit," she said, dumping the phone in her bag and her hands in her pockets.

Man, it was *cold*! And that snow... It was coming down like crazy. You lived in La La Land long enough, you forgot about snowstorms. This one was doing its best to obliterate everything.

Lissa's teeth began to chatter.

She could see the headline now. *Spring thaw leads to discovery of body of woman dumb enough to fly into a place devoid of humans. No signs of life except for vultures and bears and...*

Hell. Vultures and bears and...

And, what was that?

A light. A pair of lights.

"Yes!"

Headlights were slicing through the wall of snow.

And now she could see something. A speck. A blob of red. It was a car. No. A truck, bouncing toward her at breakneck speed, its engine howling like a demented beast.

Well, no.

It wasn't howling. It was wheezing and groaning like a creature in its death throes. And it wasn't red, it was the color of rust because, Jesus, it *was* rust. It was a pickup truck, probably older than she was.

And it was coming straight at her.

Lissa stumbled back. Felt her foot catch in something.

Grass under the snow. A tree root. What did it matter? Her foot caught and she went down on her ass.

The truck skidded to a stop a couple of feet away.

The engine stopped groaning, the sound replaced by a tick-tick-tick and by the sound of its windshield wipers. Correction. Its windshield wiper. Swish, swoosh, creak. Swish, swoosh, creak.

Lissa got to her feet.

The pickup didn't move.

The doors didn't open.

The windows didn't slide down.

Just that single wiper blade, sweeping across the windshield.

The cracked windshield.

A chill that had nothing to do with wind or snow or cold danced down her spine.

"Hello?" she said. The word came out a croak. "Hello?" she said again, louder and stronger.

The cold of this graceful Montana spring had soaked through her jeans. Her feet were wet and numb inside her canvas sneakers.

"Dammit," she said, but *louder* and *stronger* were no longer useful adverbs. Old, awful movies were flashing through her head, especially the one about the demon truck with no driver at the wheel.

Wrong.

There was a driver.

She knew that because now, the door was opening. A booted foot emerged. A denim-clad leg. Then a hand. A big hand, gloved in beat-up leather. An arm. A crutch.

A crutch?

It was definitely a crutch.

The gloved hand planted it firmly in the snow. A powerful-looking arm settled over the top.

A man swung down from the cab.

Her first impression was that he was big.

Really big.

Six two, maybe six three. Broad-shouldered. Long-legged.

In other words, big.

He was dressed in denim. Jeans faded and ripped. Jacket with a tear in the elbow. Beat-up boots. An equally beat-up Stetson pulled down so low that she couldn't see his face.

He was, in a word, scruffy. Scruffy even to her, and she'd grown up on a ranch. A real one. Cowboys, ranch hands, were not Hollywood's idea of the cool Western hero. They were often big men. They definitely wore denim and boots and Stetsons. They worked hard; you got dirty, working hard.

But this man was, well, scruffy.

And if he and his rusted truck were the duo responsible for meeting guests at the airstrip and driving them to the resort property…

Something didn't feel right.

Guests often flew into El Sueño. Friends of her father, the general. Of the family. Her brothers ran charity events a couple of times a year.

Guests were met at the airstrip by well-groomed cowboys driving well-cared for vehicles.

They weren't met like this.

The wind whipped a strand of pale blond hair across Lissa's

face. She grabbed it and shoved it behind her ear. Tried to, anyway, but her fingers were almost numb with cold. All of her was. She was minutes away from turning into Frosty the Snowman, and the guy sent to meet her had yet to say a word or reach for her suitcase. All he did was stand next to the truck, lean heavily on his crutch and stare at her. At least, she assumed he was staring. She couldn't tell because of that hat.

No way was this right.

Why hadn't she asked Marcia more questions? If she'd known the name of this place last night, she could have Googled it. She could have Googled the owner—and who, exactly, *was* the owner? She didn't know that, either. All she knew was that she didn't like the feel of things, didn't like how they were going or not going, to be accurate, and—

"Who the hell are you?"

The cowboy's voice was rough. Raw as gravel. It suited how he looked.

"I asked you a question, lady. Who are you?"

She was a woman who wanted to blink her eyes open and discover that this was just a bad dream, was who she was, but this was not a dream.

She was alone in the middle of a rapidly-worsening snowstorm with a man who looked like an extra from a really, really bad spaghetti Western.

"Are you deaf? I said—"

"I heard what you said." Lissa lifted her chin. "A better question is who are *you*?"

The man hadn't expected that response. She could tell by the way he cocked his head.

Good.

She had lived in Paris, and not in an *arrondissement* favored by tourists. She'd lived in Chicago, and not many tourists had frequented those streets, either. Even Hollywood had its dark side.

The bottom line was that she was street-smart. And showing fear was a sign of weakness. Never mind that her heart was trying to claw its way out of her chest.

She had attitude. That was all she had right now, and attitude was going to have to be enough.

"Answer the question. Who are you?"

Lissa drew herself up. "My name is Lissa Wilde."

"No."

"Yes. I am Lissa Wilde. The new chef."

"The cook?" His gaze ran over her. "The hell you are."

"I was hired last night and—" And, why in hell was she explaining herself to him? Lissa narrowed her eyes. "What is your name?"

"Why?"

"What do you mean, why? I want to know to whom I'm speaking."

He laughed. More or less. It certainly wasn't a nice sound.

"To whom?"

"To whom. Exactly. I want to know to whom I'm speaking so that I can tell your employer how insolent you are."

"It's Nick."

"Nick what?"

"Nick Bannister. You want me to spell that for you?"

"And what is the name of your employer?"

"Don't you know? You think you're the new cook, but you don't know the name of the man you'll be working for?"

Lissa felt a flush rise in her cheeks.

"As I said, I was offered the position only last night and—"

"And you jumped at it. What's the problem, Ms. Wilde? You desperate for work?"

"You aren't just insolent, Mr. Bannister, you're rude."

"And we're both going to get snowbound if we stand here much longer." Nick Bannister limped forward a couple of steps. Lissa took an automatic step back. So much for the *no fear* thing. "Hand over that suitcase."

"I'll take care of it myself."

"Sweet Jesus, lady, I'm not going to steal it. Hand the damned thing over."

"Is it possible for you to complete a sentence without using an obscenity?"

"You think those are obscenities? You've got a lot to learn. Now, give me the suitcase."

"No."

"Yes."

"No."

He cursed again, a string of words that she'd heard in some of the kitchens she'd worked back when she was just starting out. Then he closed his hand around the handle of the suitcase.

Around her hand.

His was big. It all but swallowed hers. And it was hard. Lissa had strong, hard hands for a woman. Years of chopping and slicing and handling oversized skillets had that effect on a woman's hands, but his grip was far more powerful than hers.

Still, she fought him for control of the suitcase.

"Goddammit," he said and as he did the crutch slipped and he teetered on the snow-covered ground.

Lissa reacted automatically, let go of the handle, reached out to steady him. He jerked back.

"Did I ask for your damned help?"

"Trust me," she said coldly. "I wasn't trying to help, I was trying to shove that crutch out from under your arm so you'd fall on your ass in the snow!"

There was a second of stunned silence. Then he laughed. Or, at least, he made that sound again, the one that resembled a laugh.

It made her even more angry. "You think this is funny?"

He stared at her while the seconds ticked away. Then he grabbed her suitcase and headed for the truck.

Now what?

Did she go with him to who knew where, or did she...

What?

There was no place else to go. Besides, once he dropped her off at the ranch house, the office, the main building that was surely not too far way, she'd never have to set eyes on him again.

Lissa gritted her teeth and marched to the truck, reached it in time to see the cowboy dump her case in the back, limp to the driver's door and toss his crutch inside the cab.

He climbed in. It wasn't easy; his leg was stiff as a board and he had to grab it with his hands to get his foot positioned under the dashboard.

"You can drive like that?" she said, before she could censor the words.

He looked at her.

She couldn't see his eyes, but she felt the cold rage in the look he gave her.

"I can drive just fine," he said tightly. "Now, are you getting in or am I going to leave you here?"

Head up, back straight, she went to the passenger door. The door wouldn't open. She pulled at the handle, jiggled it, but nothing happened until Nick Bannister leaned across and shoved the door open.

She climbed inside the cab.

To her surprise, it was clean. More than clean. The dashboard was polished. So was the old-fashioned leather bench seat. The cab even smelled good. Leather. Pine. Cold, clean mountain air.

"You might want to hang onto your seat. I drive fast."

"Good. The faster, the better. I can hardly wait to meet your boss and tell him—"

"—that I'm rude and, what was it? Oh yeah. Insolent. Trust me, lady. It'll be a waste of time. He already knows all about me."

"Maybe you think the fact that you got me out of the weather will save you, but I promise you, it won't."

"I'd do the same for a heifer. Damned if I want the trouble of finding you frozen stiff come the spring thaw."

Lissa swung toward him. "Just in case nobody's told you, you are one unpleasant, nasty SOB!"

"Sorry to disappoint you, Duchess, but you're not the first."

"I'm happy to hear that there are others here who are as

discerning as I am. And do not call me duchess."

"Must you always get the last word?"

"Yes."

She thought that maybe his lips twitched. She still couldn't see much of his face, just enough to know that he had a cleft chin, a square jaw, and probably a week's worth of dark stubble. Not that she gave a damn what he looked like. Count Dracula or Prince Charming, Nick Bannister was a foul-mouthed, mean-tempered piece of work.

All that mattered was reaching the lodge and meeting the person who'd hired her.

There was no point in judging the place by the isolation of the airstrip or by her surly escort.

No point at all, Lissa assured herself…

And hoped to hell that she was right.

CHAPTER THREE

IT TOOK TWENTY minutes to reach the first signs of civilization.

Actually, that was an overstatement.

What they reached was a cluster of wooden outbuildings barely visible through the heavy snowfall, and a handful of what she assumed were corrals.

On a rise in the distance, she could see glimpses of a dark structure. Was that the lodge? It was big, but not big enough to house many guests. Maybe what she was looking at was a separate building from the lodge. A dining room. A card room. A bar.

She sat forward in her seat.

"Is that the Triple G?"

"Is what the Triple G?"

She looked at the cowboy. The short exchange was the first since they'd driven away from the airstrip, but his tone of voice was that of a man who'd been beleaguered with endless questions.

"That building, of course. Is it the Triple G?"

He looked at her, then back at what she assumed was the road. It was difficult to tell because of the snow.

"You've been on the Triple G since the plane landed."

Lissa rolled her eyes. "I'm not an idiot, Bannister. I understand that we're on Triple G land. What I meant was, is that building ahead of us the hotel?"

He looked at her again.

"The what?"

God. Which one of them was the idiot?

"The hotel," she said with exaggerated patience. "The main house. The lodge. The resort. Whatever you want to call it. Is that where the guests stay? I thought it would be bigger... What?"

He was laughing. Laughing! The desire to add him to her *People She Wanted To Slug* list was strong, but so was her will to survive. Hitting a man driving an old truck far too fast through a snowstorm was probably not a good idea, and it showed just how far from reality she'd fallen that hitting a man who used a crutch didn't even enter into the equation.

"What's so funny?"

His laughter stopped as quickly as it had begun.

"Nothing."

"Don't give me that 'nothing' routine! What were you laughing at?"

She might as well have been talking to a statue. Bannister clamped his lips together—she could see that they were firm lips, nicely shaped, which was pretty amazing when you realized that nothing else about him was nice—and stepped even harder on the gas.

The truck gave an alarming lurch. The engine coughed like *Mildred Pierce's* dying daughter and really, why on earth did she watch all those old movies? The tires whined and spun before finally gripping the gravel hidden beneath what looked like several inches of snow as the cowboy, not only Insolent and Rude but also Despicable, stepped hard on the gas. The truck lunged forward, made it up the rise, through an open gate, and came to a bone-jarring stop right in front of the building.

It was a house. Just a house. Nice, but nothing remarkable about it. A house that was two stories high, a house that was made of wood, a house with a front porch...

Nick Bannister shut off the engine.

Tick, tick, tick.

Lissa took a deep breath. Held it. Then let it out.

OK. She'd misunderstood Marcia. The Triple G wasn't a resort. It was a house people rented for long pseudo-Western weekends...

Except, why would they rent a house like this? Handsome, yes, but not spectacular. Not something out of Architectural Digest. Not something that would be featured in the Sunday real estate section of a big city newspaper.

Tick, tick, tick.

Lissa was ticking, too. Be cool, she told herself. There had to be a logical explanation.

"So," she said, very calmly, "what's this? The office?"

Mr. Despicable hobbled down from the cab of the truck,

hauled his crutch from behind the seat, shoved the padded part under his arm and looked up at her.

"You getting out?"

"I asked you a question."

"You're good at asking questions."

She craned her neck, her eyes following him as he made his way to the rear of the pickup. When she saw her suitcase somersault into the snow, she opened her door and climbed down.

"And you suck at answering them. I said, is this—"

"No."

She reached for her suitcase. He brushed past her and picked it up.

"I can do that," she said.

"Do you think I can't?"

The question was filled with hostility. Lissa thought of half a dozen answers and discarded every one of them. Instead, she followed in his footsteps as he crabbed his way up the two steps to the porch. The man was spoiling for a fight and she'd be damned if she'd oblige.

"You didn't answer my question," she said.

"Which question?"

"Is this building the lodge office?"

"No."

No. That was it. All of it. Could a person actually feel her blood pressure rise?

"If it isn't the office, what is it?"

"I told you. It's the Triple G."

"Dammit, Bannister—" Lissa swallowed the rest of her

words. She drew a long, steadying breath. She had to calm down. Letting this—this unpleasant cowboy piss her off wouldn't solve anything. "What I mean is, is this all of it?"

He paused at a big, weathered wood door and turned toward her.

"What you *mean* is where are the hot tubs? The fire pit? The luxury accommodations? The candlelit dining room? The bar with its four-hundred-bucks-a-bottle vintage wines?"

There was an edge to his voice. And there was something else about his voice…

It seemed familiar.

How could that be? She'd yet to get a real look at his face, but if she'd ever met him before, she'd know it. Who could forget somebody this unpleasant? Still, he seemed familiar in other ways. His height. Those shoulders. The way he held himself. And that voice, aside from the edge to it, was, well, familiar, too. Deep. A little rough. And, despite everything, sexy.

Lissa blew a strand of snow-dampened hair out of her eyes. Ridiculous.

The man was a stranger. She'd never seen him until today.

As for what he'd just said, and with such disdain… Well, he was a cowboy. He was a man accustomed to a rugged life. Things like hot tubs and saunas wouldn't mean much to him, but they were the amenities that attracted the kind of clientele she wanted to cook for, the kind of clientele that had brought her here, and she wasn't about to apologize for that.

And, really, there was no logic in making an enemy of a man who worked on the Triple G, so she forced herself to speak pleasantly.

"You're right. I *am* wondering where those things are. I did notice several outbuildings, but where's everything else? Maybe it's the snow, but I can't see much from here."

"There's a bunkhouse a couple of hundred yards away."

"I'm not interested in the bunkhouse. It's a nice touch, though. Authentic."

He laughed again. God almighty, she *hated* that laugh! Remaining pleasant was going to be difficult.

"Oh, it's authentic, all right."

"Look, I'm not trying to pick a quarrel. I just want to know where the lodge is."

"There is no lodge."

So much for trying to be pleasant! Lissa slapped her hands on her hips.

"Are you being deliberately dense? So I'm using the wrong word. You know what I mean." The cowboy dropped the suitcase, opened the massive wooden door and kicked the suitcase through it. "And do not, I repeat, *do not* treat my luggage as if it were a—a soccer ball!"

She swept past him, snatched up the suitcase…and found herself standing in an entry hall that looked pretty much like the entry hall in lots of ranch homes back in Texas. Not El Sueño, of course; despite its prize-horse-breeding program, its cattle, its acres of land given over to oil, El Sueño was a mansion disguised as a house, but growing up she'd had friends who lived on working ranches and they'd all looked like this. Dark wood paneling. Dark wood floors. Dead animals staring glassy-eyed from the walls. The smell of coffee and the faint-but-always-there scent of horses permeating the air.

A knot formed in Lissa's belly. She heard the despicable cowboy limp up behind her, felt his presence loom over her.

"Welcome to the Triple G," he said.

He didn't say it nicely, but to hell with that.

"This," Lissa said slowly, "this is it?"

"This is it," he said, unbuttoning his denim jacket and working it off without dislodging the crutch under his left arm. "Not quite what you expected, Duchess?"

"Is it a—a boarding house?"

"It's a home. At least, it used to be. Now it's just tired house on a tired ranch."

Nick limped past Lissa Wilde and hung his jacket on a big hook in one of the pine walls. He left the Stetson on. The last thing he needed was for a woman heading back to La La Land to recognize him. There were a dozen rumors about what had happened to him and where he was; he certainly wasn't going to send the Wilde babe back to Hollywood to spread the word that she'd found the elusive Nick Gentry.

"But—but Marcia said…"

"Yeah. I can just imagine what she said. It was enough to bring you running in hopes of shaking your shapely ass for some Hollywood hotshot, but there ain't no Hollywood hotshots here."

For a long moment, nothing happened. Lissa Wilde didn't move or speak. Her disappointment was damn near palpable and he almost felt sorry for her until he reminded himself that feeling sorry for someone changed nothing.

Besides, he knew the type.

He'd dealt with it from the minute he'd earned his first box-office hit.

Small-town girl, pretty enough—this one certainly was—grows up hearing people tell her she's beautiful, wins a couple of contests—Homecoming Queen, Miss Peach Blossom, whatever—and decides she's going to be the next hot movie queen. That she has no talent doesn't mean a damn. She figures all she needs is looks and a lucky break. Getting discovered by an agent while she's waiting tables. Being noticed by a director while she's working the bar at a fancy restaurant.

A hot babe passing herself off as a cook was a new one, but, hey, you wanted to make it big, you went with whatever you figured would work.

A cook. A chef. Right, Nick thought with world-weary cynicism. If Lissa Wilde— blond, blue-eyed, great face, five four or five, a hundred ten or twenty pounds of tits, legs and ass—had cooking skills, she'd picked them up working her way west in a succession of roadside diners.

It was just his luck that he'd have to tolerate her until the storm passed. The second it did, he'd call Hank, tell him to fly back from the airport at Billings—

"You have me all figured out."

Her voice was low. Frigid. Nick shrugged, or tried to. Shrugging was another of those simple things that turned out to be hard to do with a crutch under your arm.

"Yeah, well, it's not as if your type is unique."

She spun toward him. Fire blazed in her eyes. They were, he had to admit, interesting eyes. Blue, he'd thought…but maybe they were green.

Not that he gave a damn.

"You," she said, "you are, without question…"

"Yeah, yeah. A nasty, insolent SOB. You already said that."

"Those descriptions don't even come close." She dropped the suitcase, raised her chin, pointed an index finger at his chest. "I am a classically trained chef. I plan menus. I create dishes. I run a kitchen and supervise its staff." That pointing finger found its mark in the center of his rib cage and jabbed none too gently. "I do not, *do not ever* shake my ass at anybody. You got that, cowboy?"

"Uh huh. You're not the least bit interested in being the next Jennifer Lawrence or Megan Fox or Christ knows who else, discovered waiting tables or slinging hash at *The Griddle Café.*"

"I am *not* a wannbe actress! I am a chef! You think I'd have accepted this job in the middle of the wilderness if I weren't? Although it's pretty clear that there isn't a job here." Those amazing eyes narrowed. "Which brings me to the obvious question, Bannister. Why did you tell my agent you needed a cook?"

"Because I do. I need a cook. Not a chef. Not somebody who knows how to—how to glaze a pan—"

"Pans get deglazed, cowboy. Not glazed."

"Whatever they get, that's not what I need. This is a ranch. I have six guys sweating their balls off from dawn to dusk, and I need somebody to cook for them."

"Let me get this straight. You need somebody to cook for a—a bunch of ranch hands?"

She looked—what? Stunned. Disappointed. Well, why wouldn't she? She'd come here expecting a cushy job in a cushy place where she could cozy up to Hollywood royalty. Even on the odd chance that she really was a cook, she sure as hell wasn't the kind he needed.

He had half a dozen rough-and-ready guys who needed feeding three times a day, men who wouldn't know a quiche from a casserole. You couldn't do a day's work on fettuccine and foie gras. God knew he'd spent enough time in Hollywood to know what passed for food in the land of the infamously famous.

"You told this to Marcia?"

"Who?"

"My agent. She knew this?"

Did she? He couldn't remember exactly what the conversation had been. He'd phoned the agency only because he'd been desperate; he'd Googled cooks and cooking and one of the first ads that had come up was for something called Cooks Unlimited.

"She knew," he said, because what did it matter now? He was still without a cook and he had the feeling he would be for a long time to come. If his last cook had spread the word by now, nobody in three counties would want the job.

"I want to go back to L.A."

"Yeah. I'm sure you do."

"Immediately."

"Well, Duchess, there's a little problem with that. It's called weather."

"I don't care about the weather! You hear me, cowboy? I am not spending another minute here." She drew herself up, stepped closer and jabbed her finger into the center of his chest again. "You flew me in. Now you fly me—"

She gasped as Nick grabbed her hand.

"Do not," he said through this teeth, "do not wag your finger at me again!"

"Let go!"

"And," he growled, hauling her closer, "do not ever think of giving me orders. I'm in charge here."

"You?"

"Me. This is my ranch. Got that?"

"*You* try getting this!" She pulled her hand from his. Her chin lifted to an impossible height and she glared up at him. "I don't take orders, either. Not from anybody, but especially not from you. Understand?"

Nick stared at that gorgeous face. He just bet she didn't take orders. But she would. From somebody who knew how to give them. Who knew how to change that hard glare of anger in her eyes to a soft blur of passion. Who knew how to make her want to take the kind of orders that would bring her to a soft bed, to raising her arms to the man who'd ordered her there, to opening her legs for him...

Jesus.

He turned away as fast as his limited mobility permitted.

He'd been without a woman, without sex for too long. For months. He hadn't taken a woman to his bed since the accident.

That fucking accident.

And now this.

What unkind god had dropped this latest piece of bad news into his life?

"I said—"

"I heard what you said," he growled. He swung toward her and leaned down until they were eye to eye. Hers were, indeed, green—and bright with rage.

Yeah, well, he wasn't any happier with the situation than she was.

"Here's the deal, Duchess."

"Do not call me that!"

"You are here by mistake. Yours. Your agent's. Frankly, at this point, all I know is that you're here and you'll be here until the storm ends. Trust me. I don't like it any more than you do." Unplanned, his gaze dropped from her eyes to her mouth. Her lips were slightly parted; she was breathing as if she'd run a race.

Or as if she were lying, sated, beneath a man. Beneath him, in the big, cold, empty four-poster upstairs...and what did that have to do with anything?

Tomorrow night, once she was out of his way, he'd take the truck into town. Go to one of the bars that clung to the mountains near the couple of big resorts, resorts like the one she'd hoped to find here. He'd shave, tame his dark hair with some goop, put on the kind of outfit dime-store cowboys wore—tight jeans, polished Tony Lamas, Western shirt, clean Stetson—and find himself a woman who'd be happy with a one-night fling.

And if she said what he'd already heard a couple of times—*Hey, you look like Nick Gentry*—he'd grin and give her what had become his standard answer, that the real Nick Gentry only wished he looked like him...

And then what?

How good could he be in bed?

One leg that dragged. Hell, that gave out when he least expected it.

More to the point, one leg that looked as if it had been made by Dr. Frankenstein. What woman wouldn't find that a turn-on?

Nick straightened up and took a quick step back.

"Here's the deal. I'll put you up for the—"

"Dammit, I know why you seem so familiar! You're Nick Gentry!"

"No," he said coldly. "I'm not."

"Of course you are."

"Listen, Duchess, I've been told that before. It doesn't impress me."

She raised her eyebrows.

"Why would it?"

Nick blinked. "Well, Gentry's an actor. A star."

"And?"

"Well—well, he's—he's famous."

Lissa folded her arms. "Wolfgang Puck is famous."

"Who?"

"A chef. Wolfgang Puck. He's famous."

"Is there a point to this?"

"I've dealt with a lot of actors. Stars," she said, with a curl of the lip. "Believe me, I'm long past the point of being impressed, Mr. Gentry."

"I told you, I'm not Gentry. Hell, Gentry would be happy if he looked like me." The line fell as flat as it sounded. Her fault, goddammit, for making him use it. Nick covered his irritation by lifting up her suitcase. "Take one of the spare bedrooms upstairs." His smile was all teeth. "Unless you'd rather bunk with the boys. I'm sure they'd be delighted."

Lissa flushed. "Fine. I'll stay in one of the upstairs bedrooms for the night."

He wanted to laugh. She made it sound as if she were doing him a favor. Well, she owed him a favor, all right, after all the trouble he'd gone to getting her out here.

"And since you're so determined to convince me that you know how to cook, you can repay my hospitality by making supper."

"Not on your life."

"Does that mean you prefer the bunkhouse?"

Lissa gritted her teeth. "I assume," she said, each word frosted with icy sarcasm, "you have an indoor kitchen."

"To the left, past the stairs."

"You have a menu in mind?" she asked with saccharine sweetness. "*Boeuf bourguignon*? *Poulet* à *l'orange*?"

"Very funny."

"Yes." Her smile widened; it could have killed. "I'm known for my sense of humor."

"Find something and cook it. Just be sure it'll feed a bunch of hungry men."

That took the smug smile off her face. "What hungry men?"

"I told you. This is a working ranch, Duchess. I have six guys who'll be showing up in a couple of hours, cold, tired and hungry. They'll expect something that will stick to their—"

Thud!

Lissa Wilde spun toward the closed door at the end of the hall. "What was that?"

Aw, hell!

Nick knew what it was.

It was Brutus. The Newfoundland.

He'd confined the dog in his office when he went to the airstrip. The big dog loved snow. Keeping him in the truck cab would have been impossible; keeping him from scaring the new cook would be been equally impossible. Nick had learned the hard way that there were lots of people scared spitless by a dog the size of a bear.

Thud! Thud! Thud!

The office door shuddered. Lissa looked at Nick.

"*What*," she demanded, "is making that noise?"

He thought of telling her that it *was* a bear. That it was a crazed moose. In the end, there was no time to tell her anything.

Two more thuds and the office door flew open. A black shape as big as her old VW hurtled toward Lissa, panting and drooling, nails scrabbling over the worn wood floor.

"Whoa," she said, and Brutus woofed with joy when he spotted someone deserving of a Newfoundland welcome.

Amazing, considering that the dog never offered that welcome to anyone but him, but there wasn't time to think about that; there was only time to say *Brutus* in a sharp voice...

Too late,

The dog flung himself at Lissa, paws flattened against her shoulders. A long pink tongue slopped across her face.

They went down in a heap, woman and dog, and Nick

cursed and started the seemingly endless procedure that would lead to his divesting himself of the crutch, leaning it against the wall at an angle where he'd be able to reach it after he got them apart, and how in hell was he doing to do that when squatting or bending was damn near out of the ques—

"Oh, you beautiful baby," Lissa Wilde said.

Nick blinked.

Brutus's tail was wagging like a metronome gone insane.

Nick looked at his traitorous dog and the woman who wanted him to believe that she was a chef. The dog was lying on top of her; her arms were wound around his neck.

Nick felt every muscle in his body turn hard.

And decided he had to be crazy, because surely he was the first man on earth to envy a dog.

CHAPTER FOUR

H E HAD DEFINITELY been too long without a woman.

There was absolutely no other way to explain it.

He was standing in a cold, drafty hallway, watching his dog rolling around on the floor with a woman who had quickly become a pain in the ass, and he was envious of the dog.

He was crazy. Without question, Nick decided, and stood as straight as that goddamn crutch would allow.

"Brutus," he said sharply. "Come here!"

The dog looked up, flashed a doggy grin and went back to nuzzling the woman stretched out under him.

"Brutus! I said come! Dammit, dog—"

"Woof!"

Nick felt his jaw tighten. The Newf's tail was wagging even harder, fast enough for imminent takeoff. The woman was laughing and rubbing his head. Encouraging him. Urging him on. Making it clear that not even a dog had to show him respect.

Nick could all but feel his temperature rising. His blood boiling. His gut twisting, or whatever the hell happened when a man was fast losing what little remained of his composure.

Dammit, Lissa Wilde had been nothing but trouble from the get-go. Landing a job under false pretenses, because no matter what she said, he didn't for a minute believe that she was a cook. Wasting his time letting him fly her here.

He was dealing with a bunch of wranglers who thought that saying things like *Dude, I could eat an elephant* was simply a new way to start a meal.

Now, he had to deal with this.

His dog, a dog that—unfortunately—wouldn't obey any human being in the world except him, was refusing to respond to the simplest command.

Impossible, Nick decided, and narrowed his eyes.

"Let go of my dog."

Ah, man, what a stupid thing to say! The dog had the woman pinned down and he was telling her to let go of the dog?

Nick tried again.

"The dog," he said coldly, "is not a pet."

Jesus. This was going from bad to worse. The dog is not a pet? Had he really said that? Well, hell. He had to say something, didn't he? Yeah. He damn well did.

He couldn't just watch his dog make an ass of himself…

He couldn't just stand here wishing he could change places with the dog.

Try again, Gentry.

"He doesn't like to be petted."

Hell! He'd gone beyond stupid. The woman thought so, too. She gave a snort of laughter. Brutus, who liked laughter, *woof-woofed* in response. The woman looked at Nick through a tangle of her silky blond hair and the Newf's soft black fur.

"Could have fooled me," she said.

"He's a—a—" *A what?* "He's a trained guard dog. He has a job to do. And you're diverting him."

Lissa Wilde snorted again. "Do you have a job to do, sweetie?" she crooned.

Brutus moaned with pleasure. The Wilde babe clasped the dog's ears and planted a kiss on his muzzle. The dog buried his face in the curve of her shoulder and moaned again.

Nick was painfully close to making that same sound.

"Brutus," he said sharply, "dammit, dog, get off!"

"Brutus," the woman crooned, "you're a beautiful boy and it's been lovely meeting you, but now you have to be a good dog and let me get up."

"He won't obey anyone but me," Nick said.

This was far safer ground because, unfortunately, it was true.

Brutus had not had an easy life. Among other things, the nutcase who'd originally owned him had exercised his power by forcing the dog to respond only to him and, in some cases, only to code words.

Nick had worked diligently to break the habit, though not always with success.

"He won't obey anyone but you?" Lissa Wilde said with indignation. "But that's an awful thing to do to a dog. What if you weren't here? Would he eat if you didn't tell him he could?"

Until recently, no. He wouldn't. They'd finally reached the point at which Nick didn't have to use a code word to get the dog to eat, but Brutus would still only accept food from him.

And she was right. It was not a good thing. In fact, it had been one hell of a problem the weeks he'd been hospitalized, when the only way to get Brutus to do something as simple as eating had been to record the coded command so that the guy he'd hired to take care of the dog here at the Triple G could get him to eat.

He thought of telling her that, but why would he?

The dog was none of her business. She was a temporary blip on the horizon. And the dog was a fool for thinking otherwise.

Enough, Nick decided.

"Brutus," he said sharply. "Up!"

The Newf shot him an *Are you nuts?* look and went back to total adoration of Lissa Wilde.

"Dammit, dog—"

"Brutus," Lissa Wilde said softly, "you wonderful boy, up!"

The dog shuffled to his feet.

"That's my good boy. Now go to that despicable man who thinks he owns you." The dog hesitated. "Go on," the woman said, and the dog heaved a sigh and went to Nick's side.

The cook-who-almost-surely-was-not-a-cook-but-might-be-a-dog-trainer rose to her feet and slapped her jeans free of dust bunnies.

"That," she told Nick coldly, "is how it's done. You want the dog to love you, not fear you."

Nick looked from the woman to the dog and then to the

woman again.

"How did you do that?"

"I established a bond with him."

"Yeah, but how did you…" Nick stopped in mid-sentence. His eyes narrowed. "The dog doesn't fear me."

"Uh huh."

"He doesn't, goddammit!"

"Right."

He looked at the dog again. Brutus sat with his gaze glued to his new best friend.

"Brutus," Nick said, "look at me."

The dog ignored him.

"Brutus—"

Lissa Wilde put her hand on the massive black head. "He's a lovely dog," she said. "He deserves to be treated with kindness."

"I have never," Nick said through his teeth, "mistreated this dog!"

"What do you call training him only to eat only after you tell him he can?"

"I didn't—"

"You already admitted that you did. Well, it's cruel. And dangerous." Her head lifted. "Only a control freak would be into stuff like that."

He thought so, too, but this wasn't the time to admit it.

"It can be done for the safety of the dog."

She rolled her eyes.

Yes. But it could.

The vet had explained it—except, Brutus had never been a guard dog or a dog whose life, whose owner's life might depend on not obeying the orders of strangers. Aside from situations as unusual as those, the vet had said, the risks of that kind of training definitely outweighed the benefits.

And then, together, he and Nick had cursed the absent control-freak shithead whose dog Brutus had once been.

"As if," Lissa Wilde said coldly. She folded her arms over her breasts—except, damn, not quite over them. Her arms were more or less just beneath her breasts, lifting them, framing them, flaunting them. She was wearing a light jacket with the top buttons undone. He could see the rounded shape of her breasts, could imagine the sweet pucker of her nipples... "Have you heard a word I've said, cowboy?"

Nick jerked his head up. "What?"

The expression on her face was grim. She was obviously pissed off at him and that was fine because he was equally pissed off at her. These thoughts about her, about her body...

Absolutely, positively he'd drive to a glittery town, find a glittery bar, find himself a glittery woman. A high-priced call girl, the kind who could make a man forget that he paid for her favors, that none of what she said or did in his arms was real.

So what if he hated those places and felt sorry for those women? A man could put aside his scruples for a night of sex. *He* could, anyway, because sex was obviously what he needed.

"Have you?" she repeated. "Heard a word I've spoken?"

It had to be sex that he needed. Why else would a woman as unpleasant as this turn him on?

"No," Nick said coldly. "Frankly, I've been doing my best to tune you out."

"Well, it's time you tuned in. What I said was that I'd like to see my room—that is, if you're not too busy figuring out new ways to torment dogs to point me to it."

The woman had a mouth on her—a soft-looking mouth, which was amazing when you considered what came out of it.

"There's half a dozen bedrooms upstairs. Take your pick."

The glare in her eyes could have cut glass.

"Which one is yours?"

Just that quickly, he felt his body harden. Could she see what was happening to him? Shifting his weight while balancing on a crutch wasn't easy, but he managed.

"Down the hall on the right. The one with the pine pan—"

"Don't get your hopes up, cowboy. I don't give a flying fig about pine paneling. I just want to be sure to choose a room as far from yours as possible."

She was smiling. No. She was smirking. Dammit, enough was enough! Did she really think she could go on insulting him under his own roof and get away with it?

Nick took a step forward.

She didn't move.

He took another step toward her.

Not really. What he did was hobble toward her, goddamn that leg and that crutch.

She stood her ground.

It drove him nuts.

The lady needed to be put in her place. He didn't want her afraid of him, he just wanted… What? A reaction. A response. Something that said she knew she was on the losing end of this confrontation.

So he flashed a smile.

The smile that was his trademark.

It was a smile that had been described as all-knowing and all-powerful, as sexy as sin and dangerous as hell. It was a smile that promised everything a man could fear and a woman could want.

He flashed it because the maybe-cook, maybe-dog trainer, maybe-starlet-wannabe and all-around champion pain in the ass who'd invaded his life had just about driven him to the edge, flashed it without thinking about the consequences beyond the immediate pleasure of seeing her crumble—

And by the time he realized what he'd done, it was too late.

Lissa Wilde's eyes lit with recognition.

"You *are* him," she said. "Nick Gentry."

He laughed. It wasn't a very good laugh, but it was a laugh. "If only," he said.

Her eyes narrowed. "You absolutely are Nick Gentry."

"We did this bit already, remember?" Nick shook his head. "I told you, I've heard that before, but my name is Bannister."

"It's Gentry." She plopped her hands on her hips. "*Famous Movie Star Vanishes.*"

It was one of the tabloid headlines that had haunted him after the accident. Not that anybody but a handful of people knew about the accident.

"You know how to read," he said. "Wow. I'm impressed. Unfortunately, I am not—"

"Give me a break, will you? I'm not blind. You are Nick Gentry."

Nick gritted his teeth. Now what? He'd taken on the Nick Bannister persona in the first hospital; his lawyer, an old friend and one of the few people he trusted, had set the ball in motion, completed it by transferring him under the Bannister name to a hospital in the States.

At first, there'd been lots of speculation, virtually all of it as improbable as the scripts from some of his movies.

He was trekking through the Himalayas, searching for his own Shangri-La.

He was holed up someplace in Mexico with a woman he'd stolen from a drug lord.

He was hiding out in Switzerland, recovering from plastic surgery gone wrong.

Then, as was its wont, the media had forgotten him.

By the time the doctors had decided he'd keep his leg—a bad joke, considering what that leg was like—by then, heading home incognito, if you could call a place he hadn't seen in eighteen years *home*, had been easy.

A midnight helicopter ride, a couple of trusted bodyguards, nobody in what had once been his entourage in on the deal except for his lawyer.

Easy.

A few people had made him over the intervening months. No problem. This was ranching country. Saddle tramps and cowboys, real cowboys, didn't give a crap if the man who employed them was a king or a killer.

As for Lissa Wilde—

A problem. The question was how best to handle it. If he kept denying who he was, she'd never leave it alone. He knew the type. She was not a woman to give up easily.

But if he admitted his identity, if he admitted it and offered her something for her silence—

Yes. That would work.

Come morning, he'd give her a check. A big one. He'd tell her that it was hers to keep as long as she kept quiet about where she'd been and what she'd seen. If money wasn't enough, if she really was what he suspected—a girl from Smalltown, USA in search of a Hollywood career—he'd add a promise to the check.

He'd tell her that he'd be leaving here soon and if she kept her mouth shut, just as soon as he was back in L.A., he'd put her in touch with Spielberg or Scorsese or Burton.

A lie, of course.

And he'd never lied to any of the hopefuls who'd tried all the tricks of the trade to get him to wave a magic wand and kick-start their dreams. He'd had dealings with all of them over the years, from the bartender who slipped you his résumé with the check, to the cloakroom girl who tucked her card in the pocket of your coat.

But he had no compunctions about lying to this woman. She had fudged her way into his private world. She was no cook.

What she was, was clever.

Lying to her would suit him just fine.

No way would he introduce her to anyone in L.A. How could he? He had no intention of going back there, of going back to his old life. Ever.

How could he possibly, even if he'd wanted to? But if she'd lied to get to the Triple G—and he was 99 percent sure that she had—well, one egregious lie deserved another.

The more he considered it, the more workable the plan seemed.

Yes, she'd seen that he had a problem with his leg, but so what? This was a ranch. He could have fallen off a horse. Jabbed himself on a broken fence post. Torn a ligament hauling feed bags.

Besides, once he admitted that he really was Nick Gentry, he'd be dealing with an entirely different woman. All her smug, self-righteous attitude would fall away.

His career was dead and gone; he could never make it on the screen again, but one-on-one? Hell. There wasn't a woman on the planet who wouldn't turn from tigress to pussy cat for Nick Gentry. Even now.

Not until they knew the truth, at any rate. Saw it firsthand.

"You can stop trying to figure out ways to convince me that I'm wrong."

He looked up. Lissa Wilde was starting at him, her face expressionless.

Nick hesitated.

He wasn't looking his best; he knew that. He'd given up shaving more than a couple of times a week; he'd let his hair grow so damned long that it curled over the collar of his denim jacket.

Still, his was the face that had launched an even dozen box-office hits. There was no ego in the realization, there was only the cold reality of a man who knew what had brought him to where he was.

To where he had been, once upon a time, and now was not the time to go through all of that crap again.

It was a time for dealing with the situation at hand, Nick thought, and he took off his Stetson, tossed it aside and decided he might as well play the scene for all it was worth.

"What the hell," he said. "You've got me. Yes. I'm Nick Gentry. And, look, I know that changes things a little, but—"

"It changes nothing," she said. "Except that I should tell you that I never saw a movie of yours that I liked."

Nick felt his jaw drop.

She tossed her head, picked up her suitcase, moved briskly past him and went up the stairs. Halfway up, she stopped and looked back.

Not at him.

At the dog.

"Brutus," she said in a gentle voice that was completely out of keeping with the reality of what she was like, "do you want to come and keep me company?"

"No," Nick said sharply.

Too late.

The Newf gave a joyous bark and lunged for the stairs, bounded up them as if he were a puppy instead of an arthritic old man. Lissa Wilde smiled at him when he reached her side, ruffled his ears and said something soft and sweet.

Then she looked at Nick.

There was nothing soft or sweet in that look.

"Just so we have things straight, Mr. Gentry, you can stop worrying."

"Worrying about what?"

"I don't know why you're hiding out in this—this place in the middle of nowhere and, frankly, I don't care. You want to play at being a cowboy? Fine. Be my guest."

Taken aback, Nick drew himself up.

"I am not playing at anything. This place is mine. It's a real working ranch. And I—"

"And you are a real working cowboy. Got it. The point is, your secret's safe with me."

"I don't know what you're talking about, lady. There is no se—"

"Supper's at six. I don't do late kitchen duty. Not in a place like this, so tell your men to be on time if they expect the food to be hot."

Say something, Nick told himself. *For God's sake, say something! This is your house. She is your guest. Hell. She's not your guest. She's your employee, even if it's only for tonight, so, goddammit, say something!*

Too late.

The woman and the dog turned away and climbed the remaining steps to the second story landing. The woman didn't look back.

The dog did.

For one crazy second, Nick could have sworn the dog was smiling.

"Woof," the dog said softly.

Woman and dog made a left-hand turn.

And then they were gone.

* * *

Lissa walked to the end of the hall and into the last bedroom on the left.

The dog padded in after her.

"Good boy," she said, and dumped her suitcase on the floor.

The room was awful. Cabbage rose wallpaper. Faded carpet of an indeterminate color. Oak furniture, each piece so big she could only imagine that getting it upstairs must have meant hernias, sprained backs, and lots of cussing.

A porcelain pitcher and basin stood on one nightstand. She'd have shuddered at the sight but, thank goodness, she could make out a toilet, sink and tiny shower through a half-opened door just opposite the bed.

Not that the plumbing or what passed for décor mattered.

She was here for one night. It might well end up feeling like the longest night of her life, but one night was all it was.

Tomorrow, Nick Gentry's pilot would fly her back to civilization. She'd chew Marcia out for not checking things out before sending her on this—this wild-goose chase and—

And, she'd be right back where she'd been all these past weeks.

Jobless and rapidly working toward also being penniless.

"Damn," she said softly, as she sank down on the edge of the bed.

Brutus padded over and put his massive head in her lap. He gave a soft whine and Lissa stroked his head and smiled at him.

"I know," she said. "You hate that I'm in this mess."

The dog whined again. Lissa reached down and hugged him. He was the only one she could rely on, the only one who gave a damn.

Except, that wasn't true.

Her family would have done more than give a damn, had they known her situation. But she had not told them, nor would she tell them. They were all so successful: her three brilliant brothers, her two brilliant sisters, her powerful father.

They'd all have wanted to help her if they knew what a mess she'd made of things, but she couldn't let them know about it. For one thing, she'd started off with her career looking so good…

And then, when it had begun to sink a little, she'd hidden it from them.

You came from a long line of winners, you certainly didn't want to spoil the score by showing that you were a loser.

Lissa fell back on the bed.

Wildes were always successful. Always. They didn't make mistakes, they didn't make bad judgment calls, they didn't screw up their lives.

She was the only one.

The useless one.

And now she'd made matters worse, not asking Marcia the right questions, not doing what her lawyer brother, Caleb, would surely have called due diligence before blithely, blindly boarding a plane and heading out to Nowhereland.

It was all Nick Gentry's fault.

He'd lured her here with promises of a job that didn't exist, with talk of a resort where she could make her culinary skills the talk of the West.

Lissa rolled onto her belly.

Except, he hadn't done any of those things. It was Marcia's

fault, but Gentry behaved as if it were hers.

What was he doing all the way up here? Running a ranch? It seemed as if he were, but how come? He was an actor. A talented actor.

She'd lied when she'd said that she hadn't liked any of his movies.

The truth was, she'd liked them all. He had an amazing ability to make the most removed characters accessible.

And, why not admit it, he was gorgeous.

Tall. Lean. Tightly muscled. A face like a Greek god's, but with touches that humanized him: a bump in his nose, a small scar high on his cheekbone, another on his square jaw. She'd figured the scars might be phony—she knew a little about Hollywood makeup after all this time in La La Land—but now she knew that they were real.

What she'd never figured was that he'd be so unpleasant.

Well, actually, she hadn't figured on that because she'd never thought about him as anything other than an actor, but here he was, up close and personal, and he was about as pleasant as a Texas longhorn with a burr under its tail.

Was he just another walking, talking ego? Or was it, maybe, because he was hurting?

That limp. The crutch. He was in pain—she could see it etched into the lines that radiated out from those amazing eyes. Something had happened to him, but what?

All she knew was what the rest of Hollywood knew.

Nick Gentry had been making a movie halfway around the world and then, wham, he'd disappeared.

Filming had stopped. And the industry had buzzed with

rumors.

He'd been fired, he'd quit, he'd gone into rehab for—your choice—booze or drugs. He'd come down with a rare illness. He'd run off with a woman. He was in Nepal, searching for The Truth.

The speculation had dragged on for weeks. Then, gradually, it had faded away until, finally, his name was no longer mentioned.

Gentry had dropped below the radar.

Except he hadn't.

He was here, in the back end of nowhere on a ranch that was as far from being a duded-up guest lodge as the chicken place she'd worked at was from *Per Se*. She'd come all this way for a job that, it turned out, didn't exist, only to find herself faced with a Greek god who needed a shave and probably a haircut, who snarled and snapped and was a downright miserable, mean-tempered SOB.

Brutus whined.

Lisa looked at him. He was sitting beside the bed, head cocked, watching her with interest.

"What?" she said. The dog whined again. Lissa reached out and petted his big head. "Well, he is. Mean. Just look how he treats you."

The dog got to his feet and gave a soft woof. He put his front paws on the bed.

"You want to come up?" Another woof. "Well, come on. Come on, sweetheart. You're more than welcome to—"

The big dog heaved himself onto the bed. At least, he tried. But he couldn't quite make it. She could hear his hind claws scrabbling against the rug.

"I'll help you," Lissa said.

She grabbed him around his middle. Between the two of them, he finally ended up on the mattress beside her.

"Poor baby," Lissa said softly. "You're an old man, aren't you?"

Old. And sweet. And even if he'd been trained to some kind of idiotic command procedure, you could see that Gentry was good to the dog.

Lissa had put in time volunteering at animal shelters in almost every city where she'd lived and worked; sadly, she'd become good at identifying abused animals pretty quickly, and it was obvious that Gentry had not abused Brutus, that—despite what she'd said—the dog wasn't the least bit afraid of him.

Back to Gentry again. The man was a mystery.

Not a likable mystery.

Lissa sighed. Why would he be likable? To her, anyway?

This place wasn't what she'd expected. But she wasn't what he'd expected. That should have made them even, she thought as she looped her arm around the Newf, but Gentry had taken things too far.

He refused to believe that she was a chef.

What did he think she was, then? What was it he'd accused her of being? Some blond ditz hoping for stardom?

The dog blew out a noisy sigh. His head dropped to his paws.

"Really," Lissa told him, "your Mr. Gentry started the whole thing by not believing that I am a cook."

Which was, she supposed, a kind of compliment.

Not the ditz part. The part about his assuming she was a wannabe actress. Didn't that mean he thought she looked more like an actress than a cook? No, wait. All it meant was that he was foolish enough to think women chefs were unattractive. Idiot. Still, it was a kind of back-handed compliment if you figured it meant that he thought she was, well, attractive.

Brutus yawned again. So did Lissa.

Not that she wanted him to think that. Why would she care what he thought about her looks? Just because a man who spent his time surrounded by beautiful women would see her as attractive…

Brutus's big brown eyes blinked once. Twice. Then they shut. Lisa yawned.

"A fine idea," she told him.

It was mid-afternoon and she'd been up since dawn She had plenty of time for a nap, then a shower, then a trip to the kitchen to discover, no doubt, cans of beans and chili and boxes of mac and cheese and—and—

Her lashes drooped.

Seconds later, she and Brutus were both snoring.

CHAPTER FIVE

MONTANA WAS ONE of those places that drove meteorologists crazy.

One of the wranglers his father had employed when Nick was a kid used to sit in a rocker on the bunkhouse porch in the early evening, his hands busy with a pocket knife and a piece of wood, his rheumy eyes fixed on the mountains. He was an unending source of fascination for Nick, mostly because the old guy could whittle a stick into damn near anything, but also because he chewed tobacco and unerringly spat into an old tin can between offering bits of homegrown philosophy.

One of the favorites had been that old saw about changeable weather.

"If'n you don't like the weather in these parts," he'd say between chews and spits, "jes' wait a while and it'll change while you're lookin' at it."

Nick, seven or eight at the time, had been amazed at what he'd thought was the brilliance of the remark. It had taken years before he'd realized that the statement was true of lots of places though time and travel had taught him that up here, in the high mountains, the weather really could change in the blink of an eye.

This day had dawned cold and clear, but it had devolved quickly when gathering clouds had brought snow and wind.

By now, the weather was close to blizzard conditions.

Seated at his desk in what had been his old man's office, Nick looked out the window at a thick wall of steadily falling white flakes.

Visibility was close to zero. The temperature had to be close to that, too. Thankfully, it was warm inside.

The house was old and creaky, sure, but the walls were sound. Nick had, during his Hollywood days, bought enough houses to make him something of an expert on what real estate agents liked to call the bones of a house.

This one had good bones.

Fireplaces in the living room, the dining room, the kitchen, the office and the master bedroom. Beamed ceilings. Hardwood floors. Big windows that gave expansive views of the forest and mountains.

Sometimes he thought it was too bad his father had let the place deteriorate.

Mostly, he didn't care.

He had, when he was a kid.

Back then, his father had talked about restoring the place to what it had once been, but he'd lost interest in everything after Nick's mother died. What had once been a profitable if not prosperous ranch had slowly fallen apart.

Nick was bringing it back out of necessity. The house would have fallen down without some repairs. Besides, when it came time to put it on the market, who would want to buy a disaster?

So far, he'd put money into only the most vital repairs. A new roof. A new heating system. A new well. The place still looked like shit—peeling paint inside almost all the rooms, soot-stained ceilings wherever there were fireplaces, antiquated plumbing and furniture that he suspected might even be turned down by Goodwill—but the thick walls and foundation were as sound as when his who-knew-which great-grandfather had built the place in the 1840s.

It had been a four-room cabin back then.

As a boy, Nick had found it fascinating to think of the generations of Gentrys who had put so much work into the Triple G, adding outbuildings and line shacks, and expanding the original four rooms to twelve. But by time he left, the only part of the house's history that fascinated him was trying to figure out why all those Gentrys had spent time and sweat on the place instead of packing their bags and walking away.

He'd done that once and he could hardly wait to do it again.

This was not home; it had not been home for most of his life. He had no feelings of nostalgia for the land or the house, only relief that he could stay tucked away here while he tried to figure out what to do with the rest of his life.

And he'd have plenty of time to do it. The house still needed work. Plaster. Paint. Floors. Ceilings. And furniture. Yeah, it needed the whole treatment.

So did his leg, he thought, grimacing as he massaged the muscles in his thigh.

The difference was that the house would respond well to some new touches.

His leg was a lost cause.

Use it, the therapist said. Accept it, the orthopedist who might as well have been a shrink said. And the real shrink that he'd agreed to see, only once, had put it more bluntly. Stop thinking about how this happened, he said, and get on with your life.

Sure, Nick thought. No problem there, right?

As if in mournful agreement, a gust of wind howled through the surrounding aspens like hungry wolves.

It was going to be a bad night.

At least he didn't have to worry about his crew. All six had made it back to the bunkhouse; his foreman had phoned to tell him they were OK.

"We'll hang in here until supper," Ace had said. "The boys can hardly wait to see what that new cook you hired serves up."

Neither could he.

The last cook had specialized in chili. Nick had come to hate the stuff and his boys had grown to despise it, but the meals served up by Gus, a younger guy who'd been doing most of the cooking the past week, made even chili look good.

That was one of the reasons Nick had been so desperate to get a replacement, and fast.

There was just so much anybody could take of what might have been beef fried in fat until it had the taste and texture of leather.

"Dammit," he said, and he tossed aside his pen, tilted back his chair and folded his arms over his chest.

God only knew what Lissa Wilde would call a meal.

Assuming he bought into her being a chef, it might be something like *tête de veau Cordon Bleu*, a delicacy he'd had on his first movie-star trip to France. Nick had grown up eating beef, but the memory of that particular dish still made him shudder.

His best hope was that she was a cook of sorts, that she'd worked at roadside diners while she made her way west to Hollywood. If so, she'd be able to peer into the kitchen's huge pantry and freezer and put together a meal that would at least fill the bellies of hard-working, hard-living men.

His frown deepened.

Yeah, but he wasn't counting on it.

For starters, he really didn't know what was in the pantry or freezer. Cooky and then Gus had been dealing with that, not him.

Besides, no matter what the Wilde babe said, he couldn't imagine her having any familiarity with a skillet and a stove. It wasn't the way she was dressed. Her clothes were not attention-getters. Neither was her hair or makeup, assuming she even had makeup on, and he wasn't positive that she did.

It was her manner.

Her attitude.

That who-do-you-think-you-are thing. That—what was the word? That hauteur. She was the lady of the manor; he was a peasant.

The duchess, looking down her nose at a lesser mortal.

Nick snorted.

Her, a cook?

"Right," he muttered. And he was the count of Monte Cristo.

She hadn't even checked out the kitchen. Wouldn't a real cook want to see what she was going to be working with?

Not that there was all that much to check out.

The kitchen was pretty much the same as it had been when he was growing up, meaning it was probably also the same as it had been for decades before that. A huge room with a cranky six-burner gas stove, a freezer chest big enough to hold the butchered and packaged parts of a couple of deer and, with luck, even an occasional moose, a refrigerator that clanked and groaned like a creature in pain, all of that offset by a battered pine worktable made by some forgotten Gentry a century or so ago.

His old man had never made any changes to the kitchen or anything else, not after Mary Gentry died.

"What we got here is just fine," Latham would growl if anybody was dumb enough to suggest something might be improved.

If the place had been going downhill back then, it had been racing to the bottom since Nick had taken off twelve years ago.

He'd tried to help, sending increasing amounts of money to his old man as his earnings went from good to substantial to incredible. But he'd never returned home; how could he possibly have known that his father had let the place fall into such bad shape? The conditions of virtually everything had come as a shock when he'd come back a year ago for Latham's funeral.

The second shock had been discovering that Latham had

cashed all the checks Nick had sent, put the money into a separate account at the bank and not spent a penny of it.

"Bullheaded old SOB," Nick had growled to John Carter, his father's attorney.

"Takes one to know one," the normally laconic Carter had muttered.

Nick had thought about arguing the point, but what for? He and his father had parted when Nick turned eighteen.

That had changed only the physical distance between them. From his wife's death on, Latham, always a taciturn man, had pretty much ignored his son. He'd made sure Nick was clothed, fed and schooled; beyond that, he'd paid little attention to him.

After Nick was on his own, their only contact had been an occasional telephone call.

If Carter wanted to lay that off on Nick, use it as an excuse for why his client had let the Triple G move toward compete ruin, so be it.

And, Nick thought as he brought his chair forward and folded his hands on the desk, what did any of that matter now? His father was gone; the Triple G was his, and the only thing he was interested in was getting it ready for sale.

This was hardly a place of happy memories. Why treat it as if it were? Nothing that had happened to him in the years since he'd left Montana had changed his mind about ranches and ranching and the Triple G.

His fans would not have believed it, of course. His agent, his manager, the directors he'd worked with had all helped him cultivate the image of a hard-nosed loner, a modern-day cowboy adrift in a danger-laden urban landscape.

It sold a lot of tickets. And attracted a lot of women.

Nick's mouth thinned.

But not anymore.

The accident had changed everything.

He had no interest in women.

Really? his hormones said.

Nick scowled. He supposed he ought to be grateful that he'd had his first boner in months. A sign he was healing physically; it damn well had nothing to do with Lissa Wilde.

As for his attitude toward the ranch…the accident had changed that, too. Not that he'd suddenly developed warm feelings for it. No way. It was just that when it came time to leave the hospital, he'd had a place to go, a place that hardly anybody would ever associate with the Nick Gentry who owned a house in Malibu, a penthouse in Manhattan, a beachfront hideaway on Maui.

That made the ranch the perfect place to dig in until he got his life sorted out.

And, goddammit, why was that important now?

He had a storm to ride out, men and animals to worry about, and where in hell was his cook? His for-one-night-only cook and Christ knew if she could manage even that.

As if in response, the ancient grandfather clock in the corner wheezed out the time.

Five-fifteen.

Dinner, the Wilde babe had said, would be at six. Really? She was going to get into the kitchen, find what its freezer and pantry held, put together a meal for a bunch of hungry men in forty-five minutes?

He raised his eyes to the ceiling.

Far as he could tell, she wasn't even on the move yet.

He'd have heard her. Or maybe not. One thing about old houses. The walls, the floors were made of the thickest tight-grained lumber a rustic sawmill could turn out. And if she'd gone for the room he figured, the one at the ass-end of the hall, he probably wouldn't hear her stomping around up there at all.

Ten to one that was precisely the room she'd chosen.

The one farthest from his.

Nick rolled back his chair, automatically started to put his feet up on the desk and caught his breath at the sharp pain that radiated from his hip straight down to his ankle. Goddamned bones. And muscles. And tendons. And who knew what else. He'd broken or torn virtually everything that had once made his left leg usable.

He had titanium rods and steel pins and plastic in it now.

"Superman," one of the therapists had joked.

Right. He was a fucking superman, except last time he'd checked, the Man of Steel had not limped, had not needed to hobble around on a crutch, had not been reduced, at the beginning, to getting up in the middle of the night to swallow one of a dozen different pills to quiet the pain that tormented him.

"You can start getting around with a cane soon," the last physical therapist he'd seen had told him.

"What the hell's the difference?" Nick had snarled. "And I don't need advice from you."

A cane. Crutches. What the fuck *was* the difference? He was a cripple, and it was a damn good thing his temporary guest had taken a room nowhere near his.

The last thing he needed was to have a woman hear him moan, not in the throes of pleasure but in agony.

Still, this was his house. Why had he left the choice of a room to her? He should have told her which to take. And yes, it damned well pissed him off that she'd make a selection based on its distance from his.

Did she think he'd try to seduce her if she slept one wall away?

Nick snorted.

The lady had a high-flown opinion of herself. She'd turned him on, sure, but that at this point, so would a store mannequin.

And that attitude.

Was it him she didn't like? Or was it men in particular? She wasn't a lez; the vibes she gave off were pure female.

Maybe what she needed was a man.

The bra-burners would kill him for such a thought, but he'd been around. He knew it was true. He knew that beautiful women—because, OK, the truth was that the Wilde babe was beautiful—sometimes needed reminding that they were women. Not goddesses. Not untouchables. Not royalty.

Just women, made for pleasure.

He could make her remember that.

Sweet-talk her until that la-di-da expression became a smile. Ease into her space. Not too close. Just a little. Just enough so he could gaze into her eyes. Make some skin-to-skin contact. A brush of his hand on hers, maybe; a stroke of his finger along her lips.

Lean in, breathe in the scent of her hair.

Entice her into a couple of kisses.

Soft kisses, to let her sense that he wanted her.

Then he'd draw her to him, let her feel his hardness against her belly. And when she caught her breath at the sensation, he'd bring her even closer. Stroke her tongue with his. Undo the zipper of her jeans, slip his hand under the waistband, slide his fingers over the sweet, smooth skin until he felt her heat, her wetness, her desire for him against his palm…

Christ.

Nick shuddered.

He had a hard-on the size of Montana, and for a woman he didn't even like.

No problem. Not after this coming weekend. Hadn't he already decided that?

For now, he needed a cook. Correction. That was tomorrow's problem. Today's was getting a meal of some kind, of any kind, out of Lissa Wilde. If she could cook, fine. If she couldn't, which was what he expected, that was fine, too.

She could open a dozen cans of soup. Fry some eggs. A couple of pounds of bacon. She could put up a pot of coffee, couldn't she? Damn right she could—

Bong.

Nick's head came up. The clock in the hall coughed out the time. Man, it was five thirty! A meal on the table by six? Even one dumped out of cans?

"No way," he said grimly, planting the crutch hard against the oak-planked floor and struggling to his feet.

Ridiculous, this entire thing. Did she actually think she was going to avoid responsibility for this mess? Either she or her agent was the person who'd caused it and since her agent wasn't here, Wilde drew the penalty by default.

He hobbled toward the door, automatically paused to give Brutus a chance to catch up to him and then remembered that she'd somehow lured his dog upstairs.

Terrific. No cook. No dog.

"Enough," he growled.

It was a tough growl, a sexy growl; it had thrilled hundreds of millions of female fans, but right now Nick didn't give a damn about how it sounded. He only knew that his unwanted guest was about to learn that the good times were over.

Getting up the stairs was the usual endless battle of maneuvering crutch, handrail and steps. The private-duty nurse his doctors had insisted on had taken one look at the stairs and suggested he rent a hospital bed and set it up in the living room.

She'd been out the door twenty minutes later.

He didn't need hospital beds, didn't need to turn the house he already hated into a refuge for invalids, didn't need anything but to be left alone.

At last, he reached the second floor. He clomped down the corridor, taking the same direction the duchess had taken hours ago, passing open door after open door until, yeah, just as he'd figured, he reached the last door and found it closed.

He was breathing hard. From exertion. From anger. From the effing disaster his life had become, and here was this stranger, this lying-through-her-teeth female, adding to it.

He raised his hand, formed a fist, banged it against the door.

Nothing.

Hell. This was his house. Did she really think she could ignore him?

"Wilde," he said loudly.

No answer.

Nick pounded on the door again and he heard Brutus give a short, sharp bark. The Newf was a prisoner in there. Aside from everything else, did she think she could keep his dog from him?

"Wilde," Nick snarled. "Open up!"

He hit the door again. Hard. It swung open…

His heart damn near stopped.

Lissa Wilde stood in the open door of the bathroom. Steam curled in the air behind her.

Never mind that.

Concentrate on her. On the naked woman who was more beautiful than any woman he'd ever seen.

Her hair was pinned up, long wavy tendrils of it falling down and kissing her throat.

Her breasts were lush and round and, God, and perfect. Handfuls, lovely handfuls that a man could cup and caress.

Her waist was slender, her hips curved. Her thighs were firm. Creamy. The ideal frame for pale curls she had not been foolish enough to shave or wax into submission.

Nick's heart did a shuddering restart; he could hear the pulse of his blood in his ears. His brain began functioning again; it told him to turn around, go out the door, pretend that he had not seen her, that the urge to go to her, sweep her into his arms, claim her mouth, her body, was not beating through him.

"Get out!"

His gaze swept to her face. She had gone pale; as he watched, she reached behind her, grabbed a towel, covered herself with it.

"Did you hear me, Gentry? I said—"

"I heard you." Nick cleared his throat. Turned his back because, heaven help him, how could a man who'd damn near wiped himself out just climbing a flight of stairs have an erection? "Look," he said, "I didn't mean to—"

"GET OUT!"

Something sailed past his head. A book. A hairbrush. Whatever it was missed him and he stumbled into the hall.

The door slammed behind him.

He all but fell back against the wall.

What the hell had just happened?

Sex had been the furthest thing from his thoughts. Besides, weeks of celibacy or not, he wasn't a kid. The sight of a naked woman wasn't enough to do him in. He was long past the days when a Playboy centerfold could bring him to his knees.

Nick shut his eyes. It didn't help. The image of Lissa Wilde was seared on the inside of his eyelids.

He had seen naked movie stars, nipped and tucked to perfection. Lissa Wilde didn't measure up to any of them.

And yet she was more beautiful.

She wasn't a sculptor's creation or a surgeon's idealization. She was real.

And, Christ, he owed her an apology. An explanation. She'd reacted as if he'd stormed her room…

Her door opened.

An inch.

Nick looked up. Met a pair of blue-green eyes that blazed with fury. Heard a voice that was frigid with hatred.

"I am going to put a chair under this doorknob," she said. "If you try to force the door open—"

"What?" Nick shook his head. "Why would I do that?"

"If you try... There's a lamp in here made of brass. Or something. I don't know what it's made of and I don't care. All I know is, if I use it, it looks heavy enough to dent even a skull as thick as yours. You got that, cowboy?"

"Look." He stepped forward. "I didn't mean to—"

"One more foot and you're a dead man."

"Ms. Wilde. Lissa. I knocked. You didn't answer. I guess you were in the shower and you couldn't hear me, but I didn't know that so I knocked again and the door—this house is old, see, and the doors don't always—"

Lissa flung the door open. He had time to see that she was wrapped in a robe the size of a tent before she rushed him and pounded her fist into the center of his chest.

A Hollywood stunt man would have been proud of her, Nick thought, even as he stumbled back, hit the wall...

And went down.

A sharp cry of pain burst from his lips.

He collapsed at Lissa's feet.

Good, she thought grimly. Let the SOB break his stupid neck.

She stalked back into the bedroom, slammed the door, turned the lock even though Gentry had already proved that the gesture was meaningless, jumped as something big bumped against her backside.

The dog. His dog. Whining and moaning.

"Traitor," Lissa snarled.

She jerked the door open and the Newf flew to his master.

Lissa slammed the door and fell back against it, panting.

The rat. The SOB. Was this the reason he'd told her she could spend the night in his house? Did he think he could take advantage of her?

Except, he hadn't looked like a man who was up to taking advantage of anybody or anything.

Something was wrong with his leg. Something bad.

And she'd punched him. Put him flat on his ass.

Well, look what he'd done. Forced his way into her room. An accident, he'd said…

Maybe.

It was an old house. She'd had a tough time getting the door to close, the lock to work.

She turned. Put her ear to the door.

Nothing.

Lissa chewed on her lip.

She'd downed a guy who used a crutch. Who limped. Who was—to be blunt, if not PC—a cripple.

She breathed in. Breathed out. Then, carefully, she undid the useless lock, cracked the door and peered out.

What she saw was not good.

Nick Gentry was still sitting on the floor, his legs sprawled out. His crutch was half a dozen feet away. The Newf, whining piteously, stood over him.

Lissa opened the door a couple of inches.

"Are you OK?"

Gentry looked at her. Rage glittered in his eyes.

"Get the hell out of my face, Ms. Wilde."

"Mr. Gentry. I didn't mean to—"

"You have difficulty understanding English? Get away from me!"

Lissa stared at him.

That wasn't rage she saw on his beautiful face—because why pretend that he wasn't beautiful? He was, and what she saw etched in its classic lines was pain.

Despite herself, her heart twisted.

Yeah, well, so what? She'd always been a sucker for creatures that were needy and hurting…

Hell.

There was more than pain there. There was anger and the humiliation of destroyed pride.

She knew the look; she knew the anguish that went with it. She'd suffered it before, most recently, most terribly on the night Raoul had brought her dreams to a shattering end.

Of endless different emotions, humiliation was the one that could tear you apart.

She ran through what had happened again. Her, in the shower, the water pounding down. Gentry's claim that he hadn't burst in, he'd only knocked at the door she'd had trouble closing and locking. Well, he hadn't knocked. He'd banged—but he probably had knocked, first, and she hadn't answered—and hadn't much the same thing happened downstairs, when the Newfoundland had burst through that door?

OK.

The probability was that she'd over-reacted. Gentry had seen her in the raw. So what? Bodies were bodies. She had breasts, hips, all the parts every woman had, and it wasn't as if she'd never been looked at by a man before…

But not like he'd looked at her.

He'd been as shocked by the unexpected encounter as she'd been—and then she'd seen his shock turn to something else. Desire. Need. Hunger.

Lissa gave herself a quick mental shake.

Gentry was trying to get to his feet. He had both hands flat on the floor, but he couldn't stand, not without some sort of leverage.

She grabbed the crutch and held it toward him.

"Here. Use—"

The Newf shoved his big body between them, looked up at Lissa and gave a soft but distinct growl.

Et tu, Brute? she thought, but what the hell, the dog was his, and good dogs were loyal. Besides, the dog made all the difference.

Gentry grunted, worked his fingers through the dog's collar and slowly got to his feet. The expression on his face was thunderous, but she stood her ground and offered him the crutch again. He snatched it from her and jammed it under his arm.

"Mr. Gentry," she said, "I, uh, I may have misinterpreted your actions. I mean—"

"I told you my men would want supper at six."

His voice was flat. Cold. It had the sharpness of a boning knife.

"I know. It's just that... Look, about what just happened—"

"If you know, then what were you doing sashaying around naked?"

He saw her face flush. It was like watching the sun sweep across a pale sky.

She'd been behind a closed door. Naked was her business, not his. And she hadn't been sashaying. He wasn't even sure what the word meant.

The only certainty was that she'd slugged him. And it had been a slug to be proud of. It was just too bad it had taken his legs, what passed for his legs, out from under him.

That wasn't what a man wanted. Getting dumped ass over teakettle by a gorgeous, naked woman—

"Here's news that's bound to shock you," she said, her chin lifted, her eyes flashing, the color in her cheeks now a deep rose. "Most people are naked when they get out of the shower. And I wasn't sashaying. Besides, no matter what I was or wasn't doing, nothing gave you the right to beat down the door and—"

"I didn't *beat* down anything! This miserable old house is falling apart. Things collapse if you breathe on them." Nick narrowed his eyes. "And I wouldn't have had to come up here at all if you'd been doing your job."

"My job? *My job?*"

She blew a still-wet curl back from her eyes. Despite his anger, his chagrin at not being the man he'd once been, it was hard not to notice that she had beautiful hair, a dozen different shades of gold, even something he'd call champagne.

"I do not work for you, Mr. Gentry. Please keep that in

mind."

"You do work for me, Ms. Wilde."

"I most certainly do not! Tomorrow, first thing—"

"But it isn't tomorrow. Not yet. And you have a meal to cook—or did you think I wouldn't hold you to that commitment?"

So much for feeling sorry she'd embarrassed him.

"I said I'd prepare supper," she said coldly. "And I will."

"When? At midnight?"

"You said your men eat at six."

Nick raised one dark eyebrow. "And?"

"And, what? I don't need more than an hour to make a meal."

Her chin rose another notch. She took a step toward him; the enormous robe slipped off her right shoulder, exposing pale skin and a couple of errant drops of water before she righted it.

Damn.

What a time for a man's libido to decide to come back on line.

Nick shifted the crutch, hoped it would provide cover for his third erection of the afternoon—which just happened to be the third in the months since the accident.

"Your sex drive will come back," one of his doctors had told him. Not that he'd asked, but the guy had read between the lines.

Yes, but what good was a rampant libido when it involved a woman with all the charm of a badger?

"Trust me, Mr. Gentry. Supper will be ready at six. Sharp."

Nick checked his watch, looked at Lissa and flashed a grim smile.

"You must be one hell of a cook if you can have a meal on the table in less than fifteen minutes."

"What are you talking about?" She swung away, marched to the nightstand beside the bed, snatched up her watch and strode toward him. "Evidently, you're as bad as telling the time as you are at knocking on doors. Take a look. It's not even five o'clock."

A smug smile curved his mouth. "This is Montana, Duchess."

"I *hate* that name! And what's that supposed to mean, anyway?"

"It's a little matter of time zones. Mountain time versus Pacific time." The smirk faded. "It's going on five in California, Ms. Wilde," he said, with heavy emphasis on the *Ms.* "But it's going on six here."

Her eyes rounded. Her mouth fell open. He thought about what it would be like to close the couple of feet between them, bend his head and capture that mouth with his. A stupid thought, though, because he wasn't a kid and he knew that men and women didn't stop at kisses.

Kisses, real ones, the kind he wanted from her, led to bed. And bed was not a place he could afford to go.

Not with Lissa Wilde.

CHAPTER SIX

S OMETIMES, LIFE WAS like a really bad riddle, the kind Lissa's brothers had tortured her with when she was little.

Why is the finger on that statue of Davy Crockett eleven inches long?
Because if it was twelve inches it would be a foot.

When is a door not a door?
When it's ajar.

They'd done it out of kindness, to divert her from the reality of the death of her mother. Well, *their* mother, too; Jake, Caleb and Travis had loved their stepmom as much as Lissa and her sisters had, and her death had been a terrible blow.

Lissa shut one cupboard door, yanked open another, slammed it shut, spun around and glared what she'd found of the kitchen's bounty.

Four dusty cans of Spam.

Two cans of white beans.

Ketchup.

Six loaves of stale bread.

A bin of heading-for-eternity potatoes and another of mostly overgrown onions.

And a bottle of sweet chili sauce. She refused to waste time trying to figure out what in hell a staple of Thai cuisine was doing here, metaphorically rubbing elbows with Spam.

Which brought her to riddle time. The Triple G version.

Take six hungry men. Seven, if you counted Gentry and she supposed she had to. Add this stuff, stir well and what did you have?

Not much.

Certainly not the makings of a decent meal.

She'd come down the stairs minutes ago, wearing the same clothes she'd spent the day in, her damp hair pulled back in a ponytail. She'd been running because it was so late and who knew what the Master of the Triple G would do if she didn't get into the kitchen quickly enough to suit him, but when she saw him standing outside what was obviously the dining room, leaning against the wall, arms folded, face expressionless, she'd slowed to a deliberate walk.

He'd looked at her. Then he'd made a show of looking at his watch.

"You finally got here," he'd said in the kind of supposedly pleasant tone that meant there was nothing pleasant happening. "Congratulations."

Brutus had trotted toward her, wagging his tail and wearing a doggy smile.

"Turncoat," Lissa had said, but her voice had been soft and she'd touched his head lightly with her fingertips.

As for Nick Gentry… She'd completely ignored him as she strolled through the huge dining room, past the equally huge men seated around a huge table. They were all bearded and dressed almost identically in flannel shirts and jeans, and they'd stared at her as if she were an alien creature whose rocket ship had crashed on the planet Earth.

"Good evening," she'd said briskly.

Six heads had nodded. Six voices had mumbled "Ma'am" as she'd breezed past them toward an arched doorway that led into the kitchen.

Forget huge.

The kitchen was the size of a barn.

An enormous brick fireplace. A brick hearth. Soot-smudged walls. Cobwebbed ceiling. All the requisite appliances: stove, sink, fridge, freezer, dishwasher, worktable. An open pantry and endless cupboards.

That was the good news.

The bad news was that everything was old. Really old. Decades old. And even before she'd opened the fridge, the freezer, the cupboards and the pantry, a sinking feeling told her what she'd find.

Nothing.

Zero.

Nada, niente, and however else you wanted to say it.

Old Mother Hubbard had nothing on the Triple G.

The cupboards were bare of food except for the Spam, the beans and the sweet chili sauce. The fridge had yielded what she thought might be a chunk of hard white cheese hiding under a layer of green fuzz as well as what looked like a bowl of butter. A mysterious something wrapped in butcher paper, unlabeled, frozen solid and easily the size of a half a steer was in the cavernous freezer. Cupboards under the sink held a motley assortment of mismatched plates, bowls and mugs and a battery of dented pots, skillets and pans.

The pantry had been Lissa's last hope.

Men lived here. Worked here. Worked long, hard days. There hadn't been a professional cook in residence lately, but surely there was food…

And there was. Potatoes, onions, bread, ketchup, sugar.

She looked at the worktable again, where she'd laid out what she'd found, as if in hopes that a miracle might have occurred.

None had. Add to that stuff a sad-looking heap of wizened apples she'd just unearthed from darkest corner of the pantry along with small tins of garlic powder and cinnamon plus canisters of coffee, flour and—*seriously*?—lard, and she had the makings for a delectable feast.

Lissa closed her eyes.

All she needed was a magic wand, a fairy godmother, and she'd be home free.

There was a rising hum of whispers and grumbles coming from beyond the arched doorway. From the dining room, she thought, biting back a groan, where Napoleon's starving army waited to be fed.

Now, added to that came the hard click of boot heels. No.

Not Napoleon's army. This was the Mongol horde and its general was Genghis Khan.

And Genghis was standing right in back of her.

She'd heard him coming, but she'd have known it was him without that. She could sense his presence. Big. Powerful. Masculine. He'd brought with him the scent of soap, water, and man. He must have gone upstairs and showered while she was doing a desperate search through the kitchen.

A little *frisson* of something she refused to identify swept through her.

She took a breath, let it out, took another, then turned to face him.

Yes. He had showered. And shaved.

What a great face he had. That jaw. Those cheekbones. Those eyes…

"I see you've found the supplies."

His voice was cool and calm.

"Yes," she said, just as coolly and calmly.

"The men are hungry."

She nodded. His razor had missed one tiny spot on his jaw. The stubble looked—interesting. Idly, she wondered how it would feel against her skin.

For goodness' sakes, Melissa!

"I said—"

The edge in his voice jolted her back to reality.

"The men are hungry," she said. "Right. I'll bet they are. What happened here?"

Gentry's eyebrows rose. "Meaning what?"

"What do you mean, meaning what?"

"I mean, what do *you* mean by asking me what happened here?"

So much for him smelling and looking good. He was still the same idiot. Her cool and her calm were fast fading.

"Meaning, did somebody raid the kitchen and toss out all the food?"

He shrugged. "Had a grizzly do that up in a line shack, once, but not—"

"Perhaps whoever made breakfast and lunch today decided to try an experiment that involved using up everything edible."

Everything edible? Nick looked at the table. Shit. Was that really all that the kitchen held? He'd hadn't kept track of the foodstuffs, but—"

"One minute," he snapped, and headed for the dining room.

Whispers. Raised voices. More whispers. Then he was back.

"Gus tells me that Hank—my pilot—was supposed to drop off some supplies, but with the weather coming in so fast…" There it was, that high-and-mighty look on her face again. He'd had about enough of that to last a lifetime, Nick decided, and offered a brittle smile. "You say you're a chef." He jerked his chin toward the worktable. "Improvise."

Calm, Lissa told herself. *Say nothing confrontational. Either he really is a dumb cowboy or he's playing dumb. Either way, why get into a battle you can't win?*

"Ms. Wilde? You can improvise, can't you?"

Stay calm, remember? Lissa flashed a glittery smile. She could hear whispers in the dining room.

"Certainly."

"So, you're going to get started on supper?"

"Yes. Yes, I am. Tell your men it'll just be a few minutes."

"I'll tell them. Just keep in mind that they're mighty hungry."

Enough!

Lissa swung toward him.

"I know they're hungry," Lissa shouted. "In fact, I'm sure they're hungry, so why don't you tell them that if there's nothing to eat in this effing house, it's because their effing boss didn't buy any effing food!"

Brutus whined. The whispers in the dining room had stopped.

"And do not, *do not* try to lay this off on Gus, whoever he is, or Hank, or the weather gods. If this is your ranch, keeping the kitchen stocked is part of your responsibility!"

She was right. He knew it. But such fury! Such righteous indignation!

He wanted to laugh.

It was a feeling he hadn't had very often as of late. Hell, he could probably count the number of times he'd just wanted to smile on the fingers of one hand.

"Do you hear me, Gentry? I am not a miracle worker. I cannot turn pearls into swine."

"I'm pretty sure it's supposed to go the other way round," Nick said evenly.

"Hell, no! Not if you want to eat the result!"

There was an instant or two of silence. Then Nick gave up the struggle.

He laughed. And while he was still laughing, he leaned in, grabbed Lissa by the shoulders and took her mouth with his.

Lissa heard herself say *mmf*, or something close to it.

Nick held her tighter, parted her lips with his…

And she was lost.

The kiss changed.

No laughter now. Just heat. Just flame. The kiss became something wild. Out of control. It involved teeth and tongues and instead of pulling away, she leaned into him so that her body was plastered against the long, hard, wonderfully hard length of his, and now his hands were on her hips and hers were gripping his shirt, and the room was spinning, spinning, spinning…

"*Woof!*"

Brutus nudged his way between them.

They jerked apart. One long, endless, eternal minute of silence. Then Nick cleared his throat.

"I'll give them your message," he said in a hoarse voice.

"Do that," Lissa said, just as hoarsely.

Then she swung toward the table, he limped toward the door, and seconds later, the whispers from the dining room started up again.

* * *

It was amazing what you could do with Spam, onions, potatoes and—shudder, shudder—lard.

Lissa found a knife rack. She had her own knives, of course, upstairs in her suitcase, but all she'd unpacked was her toothbrush, shampoo, hairbrush, PJs, and a change of underwear.

There was no need to unpack anything else, and certainly

not her beloved knives.

Still, the one thing in the Triple G kitchen that she couldn't complain about was the knives. Well, the knife. The rack held six useless pieces of worn stainless steel and, to her surprise, one real knife. Someone had taken excellent care of the blade, and the knife itself balanced well in her hand.

And that was all she wanted to think about right now.

The feel of the knife in her hand and how well it did, dicing the Spam, slicing the onions and the potatoes.

Dice and slice.

Do not think.

Take out a skillet the size of a tabletop. Light one of the enormous burners on the old stove. Dump in some lard. Lard made for tender pasty, but it wasn't made for healthful living.

Forget healthful living.

Think about feeding those hungry cowboys.

Think about that kiss. Nick's lips on hers. So soft. So warm. So masterful…

Stop it, Lissa told herself sternly.

She sautéed the onions. Did the same with the thinly sliced potatoes. Got everything browned. Added the Spam. Let it brown, too. Added the drained cans of white beans. Beans and potatoes. Carbs and, for good measure, more carbs, really heart-healthy food, she thought wryly, but she couldn't worry about that right now.

What she needed was a platter of food that would fill empty bellies.

And would taste…well, if not good, at least acceptable.

She added a generous sprinkle of garlic powder, even

though only barbarians used powder instead of the real thing. A healthy belt of ketchup and, what the hell, a belt of the sweet chili sauce. Then she lowered the heat, slapped a cover on the pan, and reached for the loaves of stale bread.

The toaster would do only two slices at a time.

Useless for what she intended, so she lit the oven—fingers crossed as she did because it was a long time, a very long time since she'd used a pilotless gas oven that you had to light with a match—and turned to the worktable.

She sliced the loaves into thick pieces, spread them on the oven racks, toasted one side, turned and toasted the other. Then she dumped all the slices onto the table, buttered them, sprinkled them with garlic, used the really, really, really excellent knife to shave away the green yuck from what she'd hoped would turn out to be cheese, discovered that, hooray, it *was* cheese, put thin slices of it on the toast, gave the toast a quick run in the oven, took it out, sliced each piece in thirds.

Ready.

She uncovered the skillet of whatever it was she'd made, dumped the contents into an enormous bowl, lined a basket that could have held half a dozen footballs with a bunch of paper napkins she'd found on a shelf over the sink, dumped in the toast, took a deep breath...

Lissa carried the Spam du jour into the dining room and put it in the center of the table.

Nick wasn't there.

Well, why would he be? The Lord and Master probably ate by himself—

She bumped into him as she hurried back into the kitchen.

He had his crutch under his left arm; he was holding a stack of bowls, paper napkins and spoons in his right hand.

"I can do that," she said, or started to say, but the look he gave her turned her mute.

Those eyes. So blue. So hot. *So hot!*

She tore her gaze from his, moved past him, grabbed the basket of toast sticks.

By the time she returned to the dining room, he was seated with his men.

He was eating, as were they.

They looked up when she entered the room and eyed the toast warily—she figured it probably looked like delicate fare—but he reached out, snared a piece and bit into it.

"Good," he said, and six pairs of hands descended on the basket.

Lissa looked at Nick.

His eyes were still hot. Slowly, he touched the tip of his tongue to his bottom lip and licked away an errant crumb.

Her knees threatened to buckle.

Jesus!

What was she, fifteen? He was a good-looking guy. So what? A very good- looking guy...

Not fifteen. Thirteen, maybe, and all hormones.

Reality waited in the kitchen. At the stove and the worktable.

Cooking. That was why she was here; that was what this was all about. She drained everything but that from her thoughts.

Big men, hungry men needed a dessert. She still had flour. Lard. Apples. Sugar and even cinnamon.

An apple pie would take too long. Or maybe not, if she

made a lattice crust.

Peel. Slice. Sauté. Roll out the dough. Pop the pan in the oven.

Time to go back into the dining room and see how things were going.

The men looked up. They nodded, smiled, and went back to eating.

Nick looked up, too.

"Won't you join us?"

Such a simple question. So polite. But that look in his eyes…

Her heart thumped. She shook her head, made motions toward the kitchen.

"No. Thank you. I'm not hungry and I have—I have dessert in the oven…"

She caught her lip between her teeth. Nick's eyes turned midnight blue. *Oh God,* she thought, and she all but rushed from the room.

Would he come after her? Would he?

No.

He didn't, and why on earth would she have thought he would? Whatever had occurred before had been an aberration. Just a hot sexual flare. Those things happened. You didn't have to understand the reasons, not all the time. Things just happened even when you didn't particularly like somebody, and she certainly didn't like Nick Gentry and he sure as hell didn't like her.

Her sisters didn't understand that. The hot-sexual-flare thing. She was sure Emily and Jaimie just didn't get it. Well, they did, now, with the men they'd fallen for, but surely the sex thing had only happened after they'd felt some kind of emotional bond.

They'd always been the hearts-and-flowers type.

She'd taken a more logical approach. You didn't always need moonlight and roses.

Sometimes, all you needed was a man's touch. His body. His possession. *And be honest, here, Melissa, that's the gold standard and when, if ever, was the last time you really, really had that?*

She bit back a moan. Was she nuts? What was with all this soul-searching?

Nick Gentry had come on to her. She'd reacted. End of story.

She liked sex. She liked men. At least, she had, in the past, in the days before she'd realized what out-and-out bastards men were. Besides, she wasn't into one-night stands, and that, obviously, was what an encounter like this would be.

Her head was spinning. What she needed was something in her belly. She hadn't eaten since—since when? Had she even had anything this morning?

Why had she turned down Nick's suggestion that she eat with him and his men?

The pie was ready, though it had turned into more of a cobbler than a pie. She took it out of the oven, got down a bunch of bowls, put some of the cobbler in one of them, picked up a spoon and scooped up a mouthful.

She blew on it. Blew on it again. Still, when she put it in her mouth, it burned.

Like Nick's kiss.

That amazing kiss.

There was no harm in admitting it was the best kiss she'd ever experienced.

What would he be like in bed? Tender? Demanding? Exciting. She was certain of that. He would be exciting and maybe a little dangerous and—

"Ms. Wilde?"

Definitely a little dangerous. There was a hint of wildness to him. And—

"'Scuse me, ma'am. Ms. Wilde?"

The spoon fell from Lissa's fingers and clattered to the tabletop.

"Yes?" she said, forcing a smile for the cowboy with the empty Spam bowl in his hands.

"I'm sorry, ma'am. I didn't mean to startle you." He cleared his throat. "The boys and I jes' wanted to tell you that this here's the best meal we've had in a long time."

Lissa blinked.

"Why—why, that's very kind of you, but I just, you know, I just threw together whatever I found and…." She swallowed hard. She'd have accepted the compliment had it been given for a dish she'd concocted from caviar and blini; why not accept it for something she'd made out of everyday things? "Thank you. Thank you, uh…"

"Ace. I'm Ace, ma'am. And did you say somethin' about dessert?"

Lissa smiled. "I did, indeed. Do you like apple cobbler?"

"I like apple anything, ma'am."

"Please. Call me Lissa."

"Ms. Lissa. Yes ma'am. We all like apple anything."

She laughed. "That's the perfect name for what I made," she said. "Apple Anything."

Within seconds, all the men were in the kitchen, carrying their empty bowls and plates and spoons, dumping everything in the sink. Another of the men introduced himself as Gus and asked if it was all right if he put up the coffee.

"I was always better at it than Cooky."

Lissa smiled at the old-fashioned term that had been given to every ranch cook from the start of time.

"That would be great."

The others took on the job of loading the dishwasher, scrubbing pots and rinsing them.

Everybody was here, except Nick.

Where was he? Not that it mattered; she was curious, that was all. She couldn't recall seeing the ranch owners of her childhood eating with their men the way Nick had. Had tonight been a one-time occasion? Had he been checking on her ability as a cook? Was his interest over now?

Lots of questions. And no answers, but why would she need answers? She'd be out of here tomorrow. Early. The snow had tapered off to flurries; the wind had died away.

She was curious, that was all.

Nothing more.

When the kitchen was clean and neat, or as clean and neat as it was going to get without a top-to-bottom scrub, Lissa carried the Apple Anything to the dining room table. Ace followed with bowls and spoons; Gus brought in the coffee and a bunch of chipped mugs.

Shyly, Ace asked if she'd like to have her dessert with them.

She didn't hesitate.

"I'd be honored," she said.

The men sat down in their chairs. Ace shot them a fierce look and they shot to their feet.

"After you, ma'am," he said.

Lissa sat. The others did the same. Every eye was on her and she took a paper napkin from a holder and spread it on her lap. So did the men. She lifted her spoon. They lifted theirs. She dug in. So did they.

"Dee-licious," Ace said, beaming.

Lissa smiled. "I'm glad."

Everyone ate. There were a few slurps, a few burps. Lissa finished and patted her mouth with her napkin. The men did, too.

"Well," she said, and cleared her throat, "I'll leave you to your coffee."

The men scrambled to their feet as she rose from her chair. Ace shook his head when she reached for her dish.

"We'll clean up, Ms. Wilde."

"Lissa."

"Ms. Lissa. We'll take care of this. Don't you worry about a thing." He grinned. It was an endearing grin that featured a big gap between his center-top front teeth. "We want you to know how much we're lookin' forward to tomorrow, ma'am."

"To tomorrow?" Lissa's smile dimmed. "Oh. You mean…" She hesitated. How could she tell these guys that there would be no tomorrow? "Well, thank you, but—but I'm a great believer in not planning too far ahead."

Everyone laughed politely, which was what she'd intended—except that not believing in planning too far ahead was a truism, when you came down to it.

If she'd planned ahead, she wouldn't be here.

Why hadn't she asked Marcia more questions about this job? she thought as she climbed the steps to her room. The answer was simple. She'd been desperate for something that would change her life.

Well, she'd done that, all right. Changed her life—but not for the best.

She had no work at all now. The chicken place would have replaced her without thinking twice. Nick would complain to Marcia and she would make everything out to be Lissa's fault. She'd go back to Los Angeles and—

And what?

She'd been without a good job for too long. The awful truth was that the longer you were out of work, the harder it was to get work. By this time next week, frying blobs of chicken would look good.

Lissa sighed as she reached the top of the stairs. The lighting was dim, but that was OK. It suited her mood.

If only she'd stayed in L.A. If only she hadn't been so desperate.

If only she hadn't let Nick kiss her.

Where was he, anyway?

She'd half imagined he'd be waiting for her outside the kitchen just as he had been earlier, but why would he do that? He was probably in his office. Or in bed. Wherever he was, it was none of her business. *He* was none of her business.

He was—he was a bit of a puzzle; it was why she kept thinking about him. That a man so accustomed to the spotlight should be out here in the middle of nowhere, that he was obviously hurt and just as obviously hurting…

That she couldn't stop thinking about the feel of his arms around her.

She sighed. Stopped walking, kicked off her shoes, picked them up in one hand and continued toward her room. She was tired, that was all, or why would she waste her time thinking about a man she hoped never to see again?

The man she hoped never to see again stepped out of the shadows.

"Lissa."

His voice was low. Rough. She could almost feel the sound resonate against her skin.

What was he doing here? Waiting for her, obviously, but for what reason? To tell her the meal had been fine? To confirm her departure time tomorrow?

He was so big. So beautifully masculine. And the way he was looking at her, making her the clear focus of all that incredible intensity…

He took a step toward her.

"Just stay where you are, Gentry, because you and I have nothing to say to each other."

"You're right. We don't."

She nodded. "I'm glad we agree on something."

Then her shoes fell from her hand and she went straight into his arms.

CHAPTER SEVEN

THERE WERE NO preliminaries.

Lissa came to him as if this moment had been theirs from the beginning of time.

She went up on her toes as she raised herself to him and wound her arms around his neck. Her body pressed against his, and Nick groaned, bent his head and captured her mouth with his.

He hadn't expected this, but then, he hadn't really expected anything.

He'd gotten out of the dining room before dessert, knowing that staying would have been a mistake, that seeing her again would have compounded it even more than the mistake he'd already made by kissing her.

They weren't children.

When men and women kissed the way they had, it was usually the start of something that would end in more than kisses.

But then he hadn't intended to kiss her in the first place.

She was argumentative. Difficult. A flesh-and-blood embodiment of that old nursery rhyme about sugar and spice and he wasn't a man much taken with sugar and spice, but her in-your-face-honesty was irresistible. So was the way she looked, not just naked—he couldn't get that image out of his head—but right there in that old kitchen against a backdrop of pots and pans and tired old gadgets, her face free of makeup, her hair drawn back in a way that was as sexy as it was down-to-earth.

It had all come together and he'd laughed.

Then he'd looked into her eyes and it had felt as if the air had been sucked out of the room.

Without thinking, he'd reached for her. It had been the first thing he'd done on impulse in months. Everything since the accident had been planned and orchestrated.

Not that kiss.

The feel of her mouth under his, the warmth of her in his arms...

He'd have taken her right there, if not for his men sitting in the next room.

She'd have let him.

He'd seen desire blazing in her eyes, tasted it on her tongue.

Somehow, he'd let go of her.

Somehow, he'd gotten out of the kitchen.

Ace had said something to him and he'd mumbled some kind of response, but he had no idea what in hell it had been because the only part of him working had been his dick.

He'd made an attempt at eating dinner. He couldn't do any

less, not with his men seated around him.

He hadn't tasted the food, hadn't tasted anything except the memory of that kiss. The memory of the woman. He'd wanted her with an intensity that overrode all logic. Her name roared in his ears; he'd felt the imprint of her mouth on his. After months of not feeling like a man, what he'd felt in that dining room, watching her come and go, had been like finding water in the desert when you'd believed you were about to die of thirst.

Then, someplace between whatever it was she'd served and his men's increasingly delighted comments about the new cook's talent, the truth had rushed up and all but spit in his eye.

Wanting Lissa was the good news. But he couldn't possibly have her. That was not only the bad news, it was the only news that mattered.

He couldn't take a woman to bed. Not a woman who hadn't been paid to pretend she wouldn't be disgusted by what she saw once he got undressed.

He had never been vain.

Well, hell, maybe he had. Why not? He was an OK actor, maybe even a pretty good one, but he knew that he'd landed his first big part because of how he looked.

And he damn well knew what he looked like now.

So would a woman who saw him without his pants, which was why he'd left the table, walked away from the insanity of wanting what he knew he couldn't have, and everything had been fine.

Maybe fine was overstating it, but it had been all right...

Until he'd heard her footsteps on the stairs and, dammit, why lie to himself? He'd never have heard them unless he'd been listening for them, every muscle, every neuron in his body attuned to the sound of her, the scent of her, and then he'd stopped thinking, he'd simply acted, left his room, headed down the hall and now here he was…

Here he was, Lissa in his arms. Soft and sweet and perfect.

Stop now, he told himself.

Instead, he slid one big hand down her spine, cupped her bottom, lifted her into him. He knew he was hard as granite and he loved it when she knew it, too, when she moaned softly, fisted her hands in his hair and whimpered as he deepened the kiss.

Stop now.

Instead, he let the taste of her flood his senses. Coffee. Sugar. A tantalizing whisper of spice.

Stop now.

Instead, he pressed his lips to her throat and when her head fell back, he kissed the pulse that raced in the tender hollow of her flesh.

"Yes," she sighed, "yes, please, yes…"

His mouth captured hers again. And again. She was panting. So was he. He wanted her, wanted her, wanted her…

She reached back, fumbled with the doorknob, and the door, the goddamned door that had burst open a handful of hours ago, held fast.

He brushed her hand aside, gave the door one sharp rap and it flew open.

She gave a little laugh. God, he loved that laugh. Wicked.

Knowing. Full of promise. And he laughed with her as they stumbled into the room together.

He elbowed the door shut behind them.

The room was dark, illuminated only by the soft glow of the heavy snow that covered the yard and the land beyond it.

She reached for the light switch.

He caught her hand, brought it to his lips, kissed the palm. Dark was good.

She wouldn't see his leg in the dark because, yes, he was going to make love to her, yes, he was going to take her, have her, wrap her in his arms, kneel between her legs…

Kneel? You?

The little voice inside his head was low and cold and filled with venom.

Stop it, he thought again, but then Lissa clasped his face and drew his head down to hers and he saw the wildness in her beautiful eyes, saw the way her hair had come undone and tumbled around her face, and the voice faded and died.

He was still a man. The body parts that mattered worked, he thought, and he cupped her breast through the thin cotton of her T-shirt and she gasped. Her lashes fluttered to her cheeks and he groaned with pleasure, dipped his head to her breast and bit lightly through the cotton.

She moaned.

He drew back. Undid the first button on his shirt, then the next and the next.

Lissa slid her hands inside his open shirt. The feel of her fingers against his skin made him shudder.

"Wait," he growled, and he reached for her T-shirt, almost

forgetting for the moment that he had only one free hand, that he was balanced on a crutch.

Stripping off her shirt using only one hand was impossible.

The first tiny bit of reality danced into his head and he said something, low and sharp.

She silenced him with a quick kiss. Then she clasped the hem of her shirt and pulled it over her head.

Suddenly, all that mattered was looking at her.

She was beautiful. So beautiful. Skin touched with gold by the sun. Lush breasts straining above the half-cups of a white lace bra.

Nick cupped one breast. She made a sharp little sound of pleasure. His eyes locked to hers as he swept his thumb over her lace-covered nipple.

She cried out.

His erection became almost painful.

The bra had a front clasp. A man didn't need two hands to undo it, and Nick sent a silent *thank you* to whatever genius had invented it. Still, it took a couple of seconds before the damned thing came apart and her breasts tumbled free.

They were all he could have dreamed they would be.

Round. Lovely. High. And, God, her nipples… They were a deep, elegant rose.

"You are so beautiful," he whispered. "So amazingly beautiful."

Lissa felt her lips curve.

Nick's gaze was like a silken caress. Slowly, oh so slowly, he bent his head to her, drew the tip of one breast into the heat of his mouth.

Her knees all but buckled.

He wrapped his arm around her waist, supported her as he sucked on her nipple, licked at it, rolled his tongue around it until she sobbed his name. She clasped the nape of his neck and he groaned and moved against her, his erection pressing hard into her belly.

Her thighs were wet.

She was, oh, she was soaked. How could that have happened so quickly? She was hot and wet and she needed him inside her, inside her, inside her…

She shoved his shirt back on his shoulders, dragged his head up, kissed him and pressed her body to his, groaning along with him when her breasts flattened against his hair-roughened chest.

She was trembling.

"Nick," she whispered.

He put his hand under her chin, lifted her face to his and kissed her. She sucked the tip of his tongue into the heat of her mouth.

"Nick," she said again, and he heard what she wanted in that one softly-spoken plea.

He put his hand between them, reached for the top button of her jeans and fumbled with it.

Dimly, she realized it might be difficult for him to manage the button one-handed and she started to push his hand away and deal with the button herself, but he shook away her hand and she let him do it, let him work the button until, at last, it came free.

Her jeans dropped to her hips and she took a few steps

back, Nick moving with her, until she felt the mattress against the back of her thighs.

She dropped onto the edge of the bed.

Her face was level with Nick's fly.

She looked up, watched his face as she put her hand over the bulge that strained behind the soft blue denim.

He sucked in his breath.

She caught hers as she felt him pulse against her hand.

Still watching him, she undid the top button of his jeans. Unzipped him. Reached for him, but he stopped her.

"I want to see you naked."

His voice was raw. It sent a rush of excitement through her. He took a step back. She rose, eyes on his, and slowly worked her jeans down her hips, down her long legs. Would Nick like what he saw? She wanted to be beautiful for him.

She could feel her excitement building under his gaze, as hot as tendrils of flame. Her breasts, her belly, her thighs... every part of her felt the stroke of his hand even though he had not touched her since he'd undone the button on her jeans.

A tremor went through her.

She couldn't remember ever feeling this way before. Breathless, almost dizzy, the anticipation building and building and building...

"Now," he said, and Lissa gave her jeans a final push and stepped free of them.

Nick gave an audible groan.

She knew what he was seeing. All of her, completely naked except for a tiny scrap of white lace.

He whispered her name.

She moved closer to him.

He traced the outline of her mouth with one finger.

She caught the tip of that finger lightly between her teeth and sucked it into her mouth.

"You're killing me," he said thickly.

She was killing herself as well, and when he withdrew his finger from her mouth, ran it down her chin, down her throat, between her breasts and down her belly, she felt the first unmistakable signs of an impending orgasm.

She was going to come.

Was that possible? Could you come just from a man's touch?

Nick slid his hand between her thighs. Cupped her, and her unspoken question was answered as a low, fierce cry burst from her throat.

She swayed on her feet and he leaned hard on his crutch so he could wrap his arm around her while his free hand continued the sweet, sweet strokes that had drawn that incredibly primal response.

He told himself to be careful.

He was close to the edge, holding her, inhaling her scent, feeling her body weep against his palm, all that wildfire and hot rain for him.

Only for him.

He bent to her, kissed her, his tongue stroking hers while his thumb slipped under that tiny vee of lace and found her clitoris.

She sobbed his name, and Nick's world spun.

He had not planned this. Had not intended to take this so far. There were logical reasons why he shouldn't and he knew them all, but her soft, primitive cry was his final undoing.

He forget everything but this.

This, he thought as his mouth plundered hers.

This, he thought as she lifted herself to him.

This, he thought, this moment, this woman, and he swept both his arms around her so he could lift her against him, feel every inch of her against him as he brought her down the length of his body.

One of his hands slid into her hair.

For one brief flash of time they stayed that way, he holding her, her hands on his shoulders, their mouths fused in a kiss so deep, so sweet, so erotic that nothing existed on the planet but them.

Then Nick swayed.

No, he thought, *Christ, no...*

The crutch toppled and fell to the floor.

And Nick went down with it. Hard. Fast. Gracelessly, like a once-mighty oak now splintered by lightning.

Pain screamed like a banshee down the length of his leg. He had never felt anything like it, not since the day the IED had gone off under the Humvee.

Bile rose in his throat; for one terrible moment, his world went black and he started to go under, but Lissa's shrill cry dragged him up and up and up, until he surfaced.

"Nick!"

He had landed on his side. Now, panting, gasping for air, he rolled onto his back. Lissa was on the floor beside him. She reached for him and he jerked away.

"I'm OK."

The words sounded like the worst possible lie, even to him. To her, too, because she shot to her feet.

"Where are you going?"

"For help. I'll get somebody—"

He grabbed her hand. "No."

"But your leg—"

"I'm fine."

"Nick. Please. I'll go the bunkhouse. Ace will—"

He clamped his fingers hard around wrist.

"Find my crutch."

"Nick. Let me help you—"

"Find the fucking crutch," he snarled.

He raised his eyes to hers. She looked terrified. Why wouldn't she? One second, he'd been a man making love to her; the next, he'd become a useless hulk all but sobbing at her feet.

His belly knotted with self-disgust. All he wanted was to get away from the look in her eyes that said, more than words ever could, that he was no longer a man.

"Nick," she said helplessly, and he slammed his fist against the floor.

"The crutch, goddammit! Give it to me."

She stared at him. Then she looked away, grabbed the crutch and held it out toward him.

He wound his fingers around the padded top.

His heart was racing like a frightened rabbit's; his leg, from thigh to ankle, felt as if it had been run through with a hot spear. It took all the strength he had to jam the crutch against the floor and slowly, slowly work his way to his feet.

His vision grayed. The room swam. He could feel Lissa staring at him. Hell, why wouldn't she stare?

He was nothing but a useless, pathetic piece of shit.

How could he have forgotten that, even for a minute?

At last, after what seemed an eternity, he was fully upright. He waited, head down, dragging air into his lungs. When he took his first step toward the door, the pain screamed through him again.

He could almost feel his bones turning hollow.

Lissa's hand fell on his arm.

"Nick. Sit down for a minute."

He shook her off and kept going, putting one foot after the other. Dragging one foot after the other, if accuracy mattered.

"Nick. Dammit, are you crazy? Please—"

He blocked out her voice. Somehow, he reached the door. Grasped the knob. The thing wouldn't turn.

The door was like a bad joke.

Like his life.

Nick rattled the knob again, called it something nobody in his right mind would call a doorknob, and slammed it with the heel of his hand.

Lissa said his name again. Her voice shook. Wasn't it enough that she had seen him like this? Couldn't she have the decency to leave him alone?

She touched him again and, just as she did, the knob turned and the door swung open, but not fast enough to stop her from moving past him and blocking his departure.

The sight of her broke his heart, and wasn't that amazing, that he still had a heart?

She was still half-naked, still beautiful and he wondered what in hell had made him think he deserved her. Because he didn't. Never mind the ugliness of his leg.

He didn't deserve the kindness, the goodness he saw shining in her eyes.

He wanted to tell her all of that, but then he'd have to tell her the rest, and she sure as hell didn't need to hear it.

The best thing he could for her now was to get out of her life.

He drew a long, ragged breath.

"You want to help?"

She nodded. "Yes. Yes, of course."

"Then you'll forget this ever happened. Any of it. All of it. This place. Tonight. The whole thing never happened."

Incredulity glittered in her eyes.

"That's it?"

"Hank called a couple of hours ago. As long as the weather stays clear, he'll be back at dawn. He'll fly you out then. Now do us both a favor and step aside."

She put her hands on her hips. There she stood, wearing nothing but those tiny lace panties and a look that said he was out of his mind, and she still looked tough and determined and so lovely that she made him want things he no longer had a right to want.

"Lissa. Get out of my way."

"Dammit," she said, "what the hell is with you? You think you can—you think you can just—that you can just—"

"Yes. Exactly. I *can* 'just.' I'm Nick Gentry. I can 'just' whatever I like."

Her eyes were filled with questions. And with pity. What else could that be but pity? It made him feel sick. He didn't need her questions, and he sure as hell didn't need her pity.

"You don't mean that."

Rage, despair, emotions he'd kept at bay for months swamped him. He didn't need to feel any of them. They were her fault, goddammit, her fault for intruding on his carefully constructed life.

"I always say what I mean, Duchess. Too bad you didn't get that the first time, when I told you that the only payment I wanted for your room and board was a meal."

She stared at him, the compassion in her eyes dimming.

Good, he thought, not only good but perfect.

"What's that supposed to mean?"

His mouth twisted.

"Much as I appreciate the thought, a pity-fuck wasn't necessary."

Her face went white.

He wanted to cut out his tongue. Reach for her. Draw her into his arms. Tell her that he had not meant what he'd just said, that hurting her had been, in some ugly way, his only means of fully punishing himself for dragging her into the mess that was his life, but he stood his ground, kept his face expressionless.

The air between them hummed with tension.

He saw her hand jerk, then fist.

She wanted to hit him, but she wouldn't. She'd already done that once, and she wasn't the kind of woman who'd slug a cripple a second time.

"You're right," she said. "That's precisely what it would have been. A pity-fuck, something I could write off on my 1040 as a charitable contribution."

Any other time, he'd probably have laughed. The lady had some acting talent of her own.

But this wasn't a time for laughter. Nick had been around Hollywood long enough to know a great exit line when he heard it, even if the line wasn't his.

She stepped aside.

He hobbled past her.

The door slammed behind him, hard enough to make the house shudder.

He made his way down the hall to his own room, slammed his own door with equal vigor, dumped his crutch against a chair and fell heavily into bed, fully-dressed and wide-awake. There was a half-full bottle of bourbon on the table next to the bed and he reached for it, unscrewed the cap, brought the bottle to his lips and took a long drink.

His poison of choice.

"Be careful with the pain pills," the docs had advised when he left the hospital. "You ache, you're depressed, the Vicodin can become a problem."

"The hell I'm depressed," he'd said, and by then, the docs had given up arguing.

The pills hadn't become a problem. He'd used them the first couple of months, but only when the pain had been unbearable.

Besides, he'd discovered that booze was better.

Drugs sailed him into a never-never land where the world was dreamlike and peaceful.

Booze just took him under, where the world was non-existent.

Much better.

Still, it didn't work that well tonight. He didn't drop into exhausted sleep until the old clock downstairs had tolled four, and that sleep didn't last very long.

He was awakened not by the roar of the returning plane but by the roar of the returning storm, which had doubled back and finally, inexorably, turned itself into a blizzard.

CHAPTER EIGHT

A FEW MINUTES after dawn, Lissa stood by the bedroom window, her expression glum as she stared out at the storm that held her prisoner.

She knew it was ridiculous to think of it that way, but she couldn't help it.

The storm was like a great beast, roaring through the trees and around the house.

The snow was coming down like a thick white curtain adding inches to what had fallen yesterday, and according to the weather service, there was more to come. The wind was as fierce as any she'd ever experienced.

Who knew when she'd finally get away from this horrible place and this horrible man?

You couldn't go anywhere in a blizzard.

Outside, the trees bent and swayed under the power of the wind. Nothing else moved against the stark white landscape except for a big black shape that had plowed through the snow a few minutes ago.

Brutus.

That, at least, had made her smile.

Brutus clearly loved the snow.

She'd watched as he rolled in the stuff, bit at it, flung it through the air. Then he'd stopped, cocked his head and looked back toward the house. Someone had to be calling him.

Gentry, probably.

At least he hadn't let the dog out alone.

It was painfully easy to get lost in a storm like this one.

Yes, but Gentry wouldn't let that happen to his dog. He cared for the Newf. Even more telling, the Newf cared for him. There was a time Lissa had believed that if a dog loved somebody, that somebody couldn't be all bad.

"To hell with that theory," she muttered as she turned away from the window, plopped down on the edge of the bed and tied her sneakers.

Gentry was a mean-tempered, nasty piece of work. What had happened last night proved it. He'd been making love to her and he'd fallen. She'd worried that he'd hurt himself, but his reaction—all that anger, how he'd refused her concern as well as her help, his attitude…

Ugly.

And then that vicious crack about why she'd been on the verge of having sex with him—and that was what it would have been, sex, nothing as prettified as making love, assuming *prettified* was a word and if it wasn't, it sure as blazes should be.

That horrid remark.

What sort of woman did he think she was?

It didn't matter.

The entire incident had been one huge, terrible mistake. Nick Gentry was not the kind of man she'd ever sleep with; hadn't she had enough of self-important Hollywood pretty boys?

There it was again. That word, pretty. A word, a concept to be avoided.

If only she could avoid Gentry.

It was going to be embarrassing to see the man. To be hit with the image of herself, naked in front of him, naked and kicked to the side of the road like—like trash.

Dammit.

"Get hold of yourself, Melissa," she said.

Or at least keep your metaphors straight. She had not been kicked to the side of the road, not even metaphorically. She had been treated to an ugly display of male ego. The man had a banged-up leg, it had given way and instead of dealing with it, he'd snarled and spat and headed for his man cave.

It was good that things had not gone any further. The only thing worse than ending the night the way they had would have been actually ending it in bed.

Except—except she couldn't get the memories out of her head.

The way he'd held her.

The heat of his hands, cupping her breasts.

The taste of his mouth. Of his skin.

The hardness of him against her, all that taut male power...

Somebody pounded on the bedroom door. Lissa jumped and shot to her feet.

The door was locked. Damn right it was locked, but she didn't have much confidence in either the door or the lock or—

"Wilde!"

It was Gentry. Well, who else would it be? There was nobody in the house except for the two of them and Brutus. Besides, none of the ranch hands would have banged on the door and yelled her name like that.

"Wilde. You awake?"

She drew a deep breath. Then she marched across the room and undid the lock. She considered only cracking the door, abandoned the thought and swung it wide open.

No way was she going to let him think she felt intimidated.

"Awake? After that bellow, everybody between here and Yellowstone is awake. What do you want, Gentry?"

"There won't be a plane today."

"My oh my," she said sweetly. "And here I was just about to go downstairs to wait for it." She slapped her hands on her hips. "I don't how to break it to you, but I figured that out all by myself."

"Yeah, well, you never can tell."

"No. You never can. I mean, why wouldn't I stand up to my ass in snow, waiting for Hank's plane to touch down?"

Gentry flashed a big, phony smile.

"Maybe because they don't get blizzards in L.A. And as long as we're exchanging info, that isn't Hank's plane, it's mine."

"If Hank works for you, he has my sincere condolences. And as long as we're, as you put it, exchanging info, here's some for you. I didn't grow up in L.A. I grew up in Texas. North Texas. You want to talk about blizzards? Try spending a winter there sometime."

"Try Brooklyn," he said, and he turned his back and made his way down the hall.

"Despicable SOB," she muttered as she slammed the door.

But at least he was on his feet. After that fall last night—not that she cared. For all it mattered to her, Mr. Despicable could spend the next few days in the emergency room, except that he'd never get there in weather like this.

And she'd never get out of here.

No plane.

How long before there'd be one? It depended on the weather, meaning there wasn't a thing she could do about it. Meanwhile, she was stuck here with a man who had all the charm of a mongoose and when she finally headed home, it would be to no job, not even any job prospects.

Not good. Not good at all.

But she wasn't going to let herself think about that. Or about last night. She was going to keep busy. Keep occupied.

The question was how.

Fortunately, the answer was simple.

She'd cook.

Not for Gentry. Let him scrounge for himself. She'd cook for the six ranch hands, the cowboys who had been so effusive in praise of her Spam casserole last night. They were downstairs now; she'd heard the back door open and close several times, heard the murmur of male voices.

As for what she'd cook…

She had no idea. Last night's search through the kitchen hadn't turned up much, but she'd find something and, by God, she would cook it. What was the name of that amazing food writer who'd written a book about basically turning nothing into a meal?

If M.F.K. Fisher could do it, so could she.

Lissa pulled on an extra sweater, yanked her hair into a ponytail, and headed downstairs.

* * *

She found the men milling uncertainly in the dining room, mugs of steaming coffee in their work-roughened hands.

They turned toward her as she walked briskly into the room, their weathered faces sporting immediate grins.

"Mornin', Ms. Wilde," six voices chorused.

"Good morning. I see you all managed to get here from the bunkhouse."

Ace nodded. "Yes ma'am. We got a roped path we follow. Amazin' how a body can get lost tryin' to walk twenty feet in a whiteout like this without somethin' to guide him."

Lissa nodded. That was a basic heavy-snow, blowing-wind survival skill. You grew up on a ranch or a farm in snow country, you heard all the warnings by the time you were a toddler.

"That coffee smells wonderful."

Gus blushed. "I jes' made it," he said, nodding his head at the huge pot on the sideboard. "I'd be honored to pour you a cup."

"Not just now, thank you. I want to check out the pantry. I'm hoping I missed something that I can turn into breakfast."

"Maybe there's still some flour," one of the men said hopefully, "and lard and sugar."

"Hens probably laid us some eggs," another man said.

Lissa nodded. She could turn that into pancakes of one kind or another.

"Good thinkin'," Ace said. "Let's go check the henhouse."

Both men pulled on heavy jackets and gloves and headed for the back door. Lissa headed for the kitchen. No Gentry underfoot, thank heaven. The last thing she needed was to see him again—and what was that bit about Brooklyn? What would a man like him know about—

She came to a dead stop.

He was there, right in the middle of the kitchen, leaning back against the worktable, cradling a mug of coffee in his hands.

"What are you doing here?"

He raised his eyebrows. "I live here, or hadn't you noticed?"

She ignored the fast answer, went to the pantry and retrieved the flour, sugar and lard.

"Planning on making yourself some breakfast?"

"The men are hungry."

He nodded. "Yeah. I know. I'm gonna have to get into town for supplies."

"Can you? I mean, the snow…"

"Worried about me, Duchess? I'm touched."

Lissa swung toward him, eyes narrowing when she saw the smug grin on his face.

Despicable was too kind a word for him.

What made it worse was that he didn't look despicable.

Dressed in a dark blue sweater, faded jeans and those omnipresent well-worn boots, he looked—he looked—

Dammit.

He looked gorgeous, like the movie star he was, especially with that early-morning stubble on his jaw. She'd never thought stubble sexy, but it turned out that it was.

Could a mongoose be sexy?

No, she thought coldly, it could not.

"You're in my way," she snapped.

He didn't move.

"I said—"

"Want some coffee?"

"If I do, I'll get it the next time I go into the dining room."

"There's better coffee right here."

She looked at him, followed his gaze. A Chemex half filled with dark chocolate-brown coffee was on the counter near him.

"It's my one kitchen skill. The men think it's sissified, but I have this strange thing about preferring coffee that doesn't taste like old socks."

She almost laughed. That was what she'd thought last night after she'd tasted Gus's coffee. It even smelled that way—her comment a few minutes ago about its smelling wonderful had been more a courtesy than reality.

She considered turning down his offer, but what was that old saw about cutting off your nose to spite your face? Coffee was one of the basic food groups.

There was a clean mug next to the glass pot.

"Yours," he said. "I figured you for a coffee-as-lifeblood

woman."

What he'd said was so close to what she'd been thinking that she smiled. He smiled, too, and she turned her smile into a frown as she filled the mug.

"You're very sure of yourself, Gentry. Doesn't it ever occur to you that you might be wrong?"

"Rarely."

She turned and glanced at him. He was smiling again. It was a devastatingly wicked smile, but she'd be damned if she'd respond to it.

"And when it does occur to me," he said quietly, "I've even been known to admit it."

"Really."

Her tone was flat and cool, but he knew he had her attention.

Do it, Gentry. Just say that you're sorry. You don't have to go into detail. You don't have to grovel. You just have to say two words—I'm sorry— and then you can excuse yourself, go hide in your office, put last night in a deep, dark closet where it belongs.

"I made an ass of myself last night." It wasn't what he'd intended to say, but it was accurate. "I know I must have looked like an idiot, but—"

"Excuse me?"

"Falling down the way I did. Like a clumsy—"

She slapped the mug on the counter.

"Is this an apology?"

"Well, yeah. I mean—"

"An apology about you looking foolish."

"Yes." He hesitated. She didn't seem pleased. But he'd apologized. What more did she want?

"I fell, and I know—"

"That's why you're apologizing? For falling?"

His eyes narrowed. "Didn't I just say that?"

"And the rest of it?"

"The rest of what?"

Lissa stared at him. Was he serious?

"Oh, I don't know. The way you bit my head off for being foolish enough to offer to help you."

His jaw tightened. "I didn't need help. I got up on my own just fine."

"And what you said to me. I suppose that was just fine, too."

"What I said—"

"About the reason you—you fell. About why you were in my room in the first place."

He looked blank. Then she could almost see him finally figuring it out. To her great satisfaction, color striped his high cheekbones.

"Oh. That."

"Yes," she said, her tone as cold and sharp as one of the icicles hanging outside the house. "That."

Nick put down his coffee mug. He ran his hand through his hair. The pity-fuck thing. How could he have forgotten that? Well, he knew how. What he'd said was ugly, worse than ugly, and, he knew damn well, untrue. Somehow, he'd mercifully managed to shove the memory of those words into oblivion.

What man would want to remember such stupidity?

"Obviously, I didn't mean—"

Lissa folded her arms. "You said what you were thinking."

"No. I wasn't thinking that." He raked his fingers through

his hair again. "And if I was, I meant it about me. Not about you."

"I see. So, what we almost did last night—and didn't do," she added, "thank you, God—was because you pitied me."

"What?"

"I said—"

"I heard what you said. And you're wrong. I didn't mean it that way. I meant that you—that you were only being, you know, kind—"

Shit.

He was digging himself deeper and deeper into a hole that was bound to collapse on him, and from the way she was looking at him, he'd never be able to dig himself out.

She stalked toward him, that index finger she used with the dexterity of a fencing foil outstretched.

"Get this straight, cowboy. Last night had nothing to do with pity. It had to do with stupidity. Mine. Why I ever thought I'd want to have sex with you is beyond me to—"

Someone coughed.

It was Ace, standing in the arched doorway with snow on his boots, a basket of eggs in his hands, and a look on his face that said he wished the ground would open and swallow him whole.

"Sorry. So sorry. I didn't mean to intrude."

Nick adjusted the crutch under his arm and moved toward the door at top speed. Lissa breathed deep, exhaled, forced what she hoped was a smile and took the basket from Ace's hands.

"Eggs," she said brightly. "Wonderful! Uh, Mr. Bannister

and I were just—we were just talking."

"Yes, ma'am." Ace started to turn away, hesitated and, instead, looked at Lissa. "His name is Gentry, ma'am. Nick Gentry. Latham Gentry's kid. We all know that."

She nodded as she busied herself retrieving the bowl of butter from the fridge, then finding a big bowl, a fork and a spatula. She really didn't want to discuss Nick or anything about him, but she knew that the foreman meant well.

"I mean, it ain't just that we recognized his face, it's that a couple of us knew his old man. There's been Gentrys on this land for a real long time."

She nodded again. If this was heading somewhere, she wanted it to reach its destination ASAP.

"His old man was tough. Hard as a rock. After Nick's mom passed, he clothed and fed the boy, but otherwise he pretty much ignored him."

She nodded again as she cracked the eggs into the bowl.

"Well," she said, to fill the silence, "ranching is a tough life."

"And then this here accident…"

None of this was any of her business. None of it would change Nick Gentry into a nicer man. Still, she heard herself ask the inevitable question.

"What kind of accident was it?"

"Dunno. But it was a bad one."

Yes. It must have been. If she hadn't thought that before, last night had convinced her of it.

"He come back here after he was in the hospital."

"Well," she said, opening the pantry door, taking out the flour and handing it to Ace, "he would, wouldn't he? This is his home."

Ace put the flour on the worktable. Lissa handed him the sugar.

"He hadn't been back here for years."

"But he visited, right?"

"Not unless you count his old man's funeral."

"But—"

"Ace!"

Lissa and the foreman swung toward the door that led into the dining room. Nick glared at them both, his face cold.

"Yessir."

"The snow's stopped and the wind's dying down. Might be a good time to start clearing a path to the barns, and to ride out and check on the horses."

It was a statement, but there was no mistaking it for anything but a command.

Ace nodded. "Sure thing."

"Wait!" Lissa stepped forward. "The men haven't had breakfast yet."

"Right. Because you've yet to make it. They'll come in once they've seen to their chores. Get the men moving, Ace."

Ace tipped his Stetson to Lissa and hurried away. She glared at Nick.

"You're a real charmer, Gentry."

"This is a working ranch, Wilde. You want to stand around gossiping with the help, find one of those fancy places where people hang around doing nothing all day but getting massages."

Lissa blew a strand of hair out of her eyes. "I intend to, as soon as I get away from here. When's the plane due?"

"The weather's cleared some, but not enough for getting off the ground or landing. Tomorrow, if Hank is lucky."

"You mean, if *I'm* lucky!" Lissa snapped, and turned her back on him in dismissal.

* * *

She got breakfast on the table, or an approximation of breakfast. Eggs. Pancakes topped with something she dreamed up from the remaining few apples.

The men couldn't stop praising the food.

Lissa couldn't stop smiling.

There was nothing like cooking for people who appreciated what you served them, especially when their enjoyment wasn't dependent on whether a bunch of fancy food critics or trendy magazines had first blessed you with glossy reviews.

It was almost like cooking for family. For Jake, Caleb, Travis, Emily and Jaimie. She did that whenever they were all gathered at El Sueño for a holiday or some kind of special occasion.

Or course, at El Sueño she had more to work with than, what, maybe three remaining tablespoons of lard, two cups of flour, a few eggs and, if her luck held, half a cup of sugar.

Certainly not enough to turn into a meal...

Wait. That frozen chunk of Tyrannosaurus Rex, that huge package of mystery meat was still in the freezer. She hauled it out. Not easy, considering the weight and dimensions of the thing, and wrestled it into the big sink to thaw.

Whatever it was, it was supper for tonight or tomorrow. It all depended on how fast the hawing process took.

She dried her hands on an ancient plaid cloth that had surely once been a dishtowel and looked around her. Oh, what she could do with this room! An oversized Viking range right there. A pair of Wolf wall ovens next to it. A big Bosch fridge. A Bosch dishwasher. A Miele freezer. She'd keep the worktable; all it needed was a good sanding. But the floor would have to go.

No. It wouldn't. That was oak underneath the years of neglect. She'd refinish it, put fresh paint on the walls, tear out these old Formica counters and replace them with granite or stone, finish up by using some bright terra-cotta tiles for a backsplash.

But the kitchen wasn't hers, it was Nick Gentry's, and from what she'd seen so far, he didn't have any interest in bringing this old house back to life.

He wasn't interested in anything but himself, and wasn't it a good thing they hadn't ended up in bed last night? Because if they had, she wouldn't just be disappointed in herself this morning, she'd be furious.

To think she'd let lust, down and dirty lust, carry her away like that…

"Haven't you learned anything about men Melissa?" she muttered.

The grim truth seemed to be that she hadn't.

Lissa poured more coffee into her mug, shut off the lights and headed for the stairs.

* * *

You could spend only so much time straightening a room and a tiny bath.

Make the bed. Wipe down the sink. Then what?

Lissa sighed. Unpack, was what. She was going to be here until at least tomorrow. Might as well hang up a few things.

If only she'd brought some heavier stuff with her. A more substantial jacket. Shoes that were real shoes as opposed to the ones in her suitcase, which ranged from a pair of heels to two pairs of sandals to her kitchen clogs and the sneakers that were on her feet now.

Properly dressed, she could get out of here for a while. A glance out the window confirmed that paths had been shoveled between the house and the outbuildings; somebody was clearing what looked like a million-mile driveway that probably led to the main road.

What if she added another sweater, then put on the little jacket she'd worn yesterday? Her sneakers would soak through in just a few minutes, but at least she'd breathe some fresh air.

She might even get last night and the awful, horrible, humiliating image of herself standing naked in front of Mr. Despicable out of her head, because that was becoming a serious problem, knowing that he'd seen her naked, that he'd said what he'd said about why she was naked while she was naked—

And if she kept going around and around like this, she was going to go nuts.

Lissa yanked on a second sweater, pulled on her jacket—

which wouldn't zip, dammit, not over a T and a sweater and another sweater—

"Fuck it," she said, yanked open the bedroom door and went down the stairs.

The house was quiet. The men had all gone to their chores. Gentry wasn't in sight. Good. Fine. With luck, she wouldn't have to look at his smug face again until lunchti—

"Woof!"

Brutus came galloping down the hall. She barely had time to brace herself before the big dog was on her, tail wagging madly as he covered her face with kisses.

"Hey," she said, laughing, "I'm happy to see you, too."

The dog woofed softly; Lissa squatted down, smiled as she ruffled his ears and buried her face in the deep silky fur around his neck.

"Beautiful doggy," she said. "I missed you."

"Looks as if he missed you, too."

She looked past the Newf. Gentry was coming down the hall toward her. He was dressed for the outdoors: well-worn sheepskin jacket, the omnipresent Stetson, jeans, boots, a pair of what looked like heavy gloves sticking out of one jacket pocket.

She stood up. "He's a sweetheart."

"Yes. He is."

"How old is he?"

Nick shrugged. "Nine. Ten. I'm not sure, but for a dog his size, that's old. I try not to think about it."

She looked at him. No smile on that handsome face, just a glimpse of honest emotion.

"I know," she said softly. "That's the tough thing about large breeds."

"I've been lucky so far. He's been with me for seven years."

Most people would say they'd owned the dog for seven years. She liked Nick's wording better. Too bad she didn't like Nick, but at least he had the right attitude about something.

"Well," she said briskly, "I'm going for a walk."

"A walk?"

"A walk. You know. You move one foot forward. Then you move the other foot forward. One, two, one, two—"

"Don't be stupid. It's twenty degrees outside."

So much for attitude.

"Thanks for your concern," she said coolly, "but I'll be fine."

"Like that? Oh, yeah. You'll be fine."

"I don't know how to break it to you, Gentry, but I don't have to ask your permission to take a walk."

Nick glared at her. "Didn't you bring a coat? Boots? Did you bring any warm stuff with you, or did you think Montana was on the Mexican border?"

"I thought it was in the United States," she said coldly, "where spring is a recognized season."

His lips twitched. She had a sense of humor. He'd always like that in a woman. She had a fast mouth, too. A soft mouth. He remembered that vividly from last night—except remembering last night was not the way to go.

"I'm going into town."

"Good for you."

"The highway's passable."

Her smile would have cut glass.

"Good for the highway."

"I'm going to lay in some supplies." He paused. "I want you to come with me."

She looked as if he'd just asked her to accompany him to the moon. Well, hell, he couldn't blame her. So far, he hadn't handled things between them very well. Not even that apology this morning, because maybe it hadn't come out exactly the way it should have.

"What on earth for?"

"You'll be here another day. Maybe even two."

"Let's hope not, and what does that have to do with anything?"

"There's no food in the house."

"I found a haunch of dinosaur in the freezer."

"A what?"

"There was a big, wrapped something in the freezer. It's defrosting. I'm assuming it's some kind of meat. You must have forgotten it was there."

Nick sighed. She wasn't going to make this easy and he couldn't blame her. He'd gone outside, spent almost an hour stomping around on a bum leg and a crutch, tackling chores in one outbuilding and then another, all to work off some anger.

Anger at himself, he'd finally realized, not at her.

Clomping back and forth on snow probably hadn't been the smartest thing he'd ever done, but it had helped.

By the time he came inside and took a long, hot shower, he'd come to the easy-to-reach conclusion that he'd made an ass of himself.

So here it was.

Truth time.

"The only thing I'm sure I forgot," he said, "is that I owe you an apology."

Her expression hardened.

"We went that route already, remember? You and that apology for falling down."

"Not that," he said quickly.

"Not what?"

Jesus. She wasn't going to make this easy. The woman took no prisoners. He had to admit, that was another thing he liked about her.

"I'm sorry for being such a fool last night."

Color rose in her cheeks. She turned away and started for the front door.

"I don't see any point in discussing last night."

He moved fast, came up behind her and clasped her shoulders.

"What I said to you was—it was wrong." He cleared his throat. "It was inexcusable."

"Good. Fine. You've apologized. Now let go of me."

He did just the opposite, his hands tightening on her as he turned her toward him.

"I know that what happened—what almost happened— didn't have a damn thing to do with pity."

Her face was scarlet, but her eyes were the color of ice on a high mountain lake. It was one hell of a contrast, and his gut knotted. That same hot rush of desire that had burned inside him last night flared to life again.

"I was a fool, Duchess. I was angry at myself and I let it out on you."

"I'm not interested in hearing this. Last night is history."

"I've never wanted a woman the way I wanted you."

How could a lie—because, surely it was a lie—make her feel so good? The best thing to do was make it clear that she knew he was lying.

"I'm sure that line has been a winner for you before, Gentry, but it's not gonna work this time."

"It's the truth. You think that's easy for me to admit? You think any of this is easy for me to admit?" His voice was low. Raw with emotion. "I didn't plan on anything that happened, Lissa. Not on going to your room, not on making love to you."

Her heart was beating fast and hard. She didn't want to hear this, didn't want to forgive him, but there was pain in his voice. What if there was?

It didn't change things.

He had hurt her badly last night—she knew damn well that her subsequent fury at him had actually been a way of trying to defuse that hurt.

And he was an actor. A very good actor, and she knew all about actors. For all she knew, this was Scene Two of last night's Act One. Maybe he had enough of a conscience to want absolution. Maybe he figured she'd be fool enough to welcome him into her bed again. Whatever his reason, she wasn't going to fall for the performance.

"See, that was the problem," she said with a cool smile. "Planning is everything. If you work out what you're going to do before you do it—"

She gasped as his hands tightened on her.

"Goddammit," he growled, "listen to me! I haven't been with a woman in months. I haven't wanted to be with a woman. Not since I—not since I hurt my leg. And then, there you were and you were all I could think about, and once I had you in my arms, I wanted it to be right, to be perfect, and instead I screwed up, I failed you—"

Lissa rose on her toes and put her mouth against Nick's.

For an endless moment, he didn't react. Then he groaned, slid his arm around her and responded to the kiss.

It was like last night all over again. She melted into him. Her mouth, her hands sliding up his chest, her thighs pressed against his, were all that mattered.

After a timeless interval, she flattened her hands against his chest and gave a shaky little laugh.

"So much for planning."

"Lissa—"

"You didn't fail me," she said, silencing him with a light touch of her hand to his lips. "You failed yourself, or some dumb male vision of what being a man is all about."

Nick gave a quick laugh. "Hell, Duchess, you sound like a shrink."

"You gave me a rough night, Gentry. I spent half of it worrying that you'd opened up a wound, broken a bone, did who knew what to your leg."

"What about the other half?" His gaze dropped to her lips like a caress. "Did you spend it imagining what it would have been like if we'd made love?"

"I spent it trying to keep from going into your room and smothering you with a pillow."

He grinned. "A woman of action." His grin faded. "Hell. I deserved it."

"Yes. You did. I would never, ever, not in a billion years give anybody a pity anything."

"Yeah. I know that. I knew it even when I said it. " He slipped his hand into her hair, tilted her face to his. "I'm sorry. I say things sometimes... Since the accident, I mean."

"One of my brothers went through a bad time. Jake was a pilot, but he lost an eye. It was rough."

He nodded. "Must have been hell."

"It was. I suspect there are times it still is. And he said and did some stuff right after it happened that he'd never have said or done before he was wounded."

"What happened to him?"

"He was a helicopter pilot in Afghanistan. He was wounded over there."

"In action," Nick said.

She looked up at him. His voice had gone flat.

"Yes."

"Wounded doing something brave."

"Not that he'll ever admit it, but yes, that's what happened."

Silence. Then Nick nodded and let go of her.

"So," he said briskly, "the roads are as clear as they're ever gonna get in what we laughingly refer to as early spring in Montana, and I'm heading into town for supplies. Come with me and pick up whatever we'll need for a couple of meals, OK? I don't mean you have to cook, but you'll have a better idea than I will of what the men and I can toss into a pot and eat without ending up in an emergency room."

He smiled, and Lissa revised her estimate of him as a good actor, because even she could tell that the smile was as phony as the joke.

Something had just happened. Talking about his accident—not that they'd really talked about it, but he'd mentioned it. Then she'd told him about Jake, and that had changed things. Why? She wanted to ask, but she knew she wasn't going to get an answer.

Nick wanted to change the subject? She'd go along with it. She wasn't going to be here that long. If something about his accident troubled him, he had every right to keep it to himself.

"OK," she said briskly. "I'll go with you. Heck, I'll do better than that. I'll make lunch and supper and, if I'm still here, tomorrow's breakfast. I'd just as soon keep busy. Besides, after the way your guys polished off what I gave them last night, I can only imagine how they'll react to real food."

Nick laughed. It was an easy, honest laugh, and it made her feel better.

"Trust me, Duchess. If you'd been eating what we've been eating the last few weeks—"

"Spam was a feast made for a king, huh?"

"Be it ever so humble," Nick said, and then he told her he'd scrounge up some warm stuff for her to put on, and she said that would be fine, and he looked at her and for one breathless moment she thought he was going to kiss her…

But he didn't.

And, of course, that was just as well.

* * *

It was an interesting trip, with Brutus taking up all the bench seat between them as well as most of Lissa's lap.

"You're a big baby," she told the dog softly, but she loved that Nick didn't relegate him to the open truck bed. She knew lots of truck owners did that with their dogs, but would you do that with a child?

Actually, she'd once snarled that at a jerk back in Wilde's Crossing.

She was glad she didn't have to snarl it at Nick.

It took twenty minutes to get to the nearest town. Clarke's Falls was a one-street-long collection of old buildings and storefronts. One of those was a general store, and Nick pulled to the curb in front of it.

"Stay," he told the Newf. Brutus gave a gusty sigh as Nick stepped down from the truck.

Lissa undid her seat belt and opened her door.

"Wait for me," Nick said. "There's a pile of snow on your side."

"I'm fine," she said.

Well, she probably would have been if the boots he'd found for her weren't at least three sizes too big. They started to slide off her feet as soon as she swung one leg out of the truck.

Nick was already there.

"I told you to wait," he said, grabbing the boot before she lost it and shoving it back on her foot. "Come on. Put your arms around my neck and I'll lift you down."

Lissa rolled her eyes. "The man has a short memory! We did this before, Gentry. My arms, your neck. Remember what happened?"

"Trust me, Duchess. I did a lot of practicing with this damn crutch this morning. Now, come on. Put your arms around me. That's the way. Just let me take your weight."

She did what he'd asked, and tried not to think about how good it felt as he carried her to the cleared sidewalk and set her on her feet.

"OK?" he said softly, with his arm still curved around her.

"OK," she said, trying not to sound as breathless as she felt.

"Nobody here knows who I am," he said quietly. "They all think I'm the new manager of the Triple G, a guy named—"

"Bannister. I know."

Another quick nod. Then he moved ahead of her toward the door. It swung open just as he reached it. An older man came through it, looked at her, at Nick, and tipped his Stetson.

"Mornin.'"

"Morning," Nick said.

The greeting was quick, but the look the other man flashed as Nick went past him hinted at something. It was the same look that shot across the face of the guy behind the counter.

"Bannister."

"Jessup."

It was a fast, impersonal greeting, but easy to read.

Both the men who'd just greeted Nick knew exactly who he was. The only person they were fooling was Nick. It was the kind of human courtesy you could find in small towns, and Nick, the big jerk, had no idea he was on the receiving end of it.

Lissa thought about telling him, thought better of it, and sighed.

"What?" Nick said.

"Nothing. I'm just trying to think of what to buy."

"Whatever you like. And plenty of it. Might as well lay in enough for the week, just so long as it's not going to be too complicated for me to put together."

"You?"

"Well, me and Gus."

Lissa snorted. "A pair of gourmet cooks, all right."

Nick grinned. "Just take one of those carts, Duchess, and fill it up while I check on some stuff in the back."

"Yessir, Mr. Bannister, sir."

Nick's eyes darkened. "Nice," he said in a low voice. "I like the idea of you obeying me."

Heat shot from her breasts to her belly. She felt her nipples lift and bud, felt the area between her thighs grow damp.

Crazy. That was crazy! One sentence, one swiftly-spoken sentence, and her mind filled with images so hot that she had to bite back a moan.

Blindly, she swung away, grabbed a shopping cart and all but ran down the first aisle.

* * *

Almost an hour later, she pushed the cart up the last aisle to the front counter where Nick and several big cardboard boxes were waiting. He motioned to the man behind the counter.

"This is Tom Jessup, Lissa. Tom, this is Lissa Wilde. The temporary cook—the temporary chef at the Triple G."

Tom Jessup smiled. "Find everything you needed, ma'am?"

Lissa smiled back. "Yes, thank you."

"Well, let's ring it all up, shall we?"

She'd taken Nick's suggestion to heart. She'd bought whatever she thought would keep a bunch of hungry, hard-working men filled and happy for at least a week.

Bags of sugar, of oats, of flour and rice and pasta and dried beans went from the cart to the counter to the cardboard boxes. Cans of tomatoes and vegetables followed, then packets of yeast. Cans of pineapple rings and apricots, bags of dried fruits, a couple of pounds of apples and pears as well as two ten-pound sacks of potatoes and another of onions made the same trip. Last up were quarts of milk, cartons of butter, packages of cheese, cold cuts, big bags of sandwich rolls, containers of orange juice, steaks and hamburger, chickens and turkey legs, along with a couple of pork roasts.

Nick looked bewildered.

"I won't know what to do with most of that stuff."

"I'll cook it up and freeze it. And I'll bake some bread and a couple of cakes, too. All you'll have to do is defrost and heat."

His face brightened. "Thank you."

"You're welcome. I wouldn't want you or the others to starve. Or to get ptomaine poisoning from you and Gus and your Adventures in Gastronomy."

Nick laughed. "Thanks for the vote of confidence, but I have to admit, it's probably well-placed."

She smiled as Jessup punched a bell. Two boys appeared from the storeroom at the rear and started carrying all the purchases out to the truck.

"Not that," Nick said quickly, when one boy reached for a

small box. He looked at Lissa, then jerked his chin toward a semicircle of rush-bottomed chairs that stood near a kerosene stove. "Sit down."

"What for?"

"Jesus, do you have to argue over everything?"

"I'm not arguing."

"No. But you will. I recognize that tone." Nick sighed. "Duchess. Do us both a favor. Sit down."

She sat, and her eyes widened when he opened the box and took out a pair of leather boots.

"What are those?"

"What do they look like?"

"Are those supposed to be for me?"

"No. Here. See if they fit."

"I just said, are those supposed to be for me? And you said they weren't. And now you want me to—"

"What I said was, they aren't supposed to be for you—they *are* for you. Try them on."

"Nick. Honestly—"

"You came here expecting hot tubs, fire pits and spring wildflowers. What you found was an old house, a bunch of hungry cowboys, and a snowstorm. Just give in gracefully. Try on the damn boots." He drew a breath, heaved it out. "Please."

"But I'll only be here until..." Lissa sighed. "Fine. I'll try them on."

She kicked off the three-sizes-too-big boots, easily slid her feet into the ones Nick handed her. The leather was butter-soft and the size was perfect, and she permitted herself one fleeting instant of self-indulgence, closing her eyes, giving another little sigh.

She loved good boots.

It was, she knew, something that came of growing up on a ranch.

"Good?"

Lissa blinked her eyes open.

"Very nice," she said briskly, "but I can't accept—"

"Too late."

"For what?"

"Mr. Jessup says that health department regulations won't permit him to take back boots that have been worn."

Lissa stared at the man behind the counter.

"That's ridiculous. I didn't wear them, I tried them on."

Jessup shrugged his shoulders, but she was pretty sure he was trying hard to suppress a smile.

"Nick. You're lying to me."

"Would I lie?" Nick said. He reached his hand back toward the counter. Jessup grinned and handed over a sheepskin jacket like Nick's, but half the size. "Here you go, Wilde. Try it on."

"No. Absolutely not. I cannot—"

"Neither can I. You're a temp."

"I beg your pardon?"

"You're a temporary employee, meaning you're not covered by the Triple G health insurance plan." Nick fixed her with a stern look. "You come down with pneumonia, I'm stuck with your medical bills."

She laughed. It was impossible not to laugh; he looked so serious. Tom Jessup, right behind him, was now grinning from ear to ear.

"Nick," Lissa said softly, "I can't pay you for these things. They're too expensive. And I can't possibly accept them as gifts."

"Because?"

"Because…because I just can't!"

He nodded. "Fine. Then, they're not gifts. They're payment in lieu of cash."

"Huh?"

"For all the work you've done."

"Our deal was room and board."

"For one dinner. You've already done more than that."

"Yes, but—"

"Lissa." His voice was soft. "Can't you simply say, 'Thank you, Nick. I love the boots. And the jacket.'" He paused. "Unless, of course, you don't."

"Oh, but I do! Everything is so lovely—"

He put out his hand, clasped hers, and drew her to her feet. "Turn around," he said as he tucked the crutch under his arm and held the jacket open. She slipped into it and his fingers brushed over the nape of her neck.

That breathless feeling swept through her again.

"There's a mirror on that wall… Well? What do you think?"

He was standing directly behind her. She raised her eyes, caught his in the glass.

"What I think," she said quietly, "is that you're a very kind and generous man."

A muscle knotted in his jaw.

"There are gloves in the pockets," he said. "I hope they fit."

"Nick—"

"I'm not kind, Duchess. I'm not generous." His teeth flashed in a quick, self-deprecating smile. "And as I already proved to both of us, I'm really not much of a man."

CHAPTER NINE

THEY DIDN'T TALK much during the drive back. Really, what was there to say?

Still, Lissa couldn't help glancing at Nick, at his stern profile, his hands so lightly spread on the steering wheel.

He was a man haunted by ghosts; that much was obvious, though she had no idea what those ghosts were—and what did it matter? She would never see him again after tomorrow.

And that was fine.

She had problems of her own. The last thing she wanted was to get involved with a man wrestling with demons. Not that she'd ever have become involved with him. If she'd slept with him last night, it would have been a one-time thing.

She was glad that hadn't happened.

There was no reason to sentimentalize a twenty-four-hour relationship, but sex did have a way of complicating things.

No more complications.

Not until she had her life sorted out.

And if that was a little old-fashioned, so be it.

"So be it," she murmured as Nick pulled up to the house.

"What?"

She looked at him. "I was just—I was just thinking about the weather. Any chance Hank will be able to get here today instead of tomorrow?"

Nick shook his head. "No. I spoke to him just before we went into town." He opened his door, arranged his crutch to take his weight and stepped down. Brutus jumped after him. "I know you want to get out of here, but you're going to have to wait until tomorrow morning."

"That's OK. I mean, that's fine…"

Nick wasn't listening. A couple of his men were coming toward them; they began unloading the boxes from the back of the truck. Lissa watched for a few seconds. Then she hopped down from the truck.

It was time to get to work, and that trip to town had been part of work.

It was best to remember that.

Nick's guys were carrying the boxes into the kitchen and stacking them on the big worktable. Lissa left her new jacket and boots in the hall, went up to her room for her kitchen clogs. Downstairs again, she dug around in a couple of the boxes until she'd unearthed cheese, cold cuts and a bag of rolls.

She made the men a quick lunch. Nick didn't join them. Fine. She'd be out of here tomorrow. Until then, the less they saw of each other, the better.

It would take at least an hour to put everything away. The big joint of meat in the sink was still frozen, but at least she could see that it was elk or moose. She'd get to it later. For now, she'd organize meals she'd make and freeze, then start dinner. She had a long afternoon's work ahead of her, and that was absolutely fine.

* * *

She had just put two big pans of lasagna in the oven when her cell phone chirped.

She wiped her hands on the ragged dish towel she was using as an apron and took the phone from her pocket.

Emily, said the caller ID.

Lissa took a steadying breath, pasted on a smile as if her youngest sister could see her—which, thank goodness, she could not—and said a bright, happy "Hi!"

"Liss. I've been calling and calling! Don't you ever check your voice mail?"

"What's the matter? Is somebody sick?"

"No, no, we're all fine. I just started worrying, that's all. You know. When you didn't take my calls."

"I didn't get them."

"How come?"

Because I'm not in L.A., I'm in Montana, and there was a snowstorm and I'd bet that there's zero coverage for cell phones around here when the weather closes in...

"Liss?"

"I don't know," Lissa said blithely. "You know how these cell phones are."

"Well, you should get it checked."

"I will, I will."

"Because, I mean, that's the whole purpose of having a cell phone, right? So people can reach you?"

"Right, Sure."

"I mean—"

"I know what you mean," Lissa said, a little tightly. She took a breath, eased it out. "So, what's new, Em? How are you?"

"I'm fine."

"And that gorgeous husband of yours?"

"Marco's fine, too," Emily said. "He says to send his love."

"Yeah, great, my love right back at you both. Listen, Em, I'm a little busy right now—"

"I won't keep you, Liss. I just wanted to know if you'd like a visit."

"A what?" Lissa said, trying not to sound panicky.

"You remember Nola? She and I shared an apartment in Manhattan."

Lissa didn't remember Nola. In fact, she doubted if she'd ever met her sister's former roommate. Back then, Emily hadn't let anybody within a hundred miles of where she lived, because she'd been living a lie, but why go into that now?

"What about her?"

"Well, she just called me. She's in Hollywood, some kind of audition thing, and she's only going to be there tonight and part of tomorrow, so I thought it might be cool if you guys got together."

"Now?"

"I know it's kind of last minute, but that's Nola. She doesn't always plan ahead."

"I can't," Lissa said, probably too quickly.

"OK. I know it's an imposition, but—"

"It isn't an imposition."

"How about if I tell her to give you a call and you can work out the details? Maybe just meet for a drink or—"

"I'm not in L.A., Em. I'm, ah, I'm in Montana."

"Montana? What, on location, you mean? Oh, that's exciting! Who's making a movie in Montana?"

Lissa chewed on her bottom lip. What if Emily wanted details? The movie's name. The director. The actors.

"Lissa? Did I lose you? I said—"

"I heard you. Look, I can't tell you very much except that—that I have a new job. I'm executive chef at a—at a famous ranch."

Not a lie. Not exactly. What was she if not executive chef? And surely the Triple G was famous. In Clarke's Falls, anyway.

"Oh, wow!" Emily voice rose with excitement. "I just watched something on TV about those Montana resorts. Very la-di-da, right? Hot tubs. Fire pits. The rich and the famous everywhere you turn."

Lissa sank down on a chair at the worktable. Did dreams of hot tubs and fire pits run in the Wilde DNA?

"What a perfect description of this place," she said, looking up as Brutus trotted into the kitchen and headed toward her.

He had something in his massive jaws.

What was it? A toy? A bone? What in hell… It wasn't a thing, it was a creature.

She shot to her feet. "Emily. I have to go."

"Wait! What's the name of this place? Did they ever feature

it on 'Lifestyles of the Rich and Famous'?"

Oh, God! The thing was alive. It was wiggling.

"I don't mean 'Lifestyles of the Rich and Famous.' I don't think that's on anymore, is it? But we used to watch it like crazy. Remember?"

The thing—a squirrel? A rat? A chipmunk?—had a long, swishing tail.

"We used to watch it when our nanny—which nanny was that?—when she thought we were watching the evening news." Emily laughed. "I mean, we were, what? Ten, eleven and twelve? Would we really have watched the news instead of drooling over all those movie stars?"

That was what Brutus was doing. Drooling. Tail thumping, what seemed to be his late-day snack clamped between his teeth, he sat down in front of her, his dark eyes filled with joy.

"Em. Really. This isn't a good time!"

"What? You have a soufflé in the oven?"

No. A giant dog has something in its maw.

"A soufflé! Exactly."

"Well, have fun. And good luck with that new—"

"Thanks. Bye."

Lissa slapped her phone to silence. "Nick? Nick?" Her voice rose to a shriek as she bolted from the room, skidded through the dining room and into the hall—

"Hey," Nick said.

She fell against him. His arms went around her.

"Easy," he said. "Easy, honey. What happened?"

Lissa waved her hand in the direction of the kitchen.

"Brutus has something."

Nick sighed. "Damn. I've been trying to break him of that *you can't eat anything unless you hear the secret word* crap. It's working, more or less. Couple of weeks ago, he swiped a roast off the kitchen counter. If he's done that again—"

"It's not that kind of something." Lissa shuddered. "It's a live something. He's going to kill it."

"No way. Not Brutus."

"Yes, Brutus. Come and see."

"I will," Nick said.

But neither of them moved.

His arms were hard around her. Her face was pressed against his chest. The soft wool of his sweater tickled her nose; his scent engulfed her. Hay and horse. Diesel and snow. And man. Not just man.

He smelled of Nick. Clean. Male. And wonderful.

Lissa closed her eyes.

She burrowed closer.

Nick made a low sound deep in his throat. He bent his head, pressed his lips to her hair.

"Duchess," he whispered, "about last night—"

Brutus whined.

Nick's arms dropped to his sides. Lissa stepped back. Brutus looked at them from a few feet away. The thing, whatever it was, was still in his mouth.

And still moving.

"Jesus," Nick muttered. He went toward the dog. "Brutus. Drop!"

The Newf lowered his head, opened his mouth and gently deposited the thing on the floor.

"Ohmygod," Lissa gasped. "It's a kitten!"

An extremely small kitten, pale gray and oyster white with darker gray tiger stripes. The animal wobbled to its feet and gave a piteous mew.

Brutus whined and touched his nose to it.

"Yeah," Nick said, "that's a good boy. That's a very good boy."

Lissa squatted beside the kitten. "I don't think it's more than four weeks old."

Nick thought about squatting down, too, thought better of it and reached his hand to the dog's head for a long stroke.

"I wonder where Brutus found him."

The kitten was trembling. It mewed again and fell on its side.

"It must be freezing, Nick. And terrified."

"Well, I don't know what we're supposed to do for it. I know dogs, not cats, especially not kittens."

"It's probably hungry, too."

Lissa opened the cardigan she was wearing over her T-shirt and cradled the kitten to her breasts. Nick felt a quick rush of envy, and wasn't that pathetic? They had what was probably a dying kitten to deal with, and he was envying it for being held against Lissa's silky, warm, sweetly-scented flesh.

Wonderful. A cripple, a drunk, and a pervert. Nick Gentry, Hollywood Hero.

"Nick? We need some soft towels. A shallow box."

"Duchess, listen, I don't know the first thing about kittens."

"I do. We had barn cats back home."

Home. Barns. Right. She'd said she'd grown up in Texas.

"I hope this little guy is old enough for real food. There's no way for me to improvise kitten formula with what we bought today."

"Kitten formula?" Nick said blankly.

"They can't tolerate cow's milk, but if this baby is old enough, a soft-boiled egg yolk mixed with warm oatmeal… That'll do, to start. An eyedropper will help, just in case. And we need the towels and the box."

He nodded. "I'll get the towels. And there's sure to be an eyedropper somewhere in one of the bathroom medicine cabinets."

"Fine. I have all this morning's cartons in the kitchen. I'll get one and I'll make an egg and some oatmeal and—" Her eyes widened. "Oh Lord!"

"What?"

"There's sure to be other kittens. I mean, wherever Brutus found this one…"

"Let me get the stuff you need. Then I'll see if he'll lead me to the place where he found this guy. It has to be somewhere in the house—he hasn't been outside since we got back from town."

"I hope you find them in time," Lissa said. "Otherwise, they're not going to make it."

* * *

He did find them in time, only it wasn't *them*, it was just one other kitten, pale gold with deeper peach highlights on its tiny ears.

"In the attic, of all places," Lissa said softly as she and Nick sat in the warm kitchen, each holding a sleepy, full-bellied kitten.

"The mother must have climbed up that big oak behind the house and across the roof," Nick said. "I found a hole up there. That's how she got in." The kitten lying in his big hand yawned and stretched. Nick smiled and stroked it with one finger. "I'll go up there later and fix it."

"The hole? No. Don't do that. The mom might come back."

Nick shook his head. "She won't."

"But you don't know that."

"Yeah," he said gruffly, "I do."

Lissa looked at him. "How—"

He shook his head again. He'd found blood, fur, and a couple of owl pellets. How the kittens had avoided detection was beyond him, but he didn't see any reason for going into the details.

"She's not coming back, Duchess." His voice was soft. "What matters is that these guys got lucky."

He watched Lissa process his words. She swallowed hard. Then she smiled at the bit of fluff in her hand.

"We had a tiger-striped gray-and-white cat named Louie. Well, his entire name was Louis L'Amour," she said, pronouncing *Louis* the French way, "but we just called him Louie."

Nick grinned. "Louis L'Amour? A cat with literary pretensions, huh?"

She looked at him and laughed. "Emily named him. My kid sister. Back then, she couldn't decide if she wanted to grow up to write Western stories like L'Amour or paint Western scenes like Remington."

"And today she's, what? A writer? A painter?"

Lissa grinned. "She's the VP for marketing at MS Enterprises. Her husband's company. They do international construction."

"So, why don't we call this guy Louie?"

"Let's. And what about her?" she said, nodding at the kitten sound asleep in Nick's hand.

"I'm not good at naming things."

"Everybody's good at naming things. Just look at her. Does she remind you of anybody? Of anything?"

"You're so sure she's a she?"

"Nope. It's not easy to tell when they're this little, but I'd bet your kitten is a girl."

"My kitten?"

"Yeah. Your kitten." Lissa looked at him. "She seems happy to be with you."

He looked at the cat that now lay curled like a comma in his hand.

"Dumb thing that she is," he said, but with a tenderness that made Lissa smile.

"So, come on, Gentry. Stop stalling and come up with a name."

Nick looked at the kitten, at that soft golden fur and the darker gold ears.

"She's the color of peaches," he said.

"That's what you should call her. Peaches."

He grinned. "Why not? Louie and Peaches."

Brutus, lying at their feet, raised his muzzle from his front paws and whined. Nick laughed.

"Brutus approves. In fact, he says it's perfect."

"Perfect," Lissa said, and thought, with a little rush of surprise, how right the word was to describe not just the moment, but the entire day.

* * *

She made a quick and easy supper. Meatloaf. Mashed potatoes with caramelized onions. Green beans. Dessert had taken a back seat to putting away all the groceries and dealing with the kittens, but the men reacted to a batch of chocolate chip brownies as if they were profiteroles filled with whipped cream.

Sometime after six, she set about planning what to cook for the freezer in addition to the lasagna that was cooling on the worktable. The dinosaur haunch was in the fridge, marinating in tamari, garlic, herbs and a touch of honey, ready to go into the oven first thing in the morning. She'd leave Nick directions for when to take it out and what to do after that, because she'd be gone by the time the roast was ready.

The thought made her feel a little sad. Foolish, of course, but she'd started to feel comfortable here.

She dried her hands, smiled at the kittens sleeping in their box, and heard the pad of Brutus's paws against the oak floor.

Smiling, she turned toward the dog. "Did you come to keep me comp—"

She broke off in mid-sentence. The dog wasn't alone. Nick was with him—Nick, leaning on a wooden cane instead of a crutch.

"Gentry? Are you—"

"I'm fine."

Was he? His face was a little pale. She fought back the desire to grab a chair and shove it toward him. He was a grown man. He could take care of himself.

"Stop looking at me as if I'm going to go down in a heap. I did that already, remember?" He flashed a quick smile. "A good actor never repeats a performance."

Lissa nodded. "Sure. I'm just, you know, a little surprised."

"The physio guy suggested I try using a cane a few hours a day."

"The physio guy?"

"The physiotherapist that I work with. That I was working with."

"You don't anymore?"

"No."

The "no" was hard and short. It didn't invite questions.

"Well, if you came looking for coffee—"

"I came looking for you."

"Oh." Her heart did a little stutter step. Why it should have done that was beyond her to comprehend. "Did you hear from Hank?"

"Yes."

"And?"

"And, he can be here as early as we want in the morning."

Lissa reached for a bunch of washed carrots.

"Well, that's great. I'll just finish this and—"

"You've been working all day."

"No. Not all day."

"All day," Nick repeated. He cleared his throat. "We should

settle up."

"Settle up what?"

"All the time you've put in. I wrote you a check. Tell me if it isn't enough."

Lissa turned toward him. "You don't owe me anything."

"Take it," he said, holding out the check. "And if it isn't enough, just say so."

"Gentry…"

"It's Nick."

"Nick. We said room and board, remember? And you bought me the boots and stuff today. That more than takes care of things."

"*I* said room and board, not you, and only because I was being a jerk. The boots and stuff…necessities. Go on. Take the check."

She reached for the check. Their fingers brushed and a swift electric tingle ran along her skin.

Their eyes met. A muscle knotted in Nick's jaw and suddenly the room seemed airless.

"Static electricity," Lissa said with a tight little laugh. She took a step back and stared blindly at the check. It took a while for the numbers to swim into focus. When they did, she looked up, shocked. "That's much too much!"

He smiled. "For an executive chef? It isn't enough."

"Forget the executive chef thing. All I did was cook a couple of meals."

"All you did was keep my guys from out-and-out mutiny."

"I can't possibly—"

"Yes. You can. I'm paying you what you'd have earned as an

executive chef at the kind of place you thought this would be."

"You don't know that."

Nick smiled. "Google knows everything." His voice softened. "Please. Take the check."

Lissa chewed on her bottom lip. He wondered if she knew how often she did that, or if she knew how it made him ache to soothe the tiny wound with a kiss. He wondered, too, if she knew how beautiful she looked, especially at this moment, her face flushed from the heat of the kitchen, her golden hair pulled up in the kind of knot that made a man want to take it down.

"Well…" She smiled. "Thank you. And now, if you'll excuse me—"

"No more work tonight."

"Oh, I have to! I promised the guys I'd leave some meals in the freezer and so far, all I've done is some lasagna and make a marinade for the mystery meat I told you about."

"I'm the boss, Wilde, remember?"

"Well, I know. I mean, they know that. But—"

"The boss makes the rules. And rule number one is that the night is clear, the sky is full of stars, and you can't leave Montana until you've seen a sky like this one."

He was smiling.

And, oh God, he looked so handsome.

Big. Tall. Strong. And sexy, so sexy that she wanted to throw herself into his arms and ask him if they couldn't please finish what they'd started last night, what she'd thought about all day, what she wanted, because if she couldn't leave Montana without seeing the sky on a night like this, how could she leave it without a night spent in this man's arms?

"Lissa?"

Lissa took a breath. Let it out. Then she whipped off the towel tied around her waist and gave him a dazzling smile.

"Let me get my jacket."

"And your boots."

"And my boots."

"And your gloves."

She laughed. "I promise, I won't get hypothermia."

"If you did, I'd have to save you. And the only sure way, with no hospital nearby, would be for us to get naked, wrap up in heavy blankets and hold each other until you stopped trembling."

He'd meant to say it lightly, but it didn't come out that way.

Fool, he told himself angrily, as he watched her struggle to come up with an answer, but what could a woman say to a man who'd already made such a hideous mess of things?

"So we'd both better hope that doesn't happen," he said gruffly.

If only, Lissa thought, but she smiled brightly, said, "Damn right," and went quickly past him, to the rack in the hall where she'd left her boots and jacket.

* * *

He was right.

The sky was… There had to be a better word than spectacular, but if there was, it had yet to be coined.

They stood on the back porch, faces tilted to the sky, she

inches in front of him, their breath puffing tiny clouds into the still night air.

"Oh," Lissa whispered. What else could you say when you stared into an endless black sky shot with a million night fires?

"Yeah," Nick said. "The night sky, especially after a storm, was the best thing about growing up here."

"Only that?"

"The mountains," he said, after a few seconds. "The Absaroka Wilderness. I used to hike it. Spring and fall, I'd camp overnight."

"You didn't like living on the Triple G?"

"I liked riding. Working with the horses. Checking out the line shacks. That kind of thing."

She wanted to ask him more. They'd only known each other a couple of days, but she longed to know more about him. Not about Nick Gentry, movie star. She wanted to know about Nick Gentry, the man.

She knew better than to ask.

He was not someone who would share himself easily. And she understood that; she had learned that same kind of caution over the last couple of years.

"Duchess. Look!"

"What?"

"A shooting star. And another!"

"Where? I don't see them."

"There. See that bulge in the mountain? Man, there's another!"

"This is what always happens! My brothers see shooting stars. My sisters see them. And I'm the idiot standing there saying, 'Where?'"

"Lift your head a little. Now look to the right. Here. I'll show you."

Nick clasped her shoulders. Turned her a couple of inches. "There's one now!"

"I don't see it!"

"For heaven's sake, woman!" He curved one arm around her waist and drew her back against his chest. "Follow where I'm pointing. Good. Now just give it a couple of seconds…"

Fire arced across the sky. Lissa gasped.

"Oh! Oh, how beautiful!" Another streak of light raced across the darkness. She laughed with delight. "Nick, this is wonderful!"

"Yes. It is."

His voice was low and rough. Something in it made her heartbeat quicken. Slowly, she turned her head and looked up at him. His face was shadowed; all she could see with any clarity were his eyes.

They were dark and hot.

The silence of the night gathered them in.

Nick whispered her name. He watched her lips curve in a smile as old as time, a smile that said everything a man could want to hear.

He bent his head. Brushed his mouth over hers, once, twice, and she sighed, turned in his arms, caught the collar of his sheepskin jacket in her hands and lifted herself to him, sighed again as he held her closer and deepened the kiss.

"Please," she whispered.

Please. The most wonderful word anyone had ever spoken

to him.

Another shooting star blazed across the night sky as Nick took Lissa's hand and led her into the dark house.

CHAPTER TEN

NICK'S BEDROOM WAS a shadowy oasis of ivory moon and black night.

He kissed her as they entered it, kissed her again as he closed the door. Brutus, who had followed them up the stairs, gave a plaintive woof.

"He'll be fine," Nick said softly. "It's just that I've never closed him out of this room before."

"Never?" Lissa said.

Nick shrugged off his jacket, unbuttoned hers and tossed them both aside.

"There's been nobody in this room except Brutus and me."

"Nobody?"

She was wearing a sweater with buttons over a cotton T-shirt. His hands shook a little as he undid the buttons, got rid of the top sweater, then drew the T-shirt over her head. He'd needed her help to do it last night; this time, he didn't.

The fact registered on his brain.

Surely it was a good sign.

"Nobody," he said, cupping her breasts in a pink lace bra that was, mercifully, like the white one, meaning that it, too, had a front clasp.

Lissa gave a little moan as his thumbs brushed over her nipples.

"All these months?" she whispered.

He nodded and undid the bra clasp. Her breasts tumbled into his waiting hands.

"All these months," he said, and he bent his head and took first one dusty-rose nipple and then the other into the heat of his mouth.

She gasped; her head fell back and she dug her fingers into the thick silky hair at the nape of his neck.

"Do you like that?"

"Yes. Oh yes. The feel of your mouth…"

He cupped her breasts again, worked his fingers over her nipples as he kissed her, a long, deep kiss that had her clinging to him.

"And your hands," she said, "oh, your hands…"

"Boots," he commanded.

She toed them off.

He ran one hand down her spine, pressed his palm lightly against the base and brought her into contact with his erection. She gave a little gasp and shifted against him. Her hips arched; the simple action turned him harder than he already was, harder than he'd ever imagined a man could be.

A groan rose in his throat.

As much as he'd wanted her the evening before, tonight he

wanted her even more.

Maybe it was because he knew her better now. Maybe it was because he liked what he knew.

Maybe it was both those things and more, maybe it was because he'd spent the entire night and most of the goddamned day thinking about her, about this, about how her skin would taste as he kissed her throat, how her hair would smell as it tickled his nose, how she would moan as he led her to the bed—limping, yes, but without the cane—sat down on the edge and positioned her between his parted thighs.

No way was he going to risk making an ass of himself this time.

Besides, this was better in every possible way.

She was his.

His to undress.

His to watch as he undid her jeans. As he unzipped them. As he eased them over her hips.

She had a perfect belly button. Small. Flat. Just right for kissing.

She made a soft, sweet sound as he kissed the tiny indentation, as he licked her flesh.

"Hold on to my shoulders," he said, and he drew down her jeans, helped her step free of them.

She was his now. His to touch. To taste.

To possess.

He could feel the blood thrumming in his ears, feel his balls tightening in his scrotum. Everything in him wanted her. Now. Right now. No more waiting. No more hungering for her heat to surround him, but he wanted this to last, wanted to make up to her for last night.

"Nick," she whispered.

He nipped her shoulder. Drew down her panties. She stepped free of them.

"Nick," she whispered.

He loved the way she said his name. Loved that she was breathing hard. Loved the delicate scent of her arousal.

Loved that she was naked.

He cupped her breasts again. Ran his hands the length of her body, curved them around her hips. Drew her closer. Closer.

"Spread your legs for me, sweetheart," he said.

His voice was thick. Raw. She said his name again. Sobbed it as he nuzzled her thighs apart and as soon as he put his mouth against her, she screamed.

It almost undid him.

He was at the edge. Clinging to it. His brain told him to slow down, that he wanted to make this last, but he couldn't. Not anymore. All that mattered was being inside her.

Nick pulled his sweater over his head and dropped it on the floor. He toed off his boots, unzipped his jeans, tore off the rest of his clothes, fumbled open the night table drawer, felt for the small packets he prayed were there.

His fingers closed around one.

"Wait," he said harshly, and he tore it open, freed the condom, rolled it on.

Then he reached for Lissa and she came down to him, to the bed, to his arms.

He kissed her.

She wound her arms around his neck and he tumbled her beneath him, lost in the wonder of her. The softness. The taste. The hot liquid brilliance of her desire burning against his hand as he cupped her.

She cried out against his mouth.

He couldn't last much longer. He was a man who'd always prided himself on his control, in bed and out, but need for her, for this one woman, was roaring through him, obliterating everything but blind instinct.

He swept his hands under her backside. She sobbed his name, parted her thighs, arced toward him and he moved between them, rose on his knees...

Pain rocketed through his leg.

A cry burst from his throat. He bit it back, but it was too late. Lissa had heard it, and she froze beneath him.

"Nick?"

He shook his head, fought against the knife-sharp pain.

"Nick! Wait—"

"No!" he said. "Goddammit, no!" He clasped her hands, held them tightly in his. "We're not going to stop—"

Lissa tugged her hands free, put one finger over his lips.

"Just lie back."

Her voice was soft. Her lips were curved. He hesitated, and then he fell back. She rose above him, bent and kissed his mouth. Then, slowly, slowly enough to make him groan with ecstasy, she lowered herself on his rigid length.

"God," he said thickly, "oh God..."

Lissa caught her breath.

He was big.

So big, so hard that for one breathless second, she wondered if she could take all of him inside her. But she could. Yes. Oh yes. She could.

Her head fell back. Her lashes drifted to her cheeks.

Oh, the slick, heavy feel of him! All that power. That strength.

His hands clasped her hips as she rode him.

He was claiming her. Consuming her. Taking her to the edge, the edge, the edge...

Lissa cried out. Sobbed Nick's name.

"Come for me," he said, "come for me, sweetheart," and she felt herself sliding down the long, glorious path to release.

Lights exploded behind her closed eyelids. A long, wild cry of pleasure burst from her throat and as she came, he let go and gave himself up to the night, to the whirlwind.

To Lissa.

* * *

She lay in the hard, encircling curve of his arm, her face buried against his throat.

He gave her a long, lingering kiss. Then he told her he'd be right back.

He was true to his word. One quick trip to the adjoining bathroom and he was beside her again, taking her in his arms, holding her close.

His heartbeat was still slowing.

So was hers.

She sighed.

His arms tightened around her.

"That was," she said softly, "it was—"

"It certainly was," he said, and he felt her lips curve in a smile against his shoulder.

He rolled onto his side. Her eyes were bright; her hair was a nimbus of gold against the pillows. She was, without question, the most beautiful woman he'd ever seen.

"What?" she said.

He smiled and toyed with a strand of her hair. "What what?"

She gave him a gentle poke. "What are you thinking?"

"I'm thinking what a fool I was last night."

"No. You weren't. You were upset."

"I was an asshole."

Her laugh was soft and delicious.

"OK. But you were an upset asshole."

Nick grinned. "You didn't have to agree with me, Wilde."

"Of course I did, Gentry." She touched the tip of her finger to his mouth. "I'm glad you were smarter tonight."

"Yeah. Me, too."

"Mmm," she said, and yawned.

"My very thought," he said, reaching for the duvet and drawing it up over them.

Seconds later, they were asleep.

* * *

She came awake to the feel of his mouth on the nape of her neck, the feel of his hand on her breast.

They were lying on their sides, he behind her, his swollen

penis pressing at the juncture of her thighs.

Her breath caught as her nipple pearled against his palm. Desire raced like electric current from her breasts to her belly.

She turned toward him and moved her hips against his.

"Wait," he said softly. "Let me get a condom…"

"I'm on the pill."

Had a man ever heard more welcome words? He shifted his weight. Clasped her thigh. Raised it, just a little. Just enough, she thought, gasping as the head of his engorged penis teased her hot flesh.

No. Not enough.

He was teasing her and she hated him for it, adored him for it; she was coming apart, coming apart.

"Easy," he said softly. "There's no hurry. I want to feel you taking me in. Like that." He shuddered. "Exactly like that."

He slid into her.

She cried out.

He slid deeper. Deeper. Drew her closer and she sobbed his name.

The pleasure was almost too much. It was more than pleasure, it was something new, something that made her begin to weep as he surged forward.

"Nick," she pleaded, "Nick, now. Please, now! I can't…"

He felt her begin to convulse around him.

"Yes," he growled, and he closed his eyes and took her with him to paradise.

* * *

When she woke again, the sun was just beginning to light the mountains beyond the windows.

Nick was sitting on the bed next to her, dressed in a faded blue denim shirt, the sleeves rolled to the elbows, and equally faded jeans.

His hair was damp; his jaw was dark with stubble. He was, in other words, altogether gorgeous, and her heart turned over at the sight of him.

"Hi," he said softly, smiling as he took her hand and brought it to his lips.

Lissa smiled, too. "Hi, yourself."

He bent forward and brushed his mouth over hers. She sighed and his lips moved against hers, parted hers for the stroke of his tongue.

She smiled.

"Mmm," she said. "Coffee with cream."

"Clever woman." Another kiss. "Want some?"

"That would be lovely."

"You'll have to pay the price."

Lissa fluttered her lashes. "You drive a hard bargain."

Nick grinned, clasped her hand, kissed the palm and folded her fingers over the kiss.

"I hope so."

She laughed. "OK. Let go and I'll get up, shower, get dressed—"

"You don't have to move an inch. I brought a cup for you."

"Really?"

He gave her a quick kiss, reached behind him and produced a steaming mug.

"Coffee. Light. Two sugars."

"Perfect! How did you know?"

"Magic."

Lissa sat up and reached for the mug. Nick shook his head.

"Not yet," he said softly.

"You promised!"

"I said you'd have to pay the price." His gaze dropped to her breasts; the duvet had fallen to her lap, exposing them to his eyes. "And now I know what that's going to be."

She felt heat flood her body.

"Nick," she whispered.

He put the coffee on the table and cupped her breasts in his hands. Lowered his head. Kissed the lush slopes. Kissed her nipples. Drew one into the heat of his mouth as he caressed the other between his thumb and forefinger.

Her soft moan turned him hard as stone.

"Do you like that?" he said thickly.

"Yes." She reached out, curved her hand over the bulge in his jeans. "And this," she said. "I like this, too. I like it a lot."

"Dammit, Duchess! Are you trying to seduce me?"

Her laugh was wonderful. Soft and sweet and wicked. Everything about her was wonderful, Nick thought, and he rose to his feet, all but tore off his clothes and went into her outstretched arms.

Mouth met mouth. Skin met skin.

And two mugs of coffee went very, very cold.

* * *

Nick lay on his side, watching Lissa as she slept.

Her head was on his shoulder, her hand was splayed over his heart. Her hair, a spectacular tangle of gold, covered part of her face. Carefully, he looped it behind her ear.

He liked looking at her.

What man wouldn't? She was incredibly beautiful. She was also amazing. Smart. Tough. Tender.

Damn.

Nick winced, swallowed a groan.

His leg, his damn leg, ached like a son of a bitch. Somehow or other, she'd ended up with her thigh thrown over his.

She was light as a feather, but still it was more weight than he'd handled in months. The last time he'd tried working against any kind of mass at all had been when he was still doing physical therapy, still believing the lies about regaining real use of the damaged muscles and tendons and bone. He'd worked with a machine that looked like a torture device out of the Spanish Inquisition.

His expression softened.

What Lissa looked like was a dream.

He couldn't understand why he'd been so hard on her that first day.

Sure, he'd been expecting a cook and one look had made it clear she was anything but…

Except, that wasn't true.

She'd cooked up a storm and everything she'd made had been delicious.

Delicious, like her.

"Umm."

A soft sigh. A soft turn of her head against his shoulder.

His belly knotted.

He wanted to kiss her. Caress her. But that would wake her and he didn't want to do that.

The hell he didn't.

If he woke her with a touch. A whisper of his lips. If he did that, her eyes would open, she'd give him that billion-dollar smile, half temptress, half innocent, and she'd raise her arms to him, surrender to him, to herself, to whatever had happened between them during the long night...

A roar broke the early-morning silence.

Nick winced, not from the pain but from the unwelcome noise, because he knew what it was, the intrusion of a reality he had deliberately driven out of his thoughts.

The plane.

Hank and the plane, come to take Lissa away.

He eased his arm out from under her and rolled onto his back.

All good things came to an end. If the accident hadn't proved the truth of that ugly old saying, nothing would.

Time to start the day.

Get dressed. Fire up the truck and drive Lissa to the airstrip—he'd left orders for it to be plowed and he knew it would have been done by now.

Still, he lay motionless while the minutes ticked away. Foolish, of course. There was no point in putting off the inevitable.

He sat up. Swung his good leg off the bed, used both hands to get the other aligned with it.

He shut his eyes, blinked them open.

She was awake. His senses told him so. Still, when she spoke his name in a soft voice, it put a knot in his gut.

"Nick?"

"Yes?"

He felt the mattress give a delicate shift and knew it meant she was sitting up.

"Was that—was it the plane?"

He nodded. "Yes."

Silence. Then she cleared her throat.

"Right on time," she said brightly.

"Yes." Jesus, was that his entire vocabulary?

"Well," she said, even more brightly. "I'll only be five minutes. A quick shower and, uh, and I'll come right down."

He came within a heartbeat of saying "yes" again, stopped himself just in time. It didn't matter. He got the message. It was time she left, time life returned to normal, and she wanted him out of here before she rose from the bed.

"Great," he said. "I'll see you in the kitchen."

"I won't have time to make the boys breakfast. Tell them that I'm sorry, would you?"

"It's not a problem. They've gotten used to fending for themselves in the mornings."

"Fine. Good. Then—then, I'll get started."

"OK."

But he didn't move. Neither did she.

There was such a thing as after-sex protocol. His kind, anyway, and he'd already blown through most of it with this fumbled attempt at conversation.

He'd never been the kind of man to spend the entire night in a woman's bed; he'd rarely encouraged a woman to spend the night in his, and this was one of the reasons, all the early morning nonsense of *hi, how did you sleep, oh fine and how about you, I'll just head for the kitchen while you get dressed* because both parties knew that middle-of-the-night intimacy all too easily turned into early-morning embarrassment.

Nick stood up. Pulled on his clothes. Headed for the door. Opened it…

"Goddammit," he said, and he spun toward the bed, toward the woman sitting up against the pillows, the duvet clutched to her breasts, her face pale, her mouth gently swollen from his kisses. "Goddammit, Melissa," he said as he strode toward her.

"It's Lissa," she said, "not Melissa, and what are you doing?"

"It's Melissa," he said. "You can't tell me that isn't the name you were born with and, goddammit, I like the sound of it."

"Well, that's great." Her voice shook. "You like the sound of it. And everything is about you, isn't it? Everything is about Nick Gentry. What he wants, what he does and doesn't do—"

"You are not leaving me," he growled. "You got that? You-are-not, I repeat, you-are-not-leaving-me, dammit!"

"Are you crazy? I'm going back to L.A. I'm getting out of here as fast as I—"

He reached for her, pulled her into his arms.

"You are not leaving me," he said again and this time his voice shook. "You got that? You are staying right here, Duchess, where you belong." He kissed her, tasted the salt of her tears, then drew back, framed her face with his hands and looked deep into her eyes. "Tell me you're not leaving me," he said softly.

She gave a little hiccup, a sob, a laugh that went straight to his heart.

"No," she said, "I'm not."

"Damn right," Nick said, and he tumbled her back against the pillows and made love to her again. She fell asleep in his embrace.

He waited until her breathing was deep and even. Then he eased out of the bed, pulled on his jeans and opened the bedroom door.

Brutus greeted him with an exuberant woof.

"I agree," Nick said softly, rubbing the dog's ears.

He went down the stairs, the Newf at his side.

Business first.

He phoned Ace, told him to drive to the airstrip and pick up whatever stuff Hank had brought.

"He can leave after that." Nick cleared his throat. "Ms. Wilde—Lissa will be staying on."

"Yessir," Ace said, sounding happy.

Nick grinned as he ended the call. Who wouldn't be happy, knowing Lissa was not leaving?

On to the next step. A vital step.

Four bottles of bourbon were lined up on a shelf in his office. No reason to run out, he'd thought when he bought them, though it hit him now that except for the slug of the stuff he'd downed last night after he'd left Lissa's bedroom, he hadn't so much as thought about taking a drink since she'd come to the Triple G.

And it was going to stay that way.

Nick gathered the bottles in his arms and went down the hall to the kitchen, straight to the sink.

Quickly, he unscrewed all the bottle tops. An instant's hesitation. Then, one by one, he dumped the whiskey down the drain and tossed the empty bottles into the trash.

"Woof," Brutus said again.

Nick laughed. It was precisely the right comment to make.

Together, man and dog trotted up the stairs and to the bedroom. Nick opened the door carefully.

Lissa was still asleep.

The dog butted his big head against Nick's leg.

"Only if you promise to keep quiet. And to sleep on the floor, like dogs are supposed to."

The Newf wagged his tail and grinned. Nick sighed and shut the door after them.

"Down," he said sternly.

Brutus did a perfect *down* at the foot of the bed. Nick shucked his jeans, climbed under the duvet and wrapped his arm around Lissa. She was warm and silken against him, and he drew her closer and shut his eyes.

He was almost asleep when he felt the mattress shift.

Brutus was stretched horizontally across the foot of the king-size bed, his muzzle resting on his front paws.

Nick smiled.

The big dog sometimes needed help getting up here. Not this time. Tonight, he'd made it on his own.

"Good boy," Nick said softly.

And drifted into sleep.

CHAPTER ELEVEN

TWO WEEKS LATER, Nick sat at the kitchen table, a mug of steaming coffee in his hands, watching Lissa as she made bread.

He loved watching her.

Well, yeah. But what he really loved was being with her. Seeing her smile. Knowing she was happy here.

He'd done everything he could to ensure that.

The one and only tough moment had been over money.

He'd known instinctively that handing a paycheck to the woman he was living with would not go over well, especially not with a woman as independent as Lissa. So he'd played it smart, or so he'd thought, lying through his teeth, telling her that he handled all the ranch's finances through an online account.

No problem.

Marcia, the idiot agent who'd turned out to be an angel in disguise, had already provided him with Lissa's Social Security number. All he'd needed was her bank account information, and Lissa gave it to him.

Problem solved, he'd thought, smugly complimenting himself on his brilliance…until the first morning he'd put through her week's pay.

She'd stormed into his office, eyes blazing, cell phone held out like a weapon.

"What is this, Gentry?"

Nick had peered at the screen. "Your checking account?"

"My checking account. A new entry in it from you. For two thousand dollars more than what you're supposed to pay me."

"Well, yeah. Sure. I mean, now that I know you really can cook—"

"Don't you mean, now that I'm sleeping with you?"

"No," he said quickly, "of course not."

"We did not agree on this amount of money."

"Hey." He smiled, held out his arms. "C'mere."

"No. You pay me what you're supposed to pay me. That's the amount I agree to and that's what you'll give me."

She wanted to play hardball? Fine. Nick had folded his arms, narrowed his eyes and given her the same kind of look she was giving him.

"I thought I hired a cook. I didn't. I hired a chef."

"Your agreement with Marcia—"

"What would I pay you if I owned one of those chichi places in L.A. and you were my executive chef?"

"This isn't like one of those places."

"You thought it was, when you came here."

"Yes. And I still agreed to less than I'd have made if it were."

"Because?"

"Oh, for goodness' sake! I needed the job, OK?"

Nick had risen to his feet. "And I need you," he'd said softly. "You think I want you hired out from under my nose by some la-di-da lodge?"

"That's crazy. I'm not applying for jobs at…" Her eyebrows rose. "Did you actually say, 'la-di-da'?"

He'd known she was fighting against a smile. Excellent, he'd thought, and before she could move away from him, he gathered her into his arms.

"The Triple G isn't anybody's idea of a la-di-da lodge."

She laughed. He felt his heart lift.

"But it deserves the best. And now it has the best. Would you really want me to underpay its chef? Well, would you?"

"That's completely illogical," she'd said, but she'd let him draw her closer into his embrace.

"It's completely logical, and Marcia will agree when we tell her your salary has gone up."

"Marcia will be your slave for life," Lissa had said softly.

"I don't want Marcia to be my anything," Nick had murmured. "I only want you."

The discussion, the argument, whatever it was, had ended with the office door shut and the old couch against the far wall put to good use.

Changing Lissa's pay had only been the first change he'd made, Nick thought now, as he sat watching her beat the hell out of the bread dough.

New appliances lined the walls of the big kitchen.

The pantry, the cupboards, the freezer were fully stocked.

And the place was clean from top to bottom, not just the kitchen but the bedrooms, bathrooms, his office, the living room, the dining room, the den.

Lissa had started scrubbing things; he'd joined her; his men had added their muscle to the mix and finally it had dawned on him that Esther Finch might be willing to help and that she might also agree to come in every afternoon to tend to the house and help Lissa in the kitchen.

Esther had already been showing up to clean the place every couple of weeks, well, actually, whenever he got around to asking her.

It turned out that working on a steady basis suited her perfectly.

Nick drank some of his coffee.

What suited *him* perfectly was Lissa.

She was an amazing woman. Determined. Tender. Strong. Feminine. And, unlike most of the long procession of women who'd wandered through his life, she didn't play games. No pretense. She didn't back down from her own opinions; she didn't automatically defer to him.

She was a challenge, and it had been a very long time since anyone had dared challenge Nick Gentry.

Turned out he liked being challenged just fine.

They were equals.

Turned out he liked that, too.

She could beat him at gin rummy. No problem. He could beat her at chess. She rolled her eyes at Little Richard and the Rolling Stones; he rolled his at the Black Eyed Peas and Coldplay. They compromised by downloading a lot of classical guitar because it turned out they both liked it, and because, more than anything, he wanted her to be happy that she hadn't gone back to L.A.

That she had, instead, chosen to stay here. With him.

Because they were, he'd realized with mild surprise, living together.

He'd had a lot of women. More, he knew, than most men, but he had never actually lived with one. He'd always imagined that living with, being tied to one woman, her toothbrush on the sink next to his, her lipstick on his dresser, would make him feel trapped.

Wrong.

What he felt was honored. Sharing his room with Lissa, his bed, his day-to-day existence made him feel—made him feel—

"Would you hand me that pan?"

Nick blinked. "Sorry. What did you say?"

"That pan. Could you give it to me, please?"

He reached for the pan. She smiled and he felt that smile straight down to his toes.

"Got to pay the price," he said, whisking it away from her outstretched hand.

She sighed. Dramatically. "You drive a hard bargain."

"Uh huh," he said, keeping the pan just out of reach.

She sighed again, leaned in and brushed her lips lightly over his.

"Nice," he said, "but that was only a down payment."

"Nick. I am baking bread here. I have to get this last loaf ready for the ov—"

She shrieked as he tugged her into his lap.

"I know." He waggled his eyebrows. "But I'm already ready, Duchess."

"Already ready?" she said, laughing.

"Already ready," he repeated, and he put the bowl on the table, put his arms around her and kissed her.

When the kiss ended, she gave another sigh, but this one made him smile.

"See?" he said. "That wasn't so bad, was it?"

"I don't know," she said, her eyes wide with innocence. "We'll have to try it again before I can give you an answer."

She kissed him. He took the kiss deeper. His hand went under her T-shirt, cupped her breast, and she caught her breath.

"How about leaving the baking until later?" he whispered.

"Can't. Bread dough can be temperamental."

He laughed softly. "Dough can be temperamental?"

"So can Ace and the rest of the guys. I promised them sourdough bread for supper tonight."

Nick sighed. "In that case—"

He kissed her. She kissed him back, got to her feet and went back to work, kneading the final batch of dough. Every part of her was involved in what she was doing, from the angle of her head to the sway of her body.

Nick's eyes swept over her.

He knew every inch of that body. The fullness of her breasts. The gentle curve of her belly. The exquisite taste of her between her thighs.

Damn.

He shifted his weight in the chair.

Way to go, Gentry. Sit at a kitchen table, watch a woman do something as basic as make bread, and get yourself turned on.

Why not?

They were alone in the house. There was nobody else around, wouldn't be until late afternoon. They didn't have to go upstairs, and the way he felt, this wouldn't take very long. He could get to his feet, tug down her jeans, unzip his fly, bend her over the table or the back of a chair and—

"I know what you're thinking."

Nick cleared his throat. "You do?"

"You're wondering how long it'll take until the bread is ready to eat."

He laughed. "Not exactly."

"Come on, be honest. There's something about the taste of fresh bread…"

He pushed back his chair and got to his feet.

"It isn't the taste of fresh bread on my mind, Duchess."

Lissa looked up. His voice had gone low and rough; his eyes had narrowed. "No?" she said with all the innocence possible.

He shook his head. "No."

She could feel her body's response, that hot liquidity as if her bones were melting.

"Stop that," she said.

"Stop what? Can't a man walk around in his own kitchen?"

"The bread dough…"

"Temperamental. I know." He reached for her. "Well, so am I."

She laughed. It was a down and dirty laugh, and it made him harder than he already was.

"Now, Nicholas—"

"Now, Melissa."

"Nick," she said, a little breathlessly, and he loved that, the way she sounded, the way her face was flushing, he loved seeing that she wanted him as much as he wanted her. "Nick, my hands are full of flour."

Without taking his eyes from her, he scooped up a handful of flour.

"So are mine." His grin turned wicked. "Besides, it's not your hands I'm interested in right now."

"Nick—"

"What?" he said as he gathered her into his arms, one hand at the base of her spine, the other cupping the back of her head. "What?" he said again, the one word soft and filled with need.

Lissa looked up into the hard, beautiful face of her lover.

"Just that," she whispered, "just *Nick*."

His eyes went dark.

"Tell me what you want," he said thickly.

She rose on her toes and kissed him, her lips warm and parted against his.

"Is that all? Just a kiss?"

Her hand slipped between them, over his chest, his abdomen, came to rest cupped over the bulge in his jeans.

Nick's breath hissed in his throat.

"You want that, too?"

"I'm a greedy woman, Gentry. I thought you'd have learned that by now."

"How greedy?" His hands went to the button at the top of her fly. Undid it. "How greedy?" he said, as he pulled down her zipper. "Because," he said, as he began tugging down her jeans, "I can accommodate whatever it is you have in mind."

Her eyes locked with his. She undid his fly just as he had undone hers. Her hand closed around him and in that instant, he was almost undone.

He caught her wrist, brought her hand to her side.

"Turn around. Lean over the table and put your palms against the surface."

His voice was harsh. She loved the sound of it, the demand in it.

"Like this?"

"Like that. Yes. Exactly like—."

She cried out as he sank into her. She was silk; he was steel, and the world ceased to exist.

"Nick," she said in a broken whisper, "oh God, oh God—"

The room blurred around her.

She felt it happening, the orgasm building within her, the race of heat from breasts to belly, the burst of color behind her closed eyelids, the exquisite fracturing of mind and reason.

She cried out his name; he groaned hers, and when he came deep, deep inside her, her muscles contracted around him and she came a second time on a high, sweet cry that pierced his heart.

He bit the exposed nape of her neck, his claim hard and savage and exquisite. Then he turned her to him, held her, kissed her hair, her eyes, her lips, and as she clung to him and wept with ecstasy, Nick knew that something was happening to him, something that was as wonderful as it was terrifying.

* * *

A long time later, he adjusted her clothes and his, sat down and drew her into his lap.

"You OK?" he said softly.

She laughed, wound her arms around his neck and kissed him.

"I am very OK."

He drew her closer. She sighed and pressed her lips to his throat. She'd had sex with enough other men to know that this, what she felt with Nick, was different.

Different?

It was what she'd thought might not exist. It was sex that made the world tilt under your feet, that made you understand why the French called the last seconds of passion *la petite mort*—the little death. It was joy so wild, so sweet that it turned you inside out.

Was this what her sisters felt after sex? After being with the men they loved?

Not that this had anything to do with love. She didn't love Nick, she wasn't falling in love with him, she wasn't, she wasn't...

The room spun.

She sat up straight.

"What?" Nick said.

"I—I have to get that bread into the oven pretty soon."

"Right now?"

"Right now." She swallowed drily, then smiled. "I am a practical woman."

"You are," Nick said, "an incredible woman."

One last, quick kiss and he let go of her. She went to the sink, washed her hands and then went back to work, shaping the dough. It was mindless stuff and that was what she needed right now.

Nick watched her for a couple of minutes. Then he walked over to her, swept aside her hair and kissed the nape of her neck.

"Thank you," he said softy.

She leaned back against him, closed her eyes and he kissed the back of her neck again.

"For what?"

"For being here. For who you are. For making me happy." He paused and cleared his throat. "I haven't been happy in a long, long time, Duchess. I'd almost forgotten what it's like."

Lissa turned in his arms.

"Nick," she said, rushing his name, rushing the words because he had never before revealed this much of the darkness that she knew haunted him, "whatever happened… Your accident… If you ever want to talk about it…"

He silenced her with a kiss.

"No," he said, with a finality that sent a chill through the room. A muscle knotted in his jaw. Then he kissed her again. "See you for drinks on the back porch at five."

She nodded. "Drinks" meant Cokes or ginger ale. Nick had said, casually, that he was sticking with soft drinks for a while, but she was welcome to have wine if she preferred. She'd said that ginger ale was fine. What she'd really wanted to say was that maybe sharing his secrets with her would help him.

She sighed as she watched him walk away.

Her lover was a man of secrets.

He shared all the bits and pieces of his life with her, from caring for the kittens to his plans for restoring the house, but he never mentioned his wounds or the accident that had left his leg so horrendously damaged.

He would not talk about any of it.

But he was healing. She could see that for herself.

He'd switched from the crutch to the cane; there were times he didn't need it at all. There wasn't the same darkness in his eyes, either, but something still haunted him.

She knew a little about injured legs. She'd even had a fracture herself when she was sixteen. Her horse had thrown her, but she'd gotten off easy with what the doctor had called a malleolus fracture, which sounded a hell of a lot more dramatic than it had actually been.

You grew up in ranching country, you saw breaks that were far worse. Splintered tibias and compound fractures, even fractures of the femur, that biggest, heaviest of the bones in the leg.

Taming horses, riding them day after day over rough terrain, was not for the fainthearted. Movies romanticized ranch life; reality was far from romantic.

Nick's leg had been more severely damaged than she would have thought possible.

She'd seen the scars.

They were terrifying. Brutal. She'd wanted to weep the first time, but she'd known that it had been difficult enough for him to let her see them. Instead, she'd kissed them. The purple ridge high on his thigh. The evil-looking row of what she was sure had been staples that ran the length of his calf. The jagged line that almost encircled his ankle.

Nick had flinched at the first brush of her lips. He'd tried to stop her.

"Am I hurting you?" she'd asked.

"No. No. I just—I just didn't want you to—to see—"

She'd put her mouth to his leg again. He'd shuddered. Sighed. And, gradually, she'd felt his taut muscles relax.

Lissa shaped the last of the dough into a loaf.

She hated people who went in for amateur psychiatry, but you didn't have to be a shrink to know that Nick was hurting in more ways than one. She wanted to help him. To ease that hurt.

To make the shadows that occasionally still darkened his eyes disappear.

Maybe she had to be satisfied knowing that she made him happy.

For now, it was enough.

* * *

Lissa and Esther had established a pattern.

Esther showed up at noon, did whatever needed touching up around the house, and joined Lissa in the kitchen around two.

Together, they readied things for the next day's breakfasts; they put up the lunches the men would carry with them the following morning, and Esther played sous chef as Lissa made dinner. The men ate at six; Esther tidied up and loaded the dishwasher.

That left Lissa free to relax with Nick before the fire in his office over glasses of ginger ale topped with slices of lime before they had dinner together. If the weather was warm enough, they had their drinks on the back porch.

First, though, there was what had become the dinner ritual. Tonight was no exception.

The men trooped in, clean-shaven, hands and faces shiny and scrubbed. As always, Ace was their spokesman.

"'Evenin', ma'am."

"Good evening, Ace. How was your day?"

"Excellent, ma'am. Truly fine."

"I'm happy to hear it. Everything's on the sideboard, but if you need anything, Esther's right in the kitchen."

"We'll be fine, ma'am. You jes' go on and join the boss. He'll be waitin' on you." He blushed. "I mean, there's no need to worry about us."

"Thank you," Lissa said politely. She went back into the kitchen, took off her apron, grabbed her sweater, said goodnight to Esther and headed out to the back porch that extended the length of the house. As she shut the kitchen door, the door to Nick's office opened and he stepped outside, too.

Her heartbeat skittered. Was it really going to do that each time she saw him?

"Hey," he said softly.

She smiled. "Hey, yourself."

Brutus greeted her joyously.

"He acts as if we've been apart for ages," she said, laughing.

"Yeah," Nick said. "I know just how he feels." He cupped Lissa's face with his hands and lifted it to his for a tender kiss. "For instance, it seems forever since I did that."

Lissa touched the tip of her finger to his mouth.

"Two hours and twenty-two minutes." She smiled again. "Not that I'm counting."

He linked his hands at the base of her spine.

"I figured it was too cool out here tonight. How about if we have our drinks in the living room for a change?"

"We'd have to go through the kitchen to get to the living room."

"So?"

"So, it turns out your crew is keeping an eye on us."

"I'm afraid to ask. What'd they say?"

Lissa did a creditable imitation of Ace. Nick laughed.

"OK. We'll have to detour. Go in through my office—"

"—sneak down the hall…." She sighed. "I haven't sneaked around with a boy since I dated Jefferson Beauregard the Third."

"Jefferson Beauregard the Third?"

"The Third. He'd take a fit if you were foolish enough to forget that number!"

"And he made you sneak around, huh? Doesn't sound like a southern gentleman to me."

"Oh, I liked the sneaking-around part." She grinned. "Hey, I was a teenager! But the southern-gentleman thing? Trust me. He wasn't."

Nick gave a mock growl. "I ever stumble across old Jeff, he'll be in trouble."

"He already is." Lissa giggled. "He's on wife number three."

"I guess he likes that number."

She giggled again. He smiled.

"You have a great laugh, Duchess."

"When we were kids, my brother Jake used to say that I sounded like a donkey braying."

"I'll have to add him to that guys-who-are-in-trouble list."

Lissa smiled. "Actually, you'd like each other."

"Jake. Didn't you mention him before?"

"Yes." She hesitated. "I told you that he'd been wounded."

She could almost feel Nick's quick mood change.

"In Afghanistan, right? Doing something heroic."

"He'd never say it was heroic, but yes, it was."

"Most of the guys who are heroes don't think of themselves that way." He cleared his throat. "What did you say happened to him?"

"He lost an eye. He piloted a Black Hawk and he was trying to rescue some men who'd been trapped in a firefight. His chopper went down and—and he was lucky he got out alive."

Nick stepped away from her and tucked his hands into the back pockets of his jeans.

"I'm glad he made it home."

"Yes. We are, too."

An owl cried out from somewhere in the gathering darkness. The sound was mournful, eerie, and it made Lissa shudder. Deliberately, she searched for something that would bridge the sudden silence.

"So," she said brightly, "what about that ginger ale?"

The silence stretched on. Then Nick cleared his throat.

"It's Coke tonight. We're all out of ginger ale." He brought her hands to his lips and kissed them both. "And I'm sorry."

"There's no need," she said, deliberately misunderstanding him. "I like Coke."

He laughed, exactly as she'd hoped he would, and the mood lightened.

"I keep forgetting all that fancy training of yours. But we'll have to hurry. It's almost time for us to head out."

"Out?"

"We have a seven-thirty reservation at the dining room at *Clearwater Pass*. It's about an hour's drive from here."

The swift look of delight on her face was everything he'd hoped for.

"*Clearwater Pass*? The new lodge? I've read about it. The restaurant is supposed to be wonderful."

"Well, we're going to find out."

"Oh, that's lovely! Really lovely." Her smile tilted. "Except—"

"Except what?"

"I know that you—that you've been keeping a low profile."

"You mean, I've been hiding."

"It's just that people are sure to recognize you at a place like *Clearwater Pass*. And if you're doing this for me…" Lissa looked into her lover's eyes. "We don't have to go anywhere. I'm happy right here."

Nick drew her to him.

"Are you?"

"Yes," she said simply, "I am."

He bent his head and kissed her.

"Me, too. But we're going out tonight, sweetheart. It's time you had a break."

"Esther's been doing the meals on weekends."

"Do not argue with me, woman," he growled, and softened the teasing words with a smile. "Besides, I want to show you off."

"But—"

"No *buts*," he said firmly. "It's time I left the cocoon. And you need a change of scene and somebody to serve you once in a while." He sighed and rested his forehead against hers. "We're going to have to do something about the setup here, Duchess. We need more privacy. More help for you."

"Not for me, but the privacy idea sounds wonderful idea. How are you going to do it?"

"I have some thoughts."

"That sounds mysterious."

"A little mystery can be a good thing." He smiled. "Besides, it's getting late. We have to get moving."

"Especially since I have to change for dinner."

"Change? You look just right to me."

"Men," Lissa said, leaning up to kiss him again. "What do men know about women and clothing?"

"We know how to separate them from it," Nick said gruffly. She leaned back in his arms.

"You just said it was getting late."

"Trust me." He caught her hand, brought it between them, and she caught her breath. "As long as you're willin', ma'am, this ain't gonna take very long."

"Why, cowboy," she said, batting her lashes, "I thought you'd never ask."

* * *

They made love with sweet urgency, showered together, dried each other off and dressed for the evening.

She put on one of the two just-in-case outfits she'd packed: the black cashmere sweater and the long, embroidered denim skirt, plus the boots Nick had bought her.

He changed to more formal jeans—"No holes in the knees," he said—and a black turtleneck topped by a black leather blazer, and a pair of well-worn but handsome Tony Lamas.

Brutus moaned piteously when Nick told him he'd have to stay home.

"Go keep Louie and Peaches company," Lissa said, "and if you're a really good boy, we'll bring you a treat."

"He'll expect one, you know," Nick said as they got into a truck she'd never seen before, a shiny black behemoth with glove-leather bucket seats, and headed for the main road. "He's a smart boy. Understands every word he hears."

"He took a cookie from me this afternoon," Lissa said. "Without you there to say the secret word."

Nick sighed.

"The secret word is *dynamo*. And I'm glad as hell he did that." He hesitated. "Teaching him that crap, not to eat unless a special person says a special word, was not my idea."

Lissa put her hand on his arm.

"The guy who did—I have no idea where he is right now. I can only hope he doesn't own another dog."

"What happened?"

A muscle knotted in Nick's jaw.

"We were shooting a movie in Toronto. This guy came along—he was a friend of one of the grips. That's a guy who—"

"—works with the lighting and electrical stuff. I know. You can't survive in La La Land without picking up some of the lingo."

"So this guy started hanging around. There was an animal trainer on the set because we were using horses. And this jerk asked the trainer if he wanted to see a really well-trained animal. The guy said sure, and the next day, he showed up with Brutus."

"And?"

"And," he said, his tone hardening, "Brutus was big and beautiful, smart as hell—and defeated. He kept his tail between his legs. He flinched when anybody tried to pet him. He obeyed what seemed like thousands of commands. His owner was proudest of the feeding thing. 'He'd starve to death if I weren't there to tell him he could eat,' he said, and I wanted to put my fist down his throat."

"Oh God, how horrible!"

"The SOB got busy, trying to cozy up to the trainer. I had some time alone with the dog. It took hours, but he finally let me pet him. Not pet him, exactly. He let me touch his head. The piece of shit who owned him saw it happen. He was furious. He shouted at the dog and raised his fist to him and I—I got between them and… Let's just say I put a stop to it."

"That bastard!"

"I called him far worse than that. Then I told him he was going to sell the dog to me, that he'd tell me the secret word and he'd see to it that the dog understood that it was going to be OK to let the eating command come from me from that day on." Nick's hands tightened on the wheel. "He didn't like the idea, but I persuaded him."

She nodded. She could imagine how persuasive Nick had been.

"It took me a long time to win Brutus's trust." He looked at her and smiled. "You won it in seconds. I've never seen him jump up and kiss anybody before. I mean, he's great with me, but he still hangs back with other people."

"He must have known that I fell head over heels in love with him the second I saw him."

Nick took one hand from the wheel and reached for hers.

"You know, I never believed in that love-at-first-sight thing," he said gruffly.

Lissa felt her heart stand still. She looked across the cab at Nick. His face was lit by the dashboard lights; he was looking at her, too.

"No?"

"No. Not until now."

"You mean, until you saw Brutus with me."

He brought their joined hands to his mouth and kissed her fingers.

"Something like that," he said, and just then, the road merged with the one heading for the town that was just south of *Clearwater Pass*. It was heavy with traffic and Nick let go of Lissa's hand, downshifted, and concentrated on his driving.

* * *

Their table was very private, and tucked beside a wall of glass that looked out on a grove of delicately-illuminated snow-covered aspens.

Ivory tapers in crystal holders provided just enough light; the table cloth and *serviettes* were of heavy ivory linen. The menus were handwritten with black calligraphy.

Nick had made the reservation under a pseudonym, but though they'd been treated with discretion, he knew he'd been recognized the minute he and Lissa walked in. He knew the signs: the widened eyes, the delighted greeting, the deference that went beyond the way customers were normally treated.

Identity blown, he'd thought; nothing would be the same after tonight. It scared the hell out of him, but he knew it was time.

Lissa deserved a life lived to the fullest, not one spent in the shadows.

She had changed everything, even how he looked at the world.

Once, he'd have seen *Clearwater Pass* as just another trendy venue—handsome, expensive, nothing more. Tonight, he saw it through her eyes. Its charm. Its special ambience.

Or maybe what he saw was her joy. The glow in her face, the way she looked at the menu, the candlesticks, even the heavy silver service. Some of it he recognized as female delight. Some, he knew, was the delight of a classically trained chef.

When their server brought coffee and a dish of small, exquisite pastries, Lissa asked if he'd be kind enough to wrap two of them for a very good friend.

"Brutus," she'd whispered to Nick, when the man happily

obliged.

Nick smiled. "He'll be thrilled."

She smiled, too. "Our boy deserves the best."

Our boy, Nick thought, and reached for her hand.

"Glad we came here tonight?" he asked softly.

"Oh, it's been a wonderful evening!"

"Good."

"*Clearwater Pass* could stand up to any of the most upscale restaurants in L.A. or New York. Someone took a lot of care with it, from the biggest to the smallest details. And the location! The only one I've seen that could better it is the Triple G's."

"You like the ranch's location?"

"Oh, Nick, you must know that it's amazing! The meadows. The mountains. Even the house, now that I've gotten to know it better. My sister Jaimie was in real estate for a little while. She'd say the house needs work, but that it has good—"

"—bones. Heck, I know some of that lingo myself."

"And the food here…"

"Nice?" Nick said politely.

"Amazing! Innovative! Brilliant! And beautifully presented. Even the service… It's caring, but unobtrusive."

"Caring, but unobtrusive," Nick repeated gravely. "Exactly what I was thinking."

Lissa laughed. He wanted to kiss her, but he had the feeling she wouldn't appreciate being pulled from her chair and bent back over his arm in a room filled with people.

"Do I sound crazy?"

"You sound like what you are. My gorgeous chef." He laced

their fingers together. "I'm selfish, keeping you all to myself at the Triple G."

"I'm happy at the Triple G."

"Yeah, but you'd be happier with a staff of—what? There must be a couple of dozen people working here."

"More than that. In the kitchen alone, there are probably...." Lissa rolled her eyes. "Stop me before I bore you to death."

"You could never bore me."

"It's just that, you know, this is the kind of place I've always dreamed of."

"You wouldn't change a thing about it?"

"No. Well, a little. The food was wonderful. But I'd gear the menu to the setting. The mountains, the forest, the elements. Locally produced foods, simple foods, but not simply done. You know?"

"Sure," he said, even though he was clueless. The only thing he did know was that all the other women who'd passed through his life only showed this kind of excitement over expensive jewelry and couturier labels.

"I even have a name for a restaurant like that." She caught her bottom lip between her teeth and leaned toward him "Sounds silly to have spent so much time building castles in the air—"

"What would you name it?"

"*Basic Elegance.*"

"I like it."

"Seriously?" Her teeth sank lightly into her lip again.

"Seriously." Nick cleared his throat. "And if you don't stop chewing on your lip, I'm going to pick you up and carry you out of here."

Color swept into her face, along with a look of abject delight.

"Promises, promises," she whispered.

Nick looked at her. Then he took out his wallet, dumped a stack of bills on the table, reached for his cane and stood up.

"Nick?"

"Melissa," he said, his voice low and hot and filled with an emotion that made her heartbeat quicken. "Melissa," he said again, and then he held out his hand, helped her to her feet and, *to hell with it,* curved his arm around her, drew her to him and kissed her.

A little buzz of excitement whispered through the nearest tables, followed them as they walked out the door. Outside, he kissed her again, then handed the valet the ticket for his truck.

"—Nick Gentry," an excited voice said behind them as the kid hurried away. "Really, I know it's him, but who's the—"

"Shh!" another voice said.

A couple stepped around Nick and Lissa, threw them a quick glance, and hurried along a path that led to the main lodge.

Lissa groaned and leaned her head against Nick's shoulders.

"This is going to be everywhere in twenty-four hours. Pictures of you, the fact that you're in northern Montana, and they'll surely find out about the Triple G. It's all my fault. If I hadn't let you bring me here…"

"Then we'll make the most of those twenty-four hours, sweetheart, and coming here was my idea, remember?"

The valet brought the truck to the curb. Nick thanked him

and handed him a bill. Lissa climbed into the cab. Nick got behind the wheel.

"I wanted to bring you here," he said again. "I meant what I said. It's time I moved into the world again." He stepped harder on the gas. Then he glanced at her before looking back at the road. "And there's something else."

Lissa's heart thudded. He sounded so serious. Was he going to tell her their idyll, their affair, whatever you called it, was over? If he was, as he'd put it, moving into the world again…

"What?" she said in a small voice she hardly recognized as her own.

"It's time I told you what happened to me. How I fucked up my leg." He reached for her hand and gripped it so tight that she felt each of his fingers press into the bones in her wrist. "How I fucked up everything." Nick swallowed hard. "And I'm scared shitless, because it might change how you feel about being with me."

CHAPTER TWELVE

IF EVER NICK had known a time that called for a good shot of whiskey, this was it.

But he'd poured all that bourbon down the drain two weeks back; he'd been sober ever since and he knew damn well that was a good thing.

Brutus gave them a big hello and an ecstatic wag of the tail for the delicate little pastries that vanished in two bites of his massive jaws. They checked on Louie and Peaches and found them sleeping curled together in a basket in Nick's office.

Nick let the Newf out while Lissa brewed a pot of tea. Then they went upstairs to his bedroom, to *their* bedroom, and he lit a fire on the hearth while she poured tea.

He didn't have the heart to tell her that he'd always figured tea was what you drank when you were sick. Besides, he had to admit this stuff smelled great, of cinnamon and other spices, and he needed something to warm him.

He was ice cold with fear.

He had planned on facing the world tonight, but he hadn't planned on facing Lissa.

But he knew the time was right.

They settled on the love seat before the fireplace, Brutus at their feet. Silence stretched between them.

Finally, Nick cleared his throat.

"Great tea."

"I'm a big tea fan."

"What's that taste? Cinnamon? Something else?"

"Allspice. And a little bit of orange peel."

"Ah."

More silence.

"Your own recipe?"

"I wouldn't call it a recipe. It's just something I learned to toss together years a—"

"I was on patrol with three army Rangers in Afghanistan," Nick said, the words rushed, low, spoken so quickly they ran into each other. "We were in a Humvee. We ran over an IED. I was the only one who made it out."

Lissa stared at him. He'd shifted forward, his gaze locked to the orange and blue flames on the hearth, his hands so tightly wrapped around the mug of tea that his knuckles were white.

"Oh God," she said softly, "oh Nicholas…"

"Two of them were nineteen. One was thirty. They called him Pop. He had a wife and two kids. He showed me their picture that morning."

She put her hand on his arm. She could feel the rigidity of his muscles before he shook off her touch.

"The nineteen-year-olds were from the same town in West

Virginia. One had a twin sister back home. The other was an only child."

Tea sloshed over the rim of Lissa's mug as she put it down on the small table beside her. She had to say something, but what? This was Nick's awful secret, that he'd seen three brave young men die.

"It must have been terrible, seeing that happen."

"Seeing it happen?" Nick slammed down his mug and shot to his feet. "Don't you understand? I killed them!"

The ugly words seemed to echo through the room, but even as they did, she knew they couldn't be accurate. Nick, her Nick, was incapable of hurting, much less killing, anybody.

Lissa stood up. Nick had gone to one of the windows; his hands were pressed to the sill, his forehead to the glass. She reached out her hand, then drew it back.

"Nick," she said softly.

He didn't answer.

"Nicholas. Please. Talk to me."

"I just did." His voice was low; she had to strain to hear him. "I told you that I'm the reason three men died."

"You said you killed them. And I know that you didn't."

He swung toward her. "You weren't there."

"No. I wasn't. But I know you. You'd never knowingly hurt a soul."

This far from the fireplace, the flames on the hearth limned his face in gold. She saw a muscle flexing in his jaw, saw the set of his lips, the darkness in his eyes. She said his name and put her hand on his arm again.

Progress.

He flinched, but he didn't jerk away.

"Please," she said softly. "Tell me what happened."

She waited while seconds became minutes. Just when she'd almost given up hope, Nick went back to the love seat and sat down.

"We were in India," he said. "On location in the foothills of the Himalayas, shooting a movie about an infantry unit that gets pinned down in a firefight outside Kabul." He paused, leaned forward, his elbows on his thighs, his hands knotted, and stared into the fire. "The guy who wrote the script had been a Ranger. He still had buddies in the service. A couple of them were stationed in Afghanistan. We were halfway through shooting when he said he'd been in touch with this one old friend and how much it would mean to all the guys in his unit if we paid them a visit."

"A visit? In the middle of a war?"

Nick shook his head. "The war part was over. That was the official word, anyway. We'd go in by chopper, no announcements ahead of time, no fuss, get dropped at a small base camp, I'd shake some hands, that kind of thing. Others had done it. Comics. Actors. Some with fanfare, some without." He rose again, began to pace. "The director liked the idea. The producer didn't. They joked about it, said I had the winning vote. And I voted to go."

Lissa felt a coldness seep into her bones.

"Nick. You had no way of knowing things would go bad."

"We got the necessary clearance, picked a day, a time, helicoptered in." He looked at her. "There's no way to explain what it felt like to meet those men. Some of them were on their fourth or fifth deployment. Just seeing a face from home that had nothing to do with the fucking war... You'd have thought I was Santa Claus."

"A famous face," Lissa said softly, "somebody running a risk for them the way they'd been running a risk for all of us."

"One guy said as much. I tried to explain that what we'd done that day was zero compared to what they'd been doing, what they were still doing. They said it was too bad we hadn't come in sooner. They'd gone out on patrol and I could have gone with them. And then one of them said, hey, what about going out again? What about me going with them?"

She knew it all now. She could see the awful predictability unfolding ahead of her like a road leading straight to hell.

"And I said..." He choked. "I said that sounded great. All they needed was their CO's approval and it turned out he was just heading over to meet me. They told him their idea and he said, hell, he was my biggest fan and he only wished he didn't have a meeting or he'd go with us. So we climbed into the same goddamn Humvee they just driven and headed down the same goddamn dirt road through the same goddamn field toward the same goddamn burnt-out village..."

"Nick. Don't. Please. You don't have to—"

"I don't even remember it happening. Just a lot of laughter and music blaring, and then this huge WHAM and a spear of flame and then—and then, they were gone. Two boys and a guy with a wife and kids waiting back home."

Blind instinct took her to where he stood. If he tried to push her away, she wouldn't let him. He needed her now, and she needed him.

But he didn't push her away.

He broke down, sobbing, and she took him in her arms, and there was no way of knowing where his tears began and hers ended.

* * *

The fire had died to glowing coals.

It was late. Very late, that time of night when darkness swallows the world.

It was cold in the bedroom. Lissa had drawn an old patchwork comforter from the back of the love seat; they sat wrapped within it, and within each other's arms.

"It wasn't your fault, Nicholas," she said quietly. "You must know that."

He gave a long, weary sigh.

"If I hadn't gone there in the first place, if I hadn't said yes when they suggested going out again—"

"Life is filled with ifs. That's what life is all about. The ifs. Taking a step off a curb or not taking it. Turning a corner or not turning it. Getting out of bed at seven instead of at six. All those ifs, and you can't quantify them as right or wrong because that's the thing about ifs, they aren't right or wrong, they just exist."

Nick gave a choked laugh.

"You sound like the legion of shrinks who marched through my hospital room."

"It's the truth, Nicholas, and you know it."

"Yeah." He shrugged his shoulders. "Part of me does—but

it's hard not to think how things would have gone had I made a different choice."

"You mean, how things *might* have gone *if* you'd made a different choice."

Something that was almost a smile angled across his mouth.

"Not just Psych 101. Philosophy 101."

"Reality 101. And you keep omitting that other reality. You didn't walk away from that explosion. You were wounded. Badly wounded.

"My leg," he said, "and when you get right down to it, all it is, is a leg—and look what a stinking fuss I've made over it, as if it's anything compared to what happened to those three poor bastards."

"Dammit," Lissa said heatedly, "don't minimize your wounds! They're bad. Physically, they changed your life."

He snorted.

"Right. No more skiing. No more skydiving. Talk about life-changing shit—"

"That *is* life-changing." Her voice softened. "But the real truth is that your leg is a reminder of that day. Of those men. It takes you back each time you look at the scars, or feel an ache deep in your bones. I know it does, Nick. I saw it happen with Jake. My brother. I told you, remember?"

"Yeah. He was wounded in action."

"You think that made his memories of what had happened easier to handle?"

"Your brother was a hero."

"He doesn't think so."

"Still, he was. And he was more than doing his job; he was

risking his life for others. I was—I was just along for the ride."

Lissa shook her head. "You were doing your job too, Nicholas. One of the things that makes you the actor you are, the man you are, is your ability to see what others see, feel what they feel. You understood that those men were living through something the rest of us can't begin to comprehend, and you wanted to help. You didn't have to go to that camp, or climb into that vehicle."

"Lissa. I know you're trying to help, but—"

"Nick." She took a steadying breath. "Your dad hid from life after your mom died. It didn't bring her back—all it did was hurt you."

"This isn't the same thing."

"It's absolutely the same thing! You came here to hide from life, but it won't bring back those soldiers. All it's done is hurt you and those who care for you. The people in Clarke's Falls who've known your identity all along and choose to protect you by pretending they didn't. The men who work for you—they know you're Nick Gentry, too, but they've given you space to heal." Lissa paused. "And me," she said softly. "Each time I saw the darkness in your eyes I wanted to take you in my arms and beg you to tell me what was wrong, I wanted to tell you everything would be all right, but I knew you'd push me away and—"

A deep, anguished howl broke from his throat. Lissa wrapped her arms around her lover; he wrapped his around her.

"I feel so damned guilty," he said brokenly, "knowing that I lived, that they didn't…"

"If you had died that day," she said, her voice trembling, "how would it have made things better? Four dead instead of three?" She drew back a little, just enough so she could look into his eyes. "You lived. And now you have a choice. You can honor those men by living your life for them as well as for yourself. You have to return to the world, Nicholas. You have to do the work that made millions of people happy, that made those guys happy! If you owe those men anything, you owe them that."

Tears rolled down her face, glittered in his eyes. They were both silent for a long time. Then Nick drew her hard against him and buried his face in her hair.

"This is the first time I've talked about it," he said. "I couldn't. Not with the surgeon, not with the shrinks, not with the physiotherapists."

"You can talk to me about anything," Lissa said. "Anything!"

"The truth is—the truth is, I miss working."

"I miss you working, too."

Nick looked into her eyes, the start of a smile on his lips. "Meaning, you're tired of having me around?"

"Meaning," she said, returning that smile with one of her own, "you haven't had a film out in almost two years."

"And you know this because…"

She gave a little laugh. "I know it because I've seen every movie you ever made."

Her nose was leaking; Nick drew a handkerchief from his pocket.

"Blow," he said gently, holding the square of pristine white linen to her nose. She did, and he cocked his head. "Every movie? But you told me—"

"I know what I told you. I lied. I've seen them all and I loved them all." She laughed again. "You are the toughest, tenderest, sexiest cowboy on the silver screen, Gentry."

"I don't want to boast, but I've also been the toughest, tenderest, sexiest CIA agent and NSA spy and once, the toughest, tenderest, sexiest talking-head-TV-reporter on the silver screen, Wilde—assuming there is such a word as *tenderest*."

"If there isn't, there should be. You are one hell of an actor, Nick Gentry."

"That's a matter of opinion," Nick said softly. "But here's a fact." He framed her face with his hands. "Melissa Wilde, you are the best thing that's ever happened to me."

He kissed her, and she sighed, rose on her toes and wrapped her arms around his neck.

* * *

He'd said they'd have twenty-four hours before word of his reappearance hit the news.

Wrong.

Normally, the ranch crew was just finishing breakfast when Lissa came down in the mornings. She might see one of them, perhaps two, but that next morning, all the men were waiting for her and all of them looked solemn.

"What?" she said with alarm. "Ace? What's the matter?"

"Is the boss comin' down? Not that I'd think you'd know if he was or wasn't, Ms. Lissa, but—"

It wasn't a time to stand on formalities.

"He just let Brutus out," Lissa said. "Please. What's wrong?"

"We thought you both should know, ma'am…"

"Jeez, Ace, just say it," Gus blurted. "There's a whole line of SUVs and cars comin' up the road, Miss, every last one with antennas sproutin' in all directions."

Lissa felt her stomach drop.

"Up this road? To the Triple G?"

Gus nodded. "Yes'm. I shut the upper gate so they can't come no further than that, but there's not much else we can do unless the boss tells us to go out there with shotguns and threaten to run 'em all off."

Ace cleared his throat.

"There's more. Esther called. She says to tell you she slammed her door on a reporter at dawn."

"Oh, hell," Lissa said, just as the back door opened. Brutus galloped into the kitchen straight to her, with Nick strolling after him. He smiled, but one look at Lissa's face wiped his smile away.

"Lissa? What is it?"

"We thought we'd have twenty-four hours," she said softly. "We were wrong."

"People comin'," Ace said. "Television people. Gus closed the upper gate, but there's a bunch of 'em buildin' up out there."

"Me and the boys can go out and run 'em off," Gus said. "This is private land, boss. You have every right to keep it that way."

"Thank you," Nick said. "Thank you—but they'll just head back to the main road and wait."

"You could phone Hank," Lissa said. "He could fly you out."

"They'd be waiting wherever we landed." He took Lissa's hand in his. "All of those ifs, remember? This time, they lead to the same place. I can't escape the outcome, Duchess. It's time to face reality."

She swallowed past the lump in her throat.

"What shall we do?"

"Not 'we.' Me. This is my mess. I'm the one who has to start cleaning it up."

"Nick. You don't have to do this alone."

He brought her hand to his lips.

"I do," he said softly. "I have to take a step into the world, into living my life." He smiled. "A very wise philosopher told me how important that was."

"Still, you don't have to do it all by yourself."

Nick's smile faded. "Yes. I do. The first steps have to be mine."

His gaze fell to her mouth and he leaned forward and kissed her. It was the first time they'd shared any small sign of intimacy in front of his men, and an audible sigh swept through the kitchen. After a long moment, he turned and looked at them.

"Ace. Gus. All of you. Thank you for your loyalty these past months. There's not a ranch in all of Montana with a finer bunch of cowboys than you guys. I want you to know how much that's meant to me—how much it will continue to mean to me, especially now. Those vultures out there are going to try to pick your bones."

"They ain't gonna get nothin' out of us," one man said, and

the others growled their assent.

"I know that," Nick said. "And I'm grateful." He cleared his throat. "So, let's get this over with. Ace, Gus, all of you—just go about your usual day. I'll make it clear that nobody's to bother you. I can't guarantee that'll keep them from trying—"

"It will," Ace said grimly, "if we all spend the day shovelin' manure."

Everybody laughed. Then, one by one, Nick shook hands with his men and they shuffled out of the house. Ace was the last in line.

"We all wish you only the best, boss. You an' Ms. Lissa, too."

Nick held out his hand. Ace took it in a firm grip.

"I know that, and I appreciate it more than you can imagine. And it's Nick, remember? Just Nick."

Ace grinned. "I'll remember that, boss."

"It's going to be rough," Nick said quietly, once he and Lissa were alone.

She put her arm through his and leaned her head against his shoulder.

"I know."

"There are times I think some reporters would eat their young if they could guarantee themselves a big headline."

"Wow," she said, with far more lightness than she felt, "there's an image for the ages."

Nick turned her toward him and took her hands. "Stay inside. With luck, maybe nobody figured out who you are."

"I'm not worried about me! I don't want you to have to face this alone."

"And I don't want you dragged into this. Stay inside. Don't

even go to the window. I'll deal with them." He hesitated. "I'm going to call Hank. Unless someone's found that landing strip, he should be able to touch down and get you out of here, fast. I'll tell Ace to use his own truck, and to take the back road that goes through the woods."

Lissa's heart thudded. "You're sending me away?"

"Didn't you hear what I said? I don't want you pulled into this."

"Nicholas—"

"You call me that every once in a while. Nicholas. Is there a reason?"

"Why do you sometimes call me Melissa?"

"That's a great question. I don't know. Maybe because nobody else does. Maybe it's your name just for me."

She smiled back at him. Then she moved closer, her head tilted back, her eyes on his. "You don't have to protect me, you know. It isn't as if I've never dealt with the press. Well, not directly, but my father is a general."

"A general?"

"Yes. Four stars. I'm only telling you that so you understand that I didn't exactly grow up like a small-town kid. Sometimes, all of us stood for interviews."

"All of you. Three brothers."

"And two sisters."

He gave a laugh that wasn't a laugh at all. "What a moment for us to be learning about each other."

"You're right. But—but there's time…"

As if in response, a horn blared outside and then another and another until they were enclosed by a wall of sound that seemed to last forever before it finally died.

The waiting crowd was growing impatient.

"Once," Lissa whispered, "when I was little, my father was on assignment in England. He flew us over and we spent the weekend at an estate in Northamptonshire. The big event was a fox hunt. I remember the sound of the horns, the way they drove the fox into running."

Nick took her in his arms.

"I know all about running, sweetheart. I ran away from home when I was eighteen, hitchhiked to New York, shared a room in Brooklyn so awful that not even the mice or roaches would come near it, and worked odd jobs while I figured out who I was and what I wanted to do. I ran from the reality of what had happened in Afghanistan." His eyes locked with hers. "But I'm not going to run anymore, thanks to you."

"Not me, Nicholas. You did this all by yourself."

"The hell I did. You're one amazing woman, Melissa Wilde."

"And you're an amazing man, Nicholas Gentry."

They smiled at each other. Then Lissa's smile dimmed.

"This is going to change everything," she said.

He hesitated, but she was smart as a whip. There was no sense in lying to her.

"Yes," he said. "It will."

Lissa nodded. She played with the buttons on his denim shirt.

"They're going to hound you."

"I'll answer whatever questions they ask."

"You'll tell them about Afghanistan?"

"Yes." His mouth twisted. "But I won't talk about those

guys, not until I've met with their families."

Lissa smiled. "That will mean a lot to them."

"I don't know if it will or it won't. I only know it's what I have to do."

"You're a good man, Nicholas Gentry."

The cacophony of horns sounded again. Lissa flinched. Nick wrapped his arms around her.

"There's so much more I wanted to say…"

The tears she'd tried to hold back fell like rain.

"Nicholas," she whispered, "oh, Nicholas!"

He kissed her. When he raised his head, she grabbed hold of his jacket.

"No," she said, "don't go!"

Nick put her from him. "I'll call when I can."

"Nick. Nick, wait—"

"Remember me," he growled.

Then he left her.

Lissa stood in the center of the kitchen, listening as the sound of his footsteps, the tap of his cane, receded. She heard the full-throated roar of the waiting crowd as he opened the front door, then the slam of that door.

And then, silence.

He'd told her to stay away from the window, but she couldn't. She twitched a corner of a curtain aside and saw him walking toward the gate and a frenzy of reporters, cameras, flashing lights and microphones. His head was up, his stride purposeful, the limp barely perceptible.

"Nicholas," she whispered.

The awful finality of his last words echoed in her head.

Remember me. Remember me. Remember me.

"Always," she sobbed.

Always, and forever.

CHAPTER THIRTEEN

ACE DROVE HER to the airstrip.

Hank and the plane were already there, engines idling. Ace brought the truck to a skidding halt and turned toward her.

"The boys want me to tell you how much—how much we liked havin' you here," he said. "Not jes' the cookin', though that was great. We liked havin' you around, Ms. Lissa. You was—you made things better. Happier, especially for the boss."

Lissa's throat constricted. The last thing she wanted to do was break down. Poor Ace would be devastated.

"Thank you," she said. "You tell them that I loved being here. You're a fine bunch of men."

"I hope you'll be back, ma'am. We all hope it."

She nodded. "I hope so, too."

Ace stepped down from the truck. So did Lissa. She reached for her suitcase, but he kept a grip on the handle.

"Ma'am?"

"Hurry up," Hank yelled. "I don't know how much time we have before some jackal of a reporter finds this place."

Lissa looked at Ace. "I'm sorry," she said. "But I have to—"

"What you did for the boss—for Nick—was wonderful. He's a good man with a good heart. An' you found that heart inside him jes' when we all feared he'd forever lost it. We jes'—we all want you to know that."

Tears rose in Lissa's eyes. She leaned forward, hugged Ace, kissed his grizzled cheek. Then she grabbed her suitcase from him and ran blindly for the plane.

Hank took her luggage and helped her on board.

"Sorry to rush you," he said, "but the story about Nick is exploding. He wants you kept out of this. He says if you want me to fly you someplace other than LAX—"

"No. No, LAX is fine."

It wasn't fine because Nick wouldn't be there, Lissa thought as she buckled her seat belt, but where else could she go? El Sueño? Not there. Maybe, if she was lucky, nothing about this would get that far.

She'd go back to her L.A. apartment and wait to hear from Nick.

He'd phone her as soon as he got away from the people Ace had so accurately described as jackals.

* * *

Except, he didn't.

Her phone never rang during the flight and when she checked for missed calls or messages or texts, there were none.

She understood.

Nick was besieged; he had no time for anything except dealing with the mob camped out on the Triple G. He'd call when he could, and that might take a while.

The question was, how long?

There was still nothing from him when the plane landed, nothing as she hurried from the terminal. She queued up for a taxi and while she waited, she took out her phone again and went online. Why hadn't she thought of that sooner? There might not be anything there about him, not yet, but still—

Lissa gasped in shock.

Her lover's face was everywhere. *Nick Gentry Found! Nick Gentry Discovered! Nick Gentry, Hiding in Plain Sight!*

And then her knees went weak.

Her face was everywhere, too.

Had everybody in that restaurant where she'd so foolishly imagined people were being discreet done nothing all evening except snap cell phone pictures of Nick and her?

There was a shot of them at their table. A shot of them holding hands during dinner. A shot of them outside the restaurant, she in the circle of Nick's arm.

And, on every site, blowups of Nick kissing her as they'd been leaving the restaurant, of him kissing her as they'd waited for the valet to bring the truck.

Only the breathless headlines varied.

Nick's Mystery Woman.

Nick's Mystery Babe.

And, finally, on a site known for the dirt it dished: *Mystery Woman in Nick Gentry's Secret Life Identified!*

There it was. Her picture. Her name.

Her heart rose into her throat.

She felt—violated. That was the only word for it. Her name, her face out there for the world to see…

It got worse. Much worse.

Side-by-side photos of her, one in her toque and chef's coat, snapped as a publicity shot for *Raoul's*, the other of her in jeans and a T-shirt in the beat-up old kitchen at the Triple G, probably taken with a long-range lens.

And the crowning touch, the headline that tied the two together.

Lissa Wilde! She couldn't make it in Hollywood! Interview with ex-live-in, actor/restaurateur Raoul Desplaines!

The world spun. Bile rose in the back of her throat. *Don't,* she told herself. Don't throw up, don't pass out, don't, don't, don't….

"Hey!"

She jerked around. A guy had come up behind her, a quizzical smile on his face.

"Aren't you that woman, the one who helped hide that actor?"

She spoke without thinking. "He wasn't hiding."

"But you're her, right? That woman? The cook?"

A taxi pulled up beside her. Lissa grabbed for the door, flung herself into the back seat and yanked the door shut.

"Where to, Miss?"

The guy on the sidewalk was bent over, grinning like an idiot as he aimed his phone at her through the closed window.

"Anywhere," she said desperately.

"Miss. I need an address—"

"Just start driving!"

The cabbie's eyes met hers in the mirror. "Sure," he said, and pulled away from the curb.

Lissa sank back in the seat. She could hear her heart pounding. An interview with Raoul? Her live-in? Why would he say that? Hell. She knew why. That old Hollywood maxim. Any publicity was good publicity.

And the way he'd twisted things. Saying she couldn't make it in Hollywood. What would people think when they read that? Her career was already underwater...

Oh, God!

Never mind her career. What would Nicholas think? What would he say? And her family.

Lissa groaned.

Her family! Her brothers. Her sisters. Her father. They all thought she was blazing trails in the West, cooking her way towards success...

"Miss?"

"Yes."

"Where are we going, please?"

Where? Where? To a cave, where she could hide. To Nick, so she could tell him that she wasn't what Raoul had surely made her out to be. But there weren't any caves in L.A. and she had no idea where Nick was or if he was all right, and how had she forgotten that what mattered right now was Nick?

"Miss?"

Lissa swallowed hard and gave the cabbie her address.

They drove into town, into the part of Hollywood where

Lissa's apartment complex was located.

"Miss?"

Lissa looked up. The cabbie's eyes met hers in the mirror.

"You the lady they're talking about?"

She wanted to make some clever comment about that omnipresent "they," but she didn't have the energy.

"No," she said brightly, "I'm not."

"The cook? The actor's, ah, date?"

"I just told you—"

"Fine. OK. Then you won't mind that crowd over there."

Lissa looked out the window, then shrank back in her seat. A flotilla of vehicles bearing the logos of what appeared to be every TV station in the Western world was parked outside her apartment building. Reporters and photographers jammed the small courtyard.

"Keep going," she said quickly. "Don't even slow down!"

The driver grinned at her in the mirror. "Thought you might be her. Liza something, right?"

She didn't answer. She was trying to figure out where to go.

Where *could* she go? She'd really never made any close friends in L.A. It was a town full of transients. People changed jobs, changed living arrangements, changed everything all the time.

A hotel. That was her only option.

Something affordable. Not easy in this town. But she didn't have to worry about that, not for a few days, at least. Nick had overpaid her and refused to take the money back...

Nick! Was he OK? If the media was all over her, she could only imagine what it was doing to—

Her phone rang. Lissa gave a little a sob of relief, dug it out of her purse and put it to her ear without looking at the screen.

"Nick?" she said breathlessly

"So," a woman's voice said, "it's true!"

Just when you thought things couldn't get worse.

Lissa cleared her throat.

"Hello, Jaimie."

"And me," Emily said. "It's both of us, Melissa—and don't you dare hang up!"

"Why would I do that?" Lissa said, and hung up.

The phone rang again. Rang and rang. She considered shutting it off, then pictured the zillion voice mails and messages her sisters would leave. And what if Nick called and she didn't know it was him?

The sixth time the phone rang, she took the call.

"I don't want to speak to you right now," she said, before either of her sisters could speak.

"We're sure you don't," Emily said, "but we sure as hell want to speak to you."

"Em. I know you mean well—"

"What on earth did you think you were doing, Melissa?"

Lissa gave a gusty sigh.

"Look," she said, "I really don't have the time for this."

"Telling me you were the chef at a tony spa when you were chief cook and bottle washer at a broken-down horse ranch!"

"I never said a word about a spa!"

"A ranch owned by a has-been hack!"

Lissa's jaw tightened at the sound of her other sister's voice.

"Hello, Jaimie," she said coldly. "It's nice to talk with you, too. And you're both wrong. The ranch is not broken-down, and Nick is not a—"

Her eyes met the cabbie's in the mirror. If he eavesdropped any harder, his ears would flap.

"You know what?" she said. "I am not going to have this conversation."

"Yes, you are," Jaimie said grimly.

"No, I'm not. Neither of you is saying anything sensible."

"Where are you?" Emily said. "You're not in your apartment. We already know that!"

"How can you possibly know that?"

"We were there. Well, not *there*. We didn't stop and go in, not once we saw all those reporters."

"Those ghouls," Jamie said, all but hissing through her teeth.

Lissa blinked. "You mean—you mean, you're here? In Los Angeles?"

"Where the heck else would we be when our sister is in trouble?"

"What makes you think I'm in trouble?"

"We're clairvoyant," Emily said dryly. "Now tell us where you are."

"I'm in a taxi."

"*Where* in a taxi?"

Lissa peered out the window, spotted a street sign and told them what it said.

"Excellent," Jaimie said. "We're only a few blocks away." She named a hotel in Beverly Hills. "Do you know where it is?"

"Yes. But—"

"Melissa," Emily said patiently, "you can't go to your apartment and we've got the television on, so we know that your has-been actor is too busy taking care of himself to worry about taking care of you."

"Didn't I just tell you that he isn't a has-been? And he did take care of me. He had me flown here."

"Right. He sent you off into the wilderness on your own."

Lissa's belly knotted. That wasn't true. Of course it wasn't true—

Her gaze went to the mirror again. The cabbie looked away, but not soon enough. She twisted in her seat and whispered into the phone.

"OK. I'll come to your hotel, but you have to promise not to ask me any questions. Is it a deal?"

"Write down the room number," Jaimie said.

"It isn't a room," Emily said, "it's a suite. Write it down."

"Did you two hear what I said? No questions! Deal?"

"No questions," Emily said. "Not a one."

"Promise?"

"For heaven's sake, Melissa, what are we, children? No questions! We get it. Now, how about you getting this? We're in suite 1964. Can you remember that?"

"But don't come straight here," Jaimie said. "Let the cab take you to a different hotel, then grab another and take it to this one. You don't want anybody following you."

For a merciful couple of seconds, Lissa forgot everything but her middle sister's newfound interest in cloak-and-dagger stuff.

"My sister," she said, "the secret agent's fiancée."

"Zach isn't a secret agent."

"Don't be silly! Of course he is."

Lissa disconnected while they were still arguing and checked for messages again. There were none.

Nick, she thought, *oh, Nicholas, why don't you call?*

She needed him. And surely he needed her. He had to call, and soon.

* * *

When she'd first arrived in L.A. three years ago, Lissa had stayed two nights in a moderately-priced hotel on Santa Monica Boulevard while she'd looked for an apartment.

She had the taxi take her there.

Once they arrived, she paid him, added a tip, walked briskly into the hotel lobby, waited a minute or two, and just as briskly walked out again. Her suitcase made her feel conspicuous, but it wasn't very big and half the women in L.A., actresses and models, lugged around bags almost as big, so she decided not to worry about it, especially since there wasn't anything she could do to hide it.

There was a chain pharmacy across the street. She went inside, bought a ball cap and a pair of big wraparound sunglasses.

Nobody paid her any attention, not even the bored gum-chewing cashier. She paid for her purchases, stepped into a corner of the store, tore the tags off, put the glasses on and tucked her hair up under the cap.

Much better.

Once outside, she took a taxi to Rodeo Drive, got out in front of Ralph Lauren's, peered in the windows like any other shopper, did the same in front of half a dozen other shops before setting off on foot for the elegant hotel where her sisters were staying.

An elevator whisked her to their floor; a right turn took her to the door of their suite. She knocked.

"It's me," she said, knowing that one of them would be peering at her through the peephole. The door began opening. "And I'm just warning you both that I'm not staying."

She said it firmly. But once the door was fully open and she was looking at the faces of her sisters, at the love and worry in their eyes, Lissa lost the composure she'd fought so hard to maintain.

Her suitcase dropped to the floor.

"Oh, Liss," Emily said.

"Liss, sweetie," Jaimie said.

Lissa sobbed and went straight into their arms.

* * *

Emily called room service and ordered scrambled eggs and bacon, toast and three pots of herbal tea.

"I know it's way after breakfast time, but Mom used to make scrambled eggs and herbal tea whenever one of us wasn't feeling so good, remember?"

"Are you talking about me? Because I'm feeling good," Lissa said. Jaimie and Emily looked at her. "OK. Maybe not so good. But, really, I'm not very hungry."

Her sisters said well, they were, so she could just watch them eat.

Mostly, they watched her.

The truth was, she was starved—she hadn't had anything since those cups of tea the night before, and that felt as if it had been a century ago. So she tucked into the eggs and the bacon, spread strawberry jam on the toast, drank two cups of tea.

"Done?" Emily said.

"Yes. Thank you. That was—"

Jaimie whisked the room service tray aside.

"How did you end up in Montana?" she said.

"What went wrong between you and that actor, Raoul Something-or-Other?"

"The man's an idiot!"

"No worse an idiot than Nick Gentry! What was he doing in the middle of nowhere?"

"Were you actually a ranch cook?"

"And if you were, why? What happened? What went wrong?"

Emily and Jaimie fell silent. Lissa looked from one of the to the other.

"No questions," she said. "That was the deal."

"That's ridiculous! How can we help you if we don't ask questions?"

Her sisters' eyes were filled with compassion. Lissa felt her throat constrict.

"Liss. Do you have any idea what it's like to be watching the eleven o'clock news and suddenly they flash a picture and a breathless bimbo says it's a cell phone shot of the missing actor, Nick Gentry, and an unidentified woman at a restaurant in, I don't know what it was called, Back of Beyond, Montana?"

Lissa flinched.

"And you see that unidentified woman and you say, that's not an unidentified woman, that's our sister, Melissa!"

"And then, hello, your brothers start calling and asking what in hell is going on."

"They know?" Lissa whispered.

"Of course they know! You're just lucky Jake's in Spain buying horses, Caleb's in The Hague at some kind of international-law conference, and Travis is in Germany at a finance meeting that nobody can even describe, or you'd have all three of them to deal with."

"Marco and Zach, too," Jaimie said. "You think it was easy to convince them we could handle this on our own?"

"Handle what? Me? You're going to handle me?"

"We're getting off the track," Emily said. "We want to help you, but we can't do that until we know what's happening. And only you can tell us that."

Lissa gave a deep sigh. Things were already a mess. How much worse could they get?

"OK. What do you want to know?"

"You could start by explaining what you were doing working as a cook on a ranch in the middle of nowhere," Emily said, "especially after you told me that you'd taken a job as executive chef at a fancy resort."

"*I* didn't say that. *You* did."

"Yeah. But you didn't correct me. You didn't say, well, actually, I'm at a ranch outside a town nobody ever heard of, cooking for a bunch of cowhands—"

"—and for their boss, an actor most people figured was dead.""Dead, or worse."

"It's a long story," Lissa said slowly. "It'll take lots of time to tell."

"By an amazing coincidence," Jaimie said, "we happen to have nothing but time to spare today."

"Lissa. We were all going crazy, worrying over you! We promised the guys we'd report back ASAP."

Lissa looked from one sister to the other. "Report back? Am I ten years old?"

"Don't try to change the subject! You're in trouble."

"And you know this because…?"

"Why else would you have taken such a crappy job? Why else would you have holed up with a man who's been hiding from the world?"

"Is that all?" Lissa said, each word encased in ice. "I mean, why hold back? Just say what's on your minds."

"I just did."

"You're wrong. About Nick. About why I stayed at the Triple G. You've jumped to a whole bunch of conclusions about me, about the ranch, about him."

"So tell us what we have wrong," Jaimie said quietly. "And then maybe, just maybe, we can put our heads together and come up with a plan. Because you need a plan, Melissa. You absolutely need a plan."

They were right.

She needed a plan.

A way to move forward. To restore the professional

reputation she'd permitted Raoul to destroy months ago and now to destroy again. To stand up to the wild dogs circling around her.

To tell Nick that she loved him, that she would stand with him as he made his way through this, to be with him whatever he intended to do next, whether it involved running the Triple G or making another movie.

"Liss?"

She nodded. Inhaled. Exhaled. And said, "It's a long story, guys, and it begins at a place called *Raoul's*. A restaurant in Beverly Hills that I didn't tell you about because I wanted it to be a surprise…"

Actually, the story began before that. With Carlos. And with Jack. And then, finally, with Raoul.

She told them what a breath of fresh air he'd been. How she'd come to like him. Respect him.

"Trust him," she said. "That was the real big thing. I'd trusted Jack and Carlos, and that trust had been thrown in my face, and now here was Raoul, gorgeous, successful, honorable, incredibly honorable."

She told them about the offer he'd made her, the chance of a lifetime—planning an upscale restaurant, developing its menu, becoming its executive chef.

She watched her sisters' faces light with pleasure, then darken with puzzlement over what they'd read in the interview with Raoul.

"But how—"

Lissa held up her hand.

She took them through opening day. Took them to opening

night. The excitement, the diners, the food critics.

Raoul's demand.

Their delight turned to shock. To horror. To rage. And then she told them about the fish stock. About Raoul's penis. About the fish head.

There was a second of stunned silence.

"Oh…my…God," Jaimie said, and she threw back her head and howled.

Emily roared with laughter. "A fish head," she gasped, "a fish head!"

Even Lissa giggled.

"It was," she said, "a very small fish."

That set them off again.

Jaimie finally wiped her eyes, went to the wet bar and brought back three miniature bottles of pinot grigio.

"To hell with glasses," she said, handing them around.

They unscrewed the caps and clinked bottles.

"To Raoul's penis," said Emily. "Here's hoping the fish stock rotted it off."

The Wilde sisters tilted the bottles to their lips and emptied them in a few long swallows. There were a couple of errant giggles. Then Jaimie cleared her throat.

"The bastard."

"Believe me, I called him more than that."

"And you were out of a job."

Lissa nodded. "Not just that job. I was out of consideration for any good job."

"Didn't you tell people what had happened?"

"I was upset. And humiliated. That scene… I can laugh at

it now, but I couldn't, not then. The entire thing was horrible. What he'd done to me, how I'd let him play me for such a fool…"

"You mean, you kept quiet?"

"Yes. By the time I tried to speak up, Raoul had destroyed my reputation. He said that I'd collapsed under pressure, that I'd walked out in the middle of the dinner service. By the time I tried to tell someone the truth, she just gave me this look, you know, a that's-a-truly-pathetic-story look, and I knew it was all over."

"And after that?"

"After that, I took any restaurant job I could find."

"You should have called us," Emily said indignantly. "Any of us. All of us."

"Right. Just the way you called when you were broke and desperate in New York."

Emily flushed. "Point made."

"And then you saw an ad for a job at that ranch?"

"My agent called me about it. I thought it was for a chef's position at one of those pricey spas. I flew up and when I realized what the job really was, I was pissed off."

"I'll bet," Jaimie said grimly.

"I wasn't going to stay. But a huge snowstorm blew in and I was stuck, so I made a couple of meals. Well, I was there, wasn't I?" she said, skipping over the part where she and Nick had despised each other, the part where she'd agreed to trade a cooked meal for room and board.

"But the snow stopped, eventually."

"Uh huh."

"And?"

"And—and, things changed."

"You discovered your real career was in feeding a bunch of grimy cowboys?"

"They weren't grimy! And no, I didn't decide that was what I wanted to do with my life. But…"

"But?"

"But—" She looked at her sisters. "But," she said softly, "I got to know Nick."

"Know him?" Jaimie said.

Lissa flushed. "Nick wasn't hiding. He was healing."

"So he claims," Emily said. "We haven't paid attention. Something about a stunt gone wrong?"

Lissa hesitated, but there was no longer any reason to keep Nick's secret. She told her sisters what had happened, how seriously Nick had been injured, not only physically but emotionally.

"That must have been rough," Jaimie said softly.

"It was. But he's strong. He got through it. And I—"

"And you?"

"And I—I began to care for him."

"Holy crap, Melissa! You're in love with him!"

"No!"

"Don't give me that BS! You're in love with the man."

"Maybe," Lissa said softly.

"What about him? Is he in love with you?"

"For God's sakes, James, what is this? An interrogation?"

"Meaning, you don't know if he loves you or not."

"Meaning, I don't want to have this conversation."

"Dammit, Melissa—"

"What has he told you?" Emily said. "About what's going on now."

"I haven't—I haven't spoken with him since early this morning."

"Meaning?" Jaimie demanded.

"Don't look at me like that. He's busy. Incredibly busy."

"So let's get this straight. He sent you away—"

"He had to deal with the media!"

"And he hasn't called you."

"No."

Jaimie's eyes narrowed. "How about calling him?"

Lissa stared at her sister. How about that, indeed? Between worrying about Nick and checking for calls from him and then discovering that her name and lies about her were plastered everywhere, she'd missed the obvious.

She didn't have to wait for Nick's call. She could call him.

"Lissa? How about calling him?"

Lissa rose to her feet. She looked at her sisters. They looked at each other.

Emily swung away, picked up the TV remote control, turned on the enormous flat-screen set that hung over a long buffet table and turned the volume to low. Jaimie looked at the screen, too, as if she really gave a damn about watching whatever stupid program was on.

Lissa drew a long breath, let it out and walked to the far end of the sitting room, called up her contacts list and hit the icon for Nick's cell number.

It rang. And rang. And rang again. There was a faint click.

OK. Not Nick, but his voice mail…

"*Welcome to GlobalPhone. We cannot complete your call at this time. Please check the number and dial again.*"

Frowning, she disconnected. Redialed by touching the icon again. Once more, the call went through. The phone rang and rang and then, click…

"*Welcome to GlobalPhone. We cannot complete your call at this time. Please check the number and dial again.*"

Obviously, there was some kind of glitch.

She placed the call again, this time using the keypad, touching her index finger to one digit at a time.

It didn't matter.

The phone rang. The automated message came on.

She ended the call.

OK. Definitely, a glitch. Well, GlobalPhone was her carrier, too. The number for customer service was right in her contacts list. She chose it, went through the nonsense of its electronic switchboard—

"GlobalPhone," a voice said briskly. "How may I help you?"

Lissa cleared her throat. "I'm having a problem trying to reach someone." She explained it all. That she'd called three separate times, that she'd reached the same automated message each time.

"Do you happen to know the message, ma'am?"

She did. By now, she knew it by heart, and she repeated it word for word.

"The thing is, I don't understand the part about checking the number because I absolutely know the number I've called is correct."

"I'm sure it is, Miss," the rep said. "What that message means is—"

Lissa listened. And listened. She reached behind her for a chair and sat down.

"I see," she said. "Thank you. No, no, there's nothing else."

"Lissa?"

She looked across the room. Emily and Jaimie were standing with their backs to the television screen.

"Lissa," Jaimie said, "you should probably see—"

Emily elbowed Jaimie in the ribs. "What's the matter?"

Lissa's lips felt as dry as the Mojave Desert. She moistened them with the tip of her tongue.

"It's... It's..." She paused. "I called Nicholas."

"And?"

"And I got a weird message."

"What kind of weird message?"

"A recording. I thought it meant that his phone was, you know, overloaded. I mean, everybody he ever knew is probably trying to reach him, but—"

"But?"

"But what it means is that—is that the person you're calling has—has changed his number."

Jaimie's expression turned grim. "He changed his number without telling you?"

"It's probably a mistake," Lissa said. She was shaking. Dammit! She was shaking! "Just some kind of screw-up, you know?"

Jaimie and Emily looked at each other. Then Emily picked up the TV remote. She and Jaimie moved to the sides of the set as Emily turned up the sound.

"… plans are just that right now," a slightly rough, wonderfully familiar male voice said.

Lissa caught her breath, rose to her feet and whispered Nick's name. And, yes, it was Nick on the TV screen, tall and handsome with that sexy, lazy smile on his lips.

"They're still only plans, but Beverly and I are discussing what happens next, and I promise, you guys will be the first to know."

Beverly?" Lissa said in bewilderment.

"The redhead," Jaimie said. "The one plastered to his side like glue."

Lissa tore her gaze from Nick, settled it on the woman beside him, a spectacular redhead who was gazing up at him with adoration.

"Did you ever give up hope, Beverly?" a voice called out.

The redhead laughed and put her arm through Nick's.

"Never," she said.

"And you had no idea what had happened to him?"

"No. Nick didn't let any of us know. Not even me."

"Nick?" A sea of microphones and cameras swung in Nick's direction. "Is there anything more you'd like to say about what happened in Afghanistan?"

The sexy smile faded from Nick's mouth.

"Nothing beyond what I've already told you. It was an honor to have known those men. They were the true embodiment of heroism and I'll never forget them."

Voices rang out; Nick raised his hand.

"The rest is for their families. I'm going to meet with them

individually, if they'll have me, and none of it—*none* of it—
will be for public discussion or display."

Lissa felt the sting of tears in her eyes. This was the Nicholas
she knew. The real one. The man she loved.

"Nick? What about that woman? Your cook?"

Nick's expression turned to stone.

"What about her?"

"Well, those pictures of you with her… Can we have some
details about her?"

"I've told you. No, you can't."

"Looks like she was a lot more than—"

"She was kind and generous at a time when kindness and
generosity were what I—"

Lissa snatched the remote from her sister's hand. The
screen went dark.

For a very long time, no one spoke.

Could you really feel your heart breaking?

"Liss," Emily said.

Lissa's words cut across hers. "Wow," she said brightly,
"wasn't that a nice thing for him to say about me? Really
nice…"

It was no good. She couldn't pretend, couldn't maintain
the lie. She began to cry, silently, desperately. Emily moaned
and threw her arms around her. Jaimie started to, but the hotel
telephone rang and she grabbed it.

"Hello? Travis? And Jake. And Caleb. All three of you. Well,
that's—that's… Yes. We just saw…. No, no, it isn't a problem. It
was just a, you know, just a job… The photos?" Jaimie turned
away. "Could we talk about this some other time? Because

now isn't—" Her voice rose. "Jesus, are you guys dense? We are not going to talk about—"

Lissa took the phone from Jaimie's hand.

"I was an idiot," she said. Her voice shook a little, but her words were clear and decisive. "OK? Have we got that straight? I was a fool and it's over and if you really want to help me, you can just—you can let the whole thing go and—and—What? That's crazy! You were all in Europe and now you're at JFK, waiting for one of the family jets? Listen, if this is because of me, if you lunatics are flying to El Sueño because you think I'm going there, too, if any of you are dumb enough to think I'm going to behave like a—like a lovesick teenybopper and bawl my eyes out…"

Jaimie took the phone back.

"Here's what's happening," she said crisply. "We're going home. Right away. Yes. We'll meet you there. Oh, for heaven's sake, of course with Lissa! Yes, I know what she said… Look, just get in touch with Marco and Zach. Tell them… Fine. In that case, we'll see you all soon." Jaimie hung up the phone and turned toward Lissa. "Did you hear what I said? We're all going to the ranch—and neither Em nor I will put up with any arguments."

It turned out your heart could be in pieces, but you could still laugh.

"The general would be proud of you, James," Lissa said.

An hour later, one of the Wilde's jets was soaring high above the clouds heading for Texas and Wilde's Crossing, and for the sprawling kingdom called El Sueño, a place that would always be home.

CHAPTER FOURTEEN

IN THE SPRING, the lush meadows and low ridges of the Wilde ranch always looked as if they'd been touched with an artist's paintbrush.

They were bright with bluebonnets, the Texas state flower. Legend said that bluebonnets had been brought over from Spain centuries ago. It was a charming story, but like most charming stories, it wasn't true.

Bluebonnets were true Texas natives. They might look delicate, but they were strong and determined, and Lissa was trying hard to learn from them.

Be strong. Be determined. And life will go on.

She'd been at El Sueño for four days. So was all the rest of her family, well, everyone except the general, and his absence was pretty much the standard.

John Hamilton Wilde had a world to run. A good thing, right now. It meant that nothing about Lissa's situation had reached him.

But the rest of the Wilde clan—brothers and sisters and spouses, an almost-spouse and even babies—had Lissa's world to organize.

Lissa clucked softly to her roan mare as she rode the animal to the top of a ridge.

They all meant well. And she loved them with all her heart, but she'd reached the point at which she'd have given anything for an hour of solitude.

This morning, she'd sneaked out of the house in search of some.

Everybody had still been asleep; the house had held an early-morning stillness. She'd tiptoed from her room as if she were still a little girl determined to avoid the housekeeper or one of the nannies who'd traipsed through the lives of the three Wilde sisters after their mom's death, and gone to the stable.

Soft whinnies had greeted her.

She rubbed noses, said a few words to each horse. Then she'd saddled up the roan that she'd always loved and ridden here, through meadows alive with bluebonnets, past horses grazing on new spring grass, letting the roan find the way because, even after all these years, the mare knew her rider's favorite early-morning trail.

Now, they were on the top of a ridge that looked out over land that endless generations of Wildes had claimed and worked and cherished, and Lissa, who had always thought of herself as a city person who just happened to have been born in the country, found herself seeing the meadows and, beyond them, the softly rolling hills of north Texas with new eyes.

It was a beautiful view, but not as beautiful as the dense

stands of pine and aspen and, beyond them, the fierce mountain peaks that were the view from the Triple G.

She tried not to do that too often, to think about those mountains or anything even remotely connected to them, but it was hard to close your eyes at night without suddenly seeing Louie and Peaches chasing a small rubber mouse down the hall, or Brutus trundling toward her, his tail wagging so hard that she'd laugh as she got down on her knees and wrapped her arms around him. It was hard not to hear Ace's gruff voice complimenting whatever it was she'd made for dinner, hard not to see the other men coming into the dining room, looking as eager and expectant as a bunch of kids on Christmas morning.

Most of all, worst of all, it was hard not to think about Nick. To more than think about him.

To see his face in the shadows of the porch at night, to hear his voice telling her how much he wanted her, to feel his hands on her breasts, his mouth on her mouth.

When was that going to stop?

Because it had to stop. It had to, or she was going to go crazy. Or maybe her family, her wonderful family, was going to be the cause of her going crazy and, yes, she knew that they meant well.

Nobody talked about Nick. Nobody mentioned him.

Nobody raised the subject of what in hell they were all doing here when there'd been no plans for any of them to be here in the middle of March.

Instead, everybody bubbled.

There was no other way to describe it.

"Lissa!" her sisters and sisters-in-law would say when she

walked into the room, their voices and faces filled with bright and totally artificial delight.

"Liss," her brothers would say, beaming happily whenever they saw her, "you look great this morning!" Or this afternoon or this evening, because they were always there, being cheerful, being upbeat, and Marco and Zach treated her the same way because even if they didn't carry the Wilde DNA, they were the same kind of men, caring, concerned, thoughtful and loving.

Amazing, that Nick had seemed to be like that, too.

Caring. Concerned. Thoughtful. Loving—but no, not loving. He had never mentioned love, and if she'd realized one thing these past few days, it was that falling in love with him had been her doing, not his.

And the truth was, she hadn't fallen in love with him. She'd fallen in love with lust. With needing and being needed.

Nick had come into her life, or rather she'd come into his, when she'd been at a low point. No job. No future. No money. No anything to look forward to, except more worries.

And then, overnight, everything changed. She had a job. A purpose. A bunch of people to care about.

And a man.

A man who was funny and smart and sexy, who cared about her—because he had, he *had* cared about her, and whose fault was it if she'd confused that with love?

Plus, Nick had needed her. What woman didn't want to be needed?

Add it all up and she had nothing to complain about. She'd had two weeks of incredible sex with an incredible guy who'd made her feel like the most important person in his life, and now it was over.

"Over," she said briskly. The mare whinnied and tossed her head. Lissa smiled. "Exactly. I'm glad we agree."

But he could have handled the ending a little better. She understood that their two weeks hadn't been destined to have a happy-ever-after-ending because this was not a movie, but he could have shown some tact. A phone call, even an e-mail...

Really? A phone call? An e-mail? To say what?

Lissa, I wanted to thank you for everything, but I've gone back to my real life now and...

And, Lissa thought grimly, the simple truth was that if she ever had the misfortune to see Nick Gentry again, she'd tell him that she'd been right all along. He was a selfish, egotistical jerk, and if he'd ever been foolish enough to think that he'd truly meant anything to her, it was just proof of exactly how much of a jerk he was.

All she had to do now was decide where to place him on the Lissa List. Between Carlos Antonioni and Jack Rutledge? After Rutledge but before Raoul? Or maybe after Raoul. Maybe Gentry belonged in a class all his own.

Or maybe it was her.

She'd let a series of selfish men use her.

"*—kind and generous at a time when kindness and generosity were what I needed.*"

Her eyes narrowed.

He made her sound like the Red Cross.

"To hell with you, Nicholas Gentry," Lissa said, and turned the roan toward home.

* * *

They were all waiting for her in the big kitchen at El Sueño, brothers, sisters, sisters-in-law, a brother-in-law and a brother-in-law-to-be, babies, the entire enormous Wilde clan.

They all looked up when she came through the back door. She could see the worry in their faces, worry that changed to artificial expressions meant to assure her that they hadn't been worried at all.

"Having a family powwow?" she said pleasantly, slipping off her jacket, hanging it on the coatrack beside the door, smiling at babies as she headed for the coffeepot on the stove.

"Just, you know, getting the day started," Jacob said.

Was he the designated spokesman for the morning? They seemed to choose a different one each day.

Lissa poured herself coffee, added cream, added sugar, stirred, sipped, took her time while working up something she could say that would let them know how much she loved them, how much she appreciated their love for her, but how it was time for everybody's life to return to normal.

Hell. She decided she'd simply improvise.

"Listen, you guys…" They all looked at her as if they expected a message from an oracle. She cleared her throat. "I have something to tell you." No one moved. No one breathed. Even the babies were still. "I'm going home."

That did it. They all spoke at once. Different voices, different words, one message.

She *was* home!

"No," she said gently, "I'm not. What I mean is, this place

will always be home, of course. But I have a life in L.A. Such as it is, anyway." She tried a smile; unfortunately, nobody smiled back. "My apartment is there. My things. My contacts. And before you point out that the one thing I don't have there is a job, well, I'm going to do something about that."

"Like what?" Caleb said.

There was a note of belligerence in his voice. One wrong word and for all she knew, her crazy, wonderful family was capable of barring the door to stop her from another try at taking on the big, bad world.

"For starters, I'm going to visit the last place I worked. Really worked, I mean. I was executive chef there and—well, the details don't matter. What does matter is that I let people think I'd messed up and been fired. I didn't and I hadn't, and I'm going to sort that out first. Then I'm going to talk with my agent. I might look for a different kind of job. Private cook to some big-shot producer. Or start my own boutique catering service. Boutiquey stuff is big in La La Land."

She tried another smile and was rewarded with a twitch of the lips from one sister and two brothers.

"I might even decide to pull up stakes and try another city."

"How about Dallas?" Travis said.

She knew he was dead serious, so she gave a dead-serious answer.

"Maybe."

"What do you mean, maybe?" Jake said. "It's a great place— you already know that. And we know lots and lots of people who'd line up around the block to eat at a place Lissa Wilde ran."

"It's the Wilde part I'm trying to get away from," Lissa said, even though she'd never realized it until that instant. "I love our family. I'm proud of our name. But—"

"But she wants to succeed on her own," Emily said. Everyone looked at her and she blushed.

Her husband, Marco, took her hand and brought it to his lips. "And you did, *bellisima*," he said softly.

Jaimie nodded. "Making it as yourself, not as a Wilde, is really, really important."

Zach, her fiancé, slipped his arm around her shoulders.

"That's my James," he murmured, and dropped a kiss on her temple.

Lissa looked at her brothers. Their expressions were impassive. Then, Jake sighed. Travis shrugged his shoulders. Caleb nodded his head.

"Go for it, kid," he said.

Lissa laughed. She cried, too, but these were good tears.

She went from Wilde to Wilde and hugged them. "I love you all," she said.

She went upstairs and changed her clothes. She didn't even bother packing; that would have taken too long. Besides, she had a closet full of clothes back in L.A. The only thing she didn't have back there was the garish-pink goody called *Pleasure Pleaser*. It was here, still inside the suitcase she'd brought with her, and it could remain there.

She'd never gotten around to using it.

She hadn't had to use it, she thought with a little lump in her throat.

And she wouldn't, not for a while. Just now, she didn't want to think about sex, not even the do-it-yourself variety.

What mattered was that one of the Wilde jets was waiting.

After that, sink or swim, she was on her own.

* * *

Once in L.A., she didn't bother going to her apartment.

The old saying was true. The time to strike was while the iron was hot and, dammit, she was hot. She did make one quick stop at a store she'd passed a couple of times on Santa Monica Boulevard.

Then she headed for *Raoul's*.

The restaurant was almost empty. She'd figured on that; this was the standard restaurant lull between late lunch and the early dinner hour.

"Hi," she said to the maître d', and breezed past him.

"Lissa," he said, "wait—"

But she had waited too long already.

She moved quickly, through the dining room to the kitchen, past the cooks who looked up from dinner prep and blinked with surprise, through the door that led to the basement, down a short hall and straight to Raoul's office.

His door opened before she reached it. Evidently, the maître d' had called to tell him that she was coming.

Raoul's handsome face was drawn up in a dark scowl.

"I would have thought you would have more sense than to show up here again, Wilde."

Lissa smiled as she shut the door. "You mean, you thought you'd scared me off."

"Get out, or I'll call the police."

"To do what? Protect you from me? You're, what, six feet tall? I'm five four on a good day." She held out her hands. "I'm not even armed, see? No knives. No fish stock."

Raoul reddened and reached for the house phone.

"John? Come down to my office, please." He hung up and looked at Lissa. "If you're going to beg me for a recommendation…"

"A recommendation as what? As the chef who established this restaurant? Designed the kitchen, hired the staff, planned the menu, chose everything from your suppliers to the cutlery to the dishes?"

An unctuous smile curled over his lips. "Prove it," he said, folding his arms over his chest.

"Or are you going to recommend me for the blow job I didn't give you? Dammit, I wish I had a picture of you standing there with your fly open, your pathetic weeny weenie hanging out while you told me to get down on my knees and be quick about it."

His smile fled.

"You should have dropped to your knees like a stone. Being made executive chef at a restaurant like this was worth whatever price I chose to put on it."

"Including fellating you."

"Absolutely including fellating me," he said coldly. "You owed me, big-time, for giving you a break like this. Now, if you're done…" Someone knocked at the door. Raoul moved past her and opened it. "John is here to show you out."

The maître d', looking uncomfortable, stepped into the

office.

"Sorry, Lissa, but we all know how it is, that you buckled on opening night and Raoul had to fire you and—"

Lissa grinned, reached in the breast pocket of her blue silk shirt and detached what, at first look, seemed to be only a button on the shirt pocket. But it wasn't. It was a camera, cleverly attached to a tiny video recorder inside the pocket.

"Surprise," she chirped, waggling the recorder at Raoul.

He went white. "You bitch!"

She smiled. Hit a button. A picture appeared on the little screen, accompanied by Raoul's voice. Lissa let the video run for a few seconds before stopping it. "Here we go," she said happily.

"*You should have dropped to your knees like a stone. Being made executive chef at a restaurant like this was worth whatever price I chose to put on it.*"

"*Including fellating you.*"

"*Absolutely including fellating me…*"

Click! Lissa stopped the recording. Wonderful! John's jaw had fallen almost to his knees.

"That recording isn't worth a damn," Raoul said. "You can't use it in a court of law."

"How about in the court of public opinion?" Lissa said sweetly. She dropped the tiny device into her purse, patted the maître d' on the arm and strolled through the door, up the stairs, through the kitchen, where she smiled at everyone, and out into the street.

"Oh, man," she said. "Oh, man," and she did a little circle dance.

Nobody looked at her.

You could get away with that kind of thing in only two places she could think of. One was here, where bizarre behavior was close to the norm. The other was Manhattan, where people didn't make eye contact with each other, let alone with the crazies.

On the other hand, talking to yourself and dancing on the street would probably win you some stares in Clarke's Falls, Montana…

And, damn, what was she doing, thinking about that?

Montana and everything about it was history.

So was Raoul and, by extension, the other men she'd permitted to walk all over her. Was it because she'd never felt as if she'd met her father's expectations? Was it because being ditched by Tommy Suarez in kindergarten had marked her for life?

Lissa laughed.

It didn't matter.

What did matter was that falling for good-looking hunks, for actors, was over. Her future stretched ahead, bright and shiny, and someplace out there, her Mr. Nice Guy was waiting.

By tonight, the true story about Raoul and her would be in every kitchen in town.

By morning, she'd have her choice of jobs.

As for Raoul…

That deserved another little circle dance.

His name would only evoke laughter.

* * *

Her apartment was airless after all the time away from it.

She shut the door, turned what seemed like dozens of locks—it was a different world than the one she'd known in Montana, and what did that matter?

She was back where she belonged, and glad of it.

Just as she began opening windows, her cell phone rang. She plucked it from her purse, glanced at the screen and rolled her eyes.

"Jake. I am fine. Really. I am completely—"

"Lissa. He was here."

"Who was where?"

"Gentry, that SOB."

"Nick?" Lissa dropped into a chair. "Nick was there? At your ranch?"

"At El Sueño. The no-good bastard."

"I don't understand. What was he doing at El Sueño?"

"Jesus H. Christ, Melissa, what do you think? He was looking for you."

Her heart thudded against her ribs. "Why would he do that?"

"I didn't ask him. Hell, why would I? All I did was make it clear that he'd better stay away from you.'

Lissa shut her eyes. A shotgun? A rifle? Bare fists?

"Jacob. What did you do?"

"He's just damn lucky everybody else had already left. If Travis and Caleb and Zach and Marco had still been around—"

The litany of names and the possibilities that went with them made her shudder.

"Jake. Please. What happened?"

"I slugged him, that's what happened. Does he think we're fools? '*Where is Lissa? I have to see her.*'" Jake cursed. "As if that crap would impress me."

"That's what he said? That he has to see me?"

"He didn't even fight back. All those tough-guy movie roles and the SOB didn't even try to defend himself."

"Oh, Jake," Lissa whispered. "Did you hurt him?"

"I got in one straight shot to the jaw. I'd have done more, but I'm not into hitting cowards."

"How did he look?"

"His jaw's gonna be a glow-in-the-dark gem in a few hours."

"Aside from that! Was he OK? Was he using a cane? Was he limping?"

"Who gives a damn?"

"I do, you idiot," she yelled, and she knew, just that quickly, that she wasn't over loving Nicholas.

The truth was, she never would be.

Jake was cautious with her after that. She could tell that he was trying to figure out what was happening and getting no place, fast.

"Listen," she finally said, taking pity on him, "remember when you left Addison?"

"I didn't leave her. Not really. I loved her, but things got in the way." Silence. "Dammit, Liss, are you saying you—you care for this guy?"

"I'm saying," Lissa said softly, "that I'm hoping things got in *his* way because yes, I care for him and I'm willing to hear what he wants to tell me, and if you don't understand that, ask Adoré to explain it to you."

"Her name is Addison," Jake said gruffly.

"Jacob," Lissa said, "we all know that you call her Adoré because you love her, and we all know, too, that to try and understand love is something that Stephen Hawking and Einstein combined would never be able to do."

Jake's sigh traveled through the phone.

"In that case, kid, I wish you good luck." His voice hardened. "But if this guy hurts you again, he's toast. Got that?"

"Got it," Lissa said.

She ended the call smiling, but that didn't last long because she really had no idea why Nick had finally gone after her and for all she knew, here she was again, setting herself up for a fall.

* * *

She kept busy as afternoon gave way to evening, sweeping and polishing away weeks' worth of dust, saying "Yuck" as she tossed unidentifiable stuff from the fridge into the trash, and, best of all, taking calls from people in the trade who'd already heard the story of Raoul and her.

Word was spreading even more quickly than she'd anticipated, but it was a juicy tale and juicy tales usually moved like wildfire.

She smiled a couple of hours later when the doorbell rang and a kid delivered a bouquet of long-stemmed red roses from John, the maître d' at *Raoul's*, with a note that said *Brava!*

The bell rang again and a messenger handed her a box of decadent handmade chocolates and a card that said *Welcome Back* from a friend who'd been decent enough to let her fill in at his kitchen after the Raoul fiasco.

A little while after that, a courier delivered a letter informing her that a renowned East Coast restaurant group was going to open a Beverly Hills branch, and that the CEO would be honored if she'd come in to discuss the position of executive chef.

"*Honored*," she said, laughing as she read the letter.

Lovely, all of it, but nothing could keep her from thinking about Nick's visit to El Sueño. What had he wanted? Why hadn't he simply called? Why did he want to see her? For that matter, how had he learned about El Sueño? She'd told him she was from Texas, that she'd grown up on a ranch, but she couldn't recall telling him anything else.

Exhaustion caught up to her just after ten-thirty. She showered, put on a pair of comfy if raggedy sweats, realized she'd never had supper and made herself a haute cuisine quickie: peanut butter and honey on whole wheat toast, along with a cup of tea.

Then she settled in to watch the eleven o'clock news.

Exhausted or not, she was too wired to sleep.

If Nick really wanted to find her, where was he? Why hadn't he shown up here? Why hadn't he phoned her?

Wait.

Did he have her L.A. address? Did he even have her phone number? She had his because Marcia had given it to her...

No. She was starting the old routine, making excuses for a man rather than face the...

"*Good evening, and welcome to tonight's news.*"

A home invasion in Bel Air. A homicide in downtown L.A.

An accident on the 110. And coming up next, an exclusive with Nick Gentry.

Lissa sat up straight.

Her heart did that banging-against-her-ribs thing again.

There he was. Gorgeous Nicholas. No clinging vine of a redhead this time. Just him, Nick, no cane, his hands tucked into the pockets of a leather bomber jacket—and a dark smudge, a little bit of a swelling on his jaw.

"…all kinds of rumors, Nick, about you and that ranch you own in Montana. What's it called? The Double D?"

"The Triple G," Nick said. "I've heard the rumors and I want to set them straight." His mouth twitched; Lissa recognized that twitch and knew it meant he was trying not to laugh. "No," he said solemnly, "I'm not turning it into a dude ranch. I'm not selling it to the Japanese. I'm not turning it into an ostrich-breeding farm." He took a breath and so did Lissa because, foolish as it sounded, he seemed to be staring not only at the camera but straight at her. "The Triple G will continue to be a working ranch, an honest part of an honest tradition, one I hope my dad would be proud of." He paused. "But there's going to be a new road that goes through it, to a piece of land that looks out on the mountains, land someone once described as not only beautiful but amazing."

Lissa stared at the screen.

"We're building a restaurant. Something special. Handsome. Unique. And with a menu that will, I hope, match the view. It's going to be called *Basic Elegance.*"

Her mouth dropped open.

"It's going to be called what?" she said, and just as if he'd heard her, Nick repeated the name.

"*Basic Elegance.*"

Lissa punched the remote button. The TV went mute.

"Dammit," she said, "dammit to hell!"

She'd been right about Nick Gentry all along. "Selfish" didn't even come close to describing him.

Her idea. Her dream. Even her name. He'd stolen it all, he was going to use it all, and now she knew why he surely wanted to see her, because he was selfish but he wasn't stupid and he figured he might run into some legal troubles if he stole a plan, a dream of a lifetime from her.

The doorbell rang. More flowers or chocolates, and she was not in the mood for either.

"Rat," she said to Nick's image on the screen as stalked to the door, undoing the locks without first looking out the peephole, behaving foolishly and unthinkingly because she was angry, beyond angry, beyond logic or reason. "Thief!" she snarled as she pulled the door open—

"Hello, Melissa."

It was not flowers, not a letter, not a box of candy. It was Nick, and it took her all of two seconds to haul back her arm and punch him right in the gut.

CHAPTER FIFTEEN

THE LAST TIME she'd hit him, he'd fallen back against the wall and slid to the floor.

Not this time, dammit.

He went "Oof," and she knew that was mostly because she'd caught him by surprise, but he didn't fall back; he didn't even bounce. He was holding a cane in his hand—no, not a cane. A walking stick, but he wasn't leaning on it.

He just stood there, tall and broad-shouldered, long-legged and narrow-hipped, his hair ruffled by the wind, end-of-day stubble on his jaw, and the only thing that made her feel good was that other thing on his jaw, the bruise, the swelling, and what a joy to know that a Wilde was responsible for it.

"Get out of my sight, Gentry! I have nothing to say to you."

"I have things to say to you."

"Save them for your lawyer. I'm gonna sue the pants off you."

"Look, if it'll make you feel better to slug me again, go for it."

"I'm dead serious, Nick. I don't want to talk to you."

"Yeah, well, if we're being serious, Duchess, you might as well know that I don't really want to talk to you, either."

"Then what in hell are you doing here?"

"I'll show you," he said, and he let go of the walking stick, reached for her and drew her into his arms.

"Don't," she said. "Dammit, Nicholas Gentry, don't you dare—"

He kissed her.

Kissed her, slipped one hand into her wet, tangled hair, cupped the back of her head so he could gain better access to her mouth, and she was lost.

The taste of him, the feel of him were everything she'd wanted to forget.

"Lissa," he whispered, and her knees, her silly knees, buckled and he kicked the walking stick into her sad excuse for a foyer, swung her into his arms, elbowed the door shut behind him…

And staggered.

She put her hands against his shoulders. He let her down; her feet touched the floor, but he kept his arms around her and leaned his forehead against hers.

"Fine thing when a guy tries to make like Clark Gable and ends up like Dudley Do-Right."

She wanted to laugh. She wanted to cry. She wanted to hate him, but she couldn't. The best she seemed capable of was standing within the circle of his arms and framing his face with her hands.

"You stole my restaurant."

It was the least of what he'd stolen, which made it the safest accusation to make.

"It's your restaurant, or it will be, if you'll accept it."

"Mine?"

"Yours." He raised his head, smiled into her eyes, then dipped his mouth to hers for another kiss. "Did I get the name right? *Basic Elegance*?"

"Yes."

"Good. That's settled. We can move on to more important things," he said, and kissed her again.

"Don't keep doing that," she whispered, a little breathlessly, "or I'm liable to forget all the reasons that I hate you."

"You don't hate me," he said, with that arrogant confidence that drove her crazy. "You love me."

"I don't love you."

"Of course you love me." He smiled, used his thumbs to wipe away her tears. "Not as much as I love you, because nobody can love anybody as much as I love you, Duchess, but we both know that you love me."

What was the sense in denying it? Lissa decided she wasn't even going to try.

"You changed your phone number," she said.

Nick frowned. "Beverly changed it, you mean. And forgot to mention it to me. I didn't even realize it had been changed. I just kept getting calls, but I had no idea they were coming to a new number." A muscle jumped in his jaw. "And I had no idea why there weren't any calls from you."

"When did you figure it out?"

"When I became impossible to deal with, when all I talked about was the fact that you hadn't contacted me, Beverly suddenly said, oh, she'd changed my number and maybe that was the reason."

"Beverly," Lissa said.

"Uh oh."

"Uh oh, indeed. I can't hold it against her for being gorgeous and for waiting for you to come back to her, but—"

"She's my publicity rep."

"Your what?"

"Bev handles my publicity. She's furious at me for disappearing, for never taking any of her endless calls and for not contacting her, but she's accustomed to a little chaos in her life. Heck, when you have four kids and a writer husband who never tells you what he's doing from one day to the next—"

"Are we talking about the same Beverly? The one who looks at you as if you're a bowl of whipped cream?"

Nick grinned. "She looks at me as if I'm her major client, and I am." He raised Lissa's face to his. "But the only woman I want thinking of me as a bowl of whipped cream, sweetheart, is you."

"Nick. I have so many questions…"

"Ask them."

"You didn't have my phone number?"

"No. Are you old enough to remember the good old days? Real telephones? Telephone directories? You could look up somebody's phone number back then. Not anymore." His expression changed, went from teasing to serious. "In between all of that, I'd had people working on putting me in contact with the families of those guys I'd been with in Afghanistan."

"And?"

"And," he said, his eyes darkening, "I've met with them. Such nice people, Melissa. Good people, the parents proud of their boys, the older guy's wife so proud of her husband's service and valor…" He stopped, cleared his throat. "You'll like them."

"I will? You mean I'm going to meet them?"

"Yes. We're going to stay in touch. I want to, you know, do something to honor the two kids. And Bill. The older guy. The one they called Pop. His two little girls are going to need some help. Summer camp. College—"

Lissa rose on her toes and kissed Nick.

"I love you," she said.

He drew her against him. "And I love you with all my heart." She felt his mouth curve against her temple. "Brutus says to tell you that he misses you. So do the kittens."

She smiled. "I miss them, too."

"Don't you want to hear how I found that not-so-small-country you Wildes call home?"

"Tell me."

"Well, after good old Marcia flat out refused to tell me anything about you—"

"Some of the chefs signed with her call her Marcia the Mean," Lissa said, laughing.

"I said I'd get an injunction that would force her to give me what I needed." Nick grinned. "She told me to go ahead and try it. She said the reputation of her agency was at stake. She finally offered to contact you on my behalf, but just about then

I remembered something."

"What?" Lissa said, leaning back in his arms.

"I remembered you said you'd grown up in Texas. On a ranch. And then I remembered that you'd said your old man was a four-star general." He bent his head, brushed his lips lightly over hers. "Turned out to be a cinch, finding a four-star general named Wilde who owns a ranch in Texas."

Nick winced as Lissa touched her hand lightly to his jaw.

"That was courtesy of your brother Jake."

"Yes. Well, my brothers are, you know, kind of protective."

"I'm glad they are."

"And then Marcia gave you my address here?"

Nick smiled. "I called El Sueño from my plane, just before we took off from the Dallas airport. I told Jake that he had it all wrong, that I loved you and you loved me. He'd refused to let me get three words out when I saw him, but for some reason he listened to me when I called, gave me your phone number and address—and added that he and a bunch of other guys—it sounded like the roster of a rugby team—would happily take me apart limb by limb if it turned out that I was lying."

Lissa brought Nick's hand to her lips. He winced.

"What?" she said.

"Nothing."

He started to tug his hand free. She hung onto it, looked at it…

"Your knuckles are swollen."

He shrugged. "It's nothing."

"Nicholas. Why are your knuckles swollen?"

"I had a slight run-in with somebody's jaw."

"But Jake said—"

"Not him. He slugged me and I figured, from his vantage point, I deserved it."

"I don't understand. If not my brother…"

"That guy named Raoul's jaw looks a lot worse than mine."

Lissa stared at her lover. "Nick. You didn't."

"I read what he said about you." His eyes narrowed. "And I didn't like it, so I decided to pay him a little visit. I stopped at his restaurant and confronted him and, you know, one word led to another…"

Lissa began to laugh. "Raoul has had a very difficult day."

"Meaning?"

"Meaning, I don't want to talk about him now, not when I'm still trying to believe that you're really, really here."

Nick lifted her face to his.

"I'll always be here, sweetheart. You're everything I could ever need or want."

"A happy ending after all," she said softly.

"There's no other kind for us."

Lissa rose on her toes, caught his bottom lip between her teeth and bit lightly into the tender flesh.

"Prove it."

His smile became the one she loved, sexy and arrogant and filled with wicked promise.

"Ah, Duchess," he said softly, "and here I thought you were such a good girl."

"That whipped cream I mentioned…" She fluttered her lashes. "Unfortunately, I don't have any on hand, but I do have a box of delectable, delicious, easily melted chocolates."

Nick kissed her. This time, his kiss was deep and hard and it told her that everything she'd wanted, everything she'd ever imagined wanting, was right here, in her arms.

"I love you," he said. "And I love the idea of that melted chocolate." His arms tightened around her. "But first you have to say the only word that matters."

"What word?"

"Yes."

"Yes what?"

"Yes, you'll marry me. Yes, we'll grow old together. And yes, you'll let me do my best to make you happy for the rest of our lives."

Lissa sighed. "For a cowboy, you drive an awfully hard bargain, Nicholas."

He smiled. "Is that a yes, Melissa?"

Lissa wound her arms around her lover's neck and gave him her answer with her kiss.

* * *

They would have been married right away. Nick didn't want to wait and neither did Lissa, but Zach and Jaimie's wedding was scheduled for May.

They scheduled theirs for June.

Two weddings, back-to-back.

Perfect, everyone said.

Each time, the bride was beautiful. Each time, the groom was handsome.

And El Sueño was, each time, at her brilliant best, the

meadows carpeted with delicate lavender winecups when Jaimie and Zach took their vows, with crimson firewheels by the time Lissa and Nick took theirs.

Each wedding was exactly as the bride and groom had wanted it. Small, by Texas standards, with only family and friends in attendance.

Everyone was now looking forward to Fourth of July weekend at El Sueño. All the Wildes, including the general, would be home for the festivities.

He had come home, of course, in May for Jaimie's wedding and then in June for Lissa's, but only for a short time. He'd written, however, to say that he would also be home for the Fourth of July celebration, and that this time, he would stay a little longer.

And that he would be bringing a surprise.

"Some surprise," the Wilde sisters said among themselves.

He'd bring the same gift certificates he always gave his children and now his daughters-in-law and sons-in-law and grandbabies, elegant gift cards from all the best shops in Dallas, and they'd all say "thank you" even though they'd have traded all those certificates for just one thing that had meaning, that would be a part of the general himself.

The Wildes, the Santinis, the Castelianoses, and old friends His Royal Highness Sheikh Khan and his wife, Laurel, arrived two days before the Fourth.

There was lots of laughter, lots of fun. The men played touch football; the women floated in the pool. Babies crawled on the lawn and were taken for rides on the backs of the most docile of the horses.

Emily and Caleb's wife, Sage, oversaw the decorations inside the house; Jaimie and Jake's Addison did the same for the fireworks displays; Lissa and Jennie, Travis's wife, supervised the making and baking of endless goodies for the big party that would take place on the Fourth itself.

The day dawned bright, clear and, wonder of wonders, not too hot.

Jake, Caleb and Travis had arranged for a band. Two bands, really: a mariachi band and the same versatile six-piece group that had played at all the Wilde weddings. Virtually the entire citizenry of Wilde's Crossing had been invited; umbrella tables dotted the lawn.

A line of grills was fired up; big tables groaned under the weight of four kinds of chili, steaks, ribs, chicken, and something not native to Texas but delicious all the same: lobster tails.

There was only one problem.

The hours sped by and still the general had not shown up.

"He's not coming," Lissa told Emily and Jaimie.

"Frankly, who gives a damn?" Emily said, but it wasn't true.

For years, for decades, the Wilde offspring had waited for their father to turn up for birthdays, for Christmases, for every imaginable holiday.

He rarely had.

The weddings over the past few years had been exceptions to the rule. He'd been present for those, and the truth was, they'd been surprised that he had.

Now, as the hours passed, they began to accept the fact that this holiday would be no different from dozens of others.

Hard as it was to admit, they were disappointed.

Maybe it was because they were all foolish enough to keep hoping that he would change, or maybe it was simply that because all their lives had changed, they'd foolishly believed his would, too.

As the sun dipped behind the rolling hills, Jacob, Caleb, Travis, Emily, Jaimie and Lissa gathered in a small grove of trees behind the big Wilde house.

"He's not coming," Jaimie said.

"No," Lissa said, "he's not."

Emily sighed. "Well, we might as well get the fireworks started. There's no point in waiting any longer."

Jaimie nodded and used her cell phone to instruct the specialists in charge of the display that it was time to get things going.

"But wait another five minutes," she said, and she gave her brothers and sisters an apologetic smile. "Can't hurt to give it just a little more time."

"Right," Travis said, and then smiled at each of his sisters. Jake hugged them. Caleb ruffled their hair.

It was nothing new, their father making promises and not keeping them, but they all sensed a different texture to it this time, the way the air feels different when a storm is rolling in.

Perhaps that was the reason the brothers looked at each other, laughed a little self-consciously and stepped into the kind of quick bear hugs often exchanged by men who love each other but aren't great at saying it.

Zach, Marco, Nick, Sage, Addison and Jennie joined the little group. The babies were in the house, tucked away from all the noise that would accompany the fireworks.

Jaimie checked her watch. "Just another couple of minutes—"

"Here you are!"

The voice was unmistakable.

The general, resplendent in full uniform, a score of brightly polished medals and colorful ribbons pinned to his chest, was coming toward them through the rose-covered arched trellis that led into the little grove.

"Sorry we're late," he said briskly. "I hope we didn't miss the fireworks."

"We?" Lissa started to say, but as their father reached them, they could all see that he was not alone.

There were people with him. Two men, about the ages of the Wilde brothers. Two women, about the ages of the Wilde sisters. All four stood in a way that made them appear stiff and unyielding.

"Yes," the general said. "We." He gave them all a bright smile, as false as a party mask. "And we're happy to see that you're well and—"

The general's words blurred as the Wildes stared at the four unknown guests. They were strangers.

And yet—and yet, there was something familiar about them.

The height of the men. Their long, leanly-muscled bodies. Their dark hair, and the elegantly masculine bone structure of their faces.

The way the women held themselves. Their slender bodies. Their fair hair, and the shapes of their noses and mouths.

Instinctively, the Wildes drew closer together.

"…so my apologies for the delay," the general said, "but the weather in Rome—"

"*Basta!*" one of the men with him growled. "Enough! Just get to it."

"*Si*," the second man said. "*Cristo*, we have had enough of talk!"

Caleb looked at the general. "Who are these people?" he said. "What's going on here?"

The general cleared his throat. "They are—they are—"

The first man stepped forward. "I am Matteo."

The second man joined him. "I am Luca. And these are our sisters, Alessandra and Bianca."

Silence. No one moved. No one spoke. After what seemed a very long time, Travis said, "And you have come here as our father's guests?"

"We have come," Matteo said, "because we finally know the truth."

Jake folded his arms over his chest. "What truth?"

"You will not like it," Alessandra said.

Caleb flashed a cold smile. "Let us make the decision about what we will or will not like."

Bianca cleared her throat. "My sister is simply trying to warn you that—"

"She warned us," Travis said sharply. "Just get to it. What's this truth that you think we won't like?"

Matteo and Luca looked at each other. Then Matteo shrugged his shoulders.

"It is," he said, "that we, the same as you, have the misfortune of being the sons and daughters of General John Hamilton Wilde."

Beyond the ridge, the first group of fiery rockets shot into the black Texas sky and burst into a dozen glorious shades of pink, purple and blue.

THE END

Want to be notified when Sandra releases a new book?

Go http://www.sandramarton.com
and sign up for the email list.

We'll let you know when the next book arrives.

Join Sandra on Facebook:

https://facebook.com/SandraMartonAuthor

COMING SOON:

A brand new series from Sandra Marton

In Wilde Country

Book One: PRIDE

Book Two: PASSION

Book Three: PRIVILEGE

Book Four: POWER

Made in the USA
Middletown, DE
18 April 2021

37862596R00184